Evelyn

Evelyn James has always been fascinated by history and the work of writers such as Agatha Christie. She began writing the Clara Fitzgerald series one hot summer, when a friend challenged her to write her own historical murder mystery. Clara Fitzgerald has gone on to feature in over thirteen novels, with many more in the pipeline. Evelyn enjoys conjuring up new plots, dastardly villains and horrible crimes to keep her readers entertained and plans on doing so for as long as possible.

Other Books in
The Clara Fitzgerald Series

The Monster at the Window

by

Evelyn James

A Clara Fitzgerald Mystery
Book 11

Red Raven Publications
2018

Chapter One

Oliver Bankes stumbled over a log in the darkness. He fell to his hands and splashed muddy water from the ground onto his face. Blinking, briefly, he got to his feet and kept running, his terror moving his body despite the tightness in his chest and the ache in his legs.

Even as he fled in fear, his mind was repeating over and over that what he had just seen was not possible. But he could not disbelieve his eyes, or his other senses. What he had seen that night beggared belief, but that did not mean he had not seen it. The sight had scared him out of his wits, and he had turned and run for his life through the dark night, across the parkland, wildly guessing the direction to the road. He had left behind his expensive photography equipment, not that he cared in that moment. All that mattered was escape.

Another tree root threatened to topple him. He somehow kept his footing. Nearer, nearer the road drew, the landscape becoming vaguely familiar. He was sure he recognised that burned out tree, struck by lightning years ago and left as a stark reminder of the cruelty of nature.

Nature!

What creation of nature had he seen that night? Was this some sort of strange natural phenomena, explainable by science? He feared not, but he did know of one person who might be able to explain. He had at first only meant to run away as fast as possible, now he had a new idea and with it came purpose. He had to reach Clara Fitzgerald and explain this terrible night to her. Maybe she could solve this nightmare and put everyone's mind at ease. At least she would be practical about the whole thing and, right there and then, what Oliver needed most was someone practical.

The wall of the estate was in sight, just beyond would be the road. Oliver breathed a sigh of relief. It was still a long walk to Brighton, but the draw of the town with its many residents was too tempting to ignore. Oliver wanted to be among people, a lot of people. He wanted to see lights in windows and hear people laughing and shouting. That was the only way to banish this horror from his soul. He skirted the wall until he found the gate, and then he was on the road and slowing to a fast trot. He was out of puff and sore, but ahead was salvation.

He strode on into the night, determined to put as much distance between him and the monster he had just seen as was possible. Every step counted as he made the tedious journey back to Brighton.

~~~*~~~

Captain O'Harris had suggested going to the picture house. There was a horror movie playing, one based on Frankenstein. As the evening was damp and dark, autumn closing in fast, it seemed a perfect time to go to the movies and escape the real world for a bit. Clara agreed even though she was not that fussed about horror movies, she just liked being in O'Harris' company.

Clara was Brighton's first female private detective, an accolade that brought her as much grief as it did fame, but she loved her work and the help she could bring to others. If someone had told her two years ago that she would be solving murders and confronting hardened criminals she would have thought they were talking rot, but that was her life now. It was certainly not a usual career for a woman, at least not in Brighton.

Clara had first met Captain O'Harris on a case. He had been curious about the mysterious death of his uncle. The unravelling of the mystery had brought Clara close to O'Harris, a closeness she had hoped to pursue until he vanished during a record-breaking flight across the Atlantic. A whole year later he had turned up in America, so ill and traumatised he could not even state his name to those who helped him. It was only by chance that his real identity was discovered, and he was ultimately returned to England. O'Harris was still battling his demons, but at least he was home and each week that passed brought improvement. Clara had high hopes that he would soon be completely fit and back to the man she remembered. In the meantime, they were reacquainting themselves with each other, and that closeness they had barely touched upon a year ago was rapidly growing.

All of which meant that Clara was quite happy to sit in the picture house with O'Harris and watch the silent production of Frankenstein, while a pianist played appropriate accompanying music. The only thing she was not able to do was act like the other girls in the audience, who were screaming and squeaking as the monster lumbered across the screen, and ducking their heads into the shoulders of their male companions. Clara watched these antics with mild interest. She did not find the movie very frightening at all, in truth, she felt sorry for poor Frankenstein who was taking the brunt of people's misunderstandings and prejudice.

Clara didn't really do screaming or running for cover into the arms of the nearest young man. She would hardly be doing the career she did if she was so inclined. But she was beginning to wonder if perhaps it was rather expected whilst watching a horror movie to act terrified for the sake of your male companion. It seemed to give them ample excuse for indulging in heavy petting. Things were becoming a little unseemly in certain quarters.

Clara nestled herself a little closer to O'Harris, to remove herself as much as possible from the next-door couple who had given up on the movie and were now kissing with little regard for their whereabouts. Captain O'Harris glanced at Clara and smiled, then he reached out and took her hand in his, squeezing it lightly. Clara was close to explaining that she was not scared, only aiming to avoid the people next to her, but decided that would be rather tactless. In any case, she was quite happy to have her hand held by O'Harris.

On the screen Frankenstein roared mutely as the villagers chased him up to the top of a tall ravine. There, jabbed at by pitchforks and flaming torches, the tormented creature stumbled backwards and fell down into the rocky crevasse.

Around Clara people cheered. She was rather disappointed in their failure to understand. The monster was not the ugly, stomping brute who cried out in silent pain to his pursuers. The real monsters were the villagers who hunted him just because he was different and strange. Clara sighed softly to herself. People never learned.

Clara and O'Harris returned to the foyer of the picture house and the captain retrieved their coats. Outside it was pouring with rain and the pavements swirled with puddles.

"Sorry Clara, I didn't think to bring an umbrella," O'Harris grimaced as he looked at the rain.

Clara shrugged.

"No matter," she said. "Nor did I."

"We'll make a dash for it then?" O'Harris suggested, holding out his arm for Clara to take.

Clara pulled her hat firmly down on her head.

"Sounds like the best solution!" she took his arm and they darted out into the rain, laughing as they dived around puddles and splashed their way home as fast as they could. They were bound to get soaked, running did not make a difference, but they ran anyway, dodging the odd vehicle meandering along the roads and keeping to the lit streets where they could see the path clearly.

By the time they had reached Clara's house they were both drenched.

"You should come in and dry off," Clara said to O'Harris.

"I'll only have to get wet again heading for Dr Cutt's house," O'Harris remarked. "Not that I am turning down your offer lightly. I would rather sit by your parlour fire for a time, but the thought of warming up and then having to come out in the rain again gives me a chill."

"Oh, you can borrow an umbrella," Clara said cheerfully. "You shan't get wet again. At least stop for a cup of cocoa."

O'Harris did not need a lot of persuasion. He grinned.

"As long as Annie won't get cross about me dripping on her clean floors."

"Annie will putter," Clara admitted, referring to her friend and housekeeper, "but she will understand."

Clara led him into the hall of the house and took his wet raincoat. Clara's brother Tommy emerged from the parlour, having heard the front door opening and closing. He looked at the drenched pair and nodded.

"Is it raining then?"

"Not so you would notice," O'Harris responded brightly.

"You best sit by the fire and dry off!" Tommy pointed the newspaper he had been reading at them. "You'll catch your deaths."

"You are beginning to sound like Annie," Clara teased him, heading through into the parlour and poking up the fire so it blazed.

O'Harris joined her and they both gave a sigh of relief as the warmth of the flames started to get through to their bones. Annie appeared in the doorway of the room, wiping her hands on a cloth.

"You two will catch your deaths!" she declared.

"I already told them that," Tommy interjected.

"Hot cocoa at once!" Annie said, ignoring him. "Why on earth did you not take an umbrella, Clara?"

Clara could only shrug helplessly, knowing Annie would tut at her as she stalked off to make the warm drinks. Tommy shook his head at them.

"At least was the film good?"

"It was sad," Clara replied. "The poor monster was so misunderstood…"

She was interrupted by a rapid hammering on the front door. Tommy glanced at them with a frown.

"Who would it be at this hour?" he tilted his head to the clock which was already showing a quarter to ten on its dial.

The hammering came again, hard and insistent. Perplexed, Tommy went to answer it. From where she stood by the fire, Clara heard him declare;

"Oliver! Look at the state of you! Come in at once."

Tommy brought a dishevelled Oliver Bankes into the parlour. The poor man was soaked to the skin and covered in mud. He was trembling and looked fit to collapse.

"Fetch him some dry clothes," Clara instructed, grabbing a chair from the breakfast table and hastening to sit Oliver in it. "You look a state, where have you been?"

Oliver's teeth were chattering so badly he could not answer. He was not wearing a coat, only a woollen waistcoat over his shirt. Tommy started to help him take these off. Oliver's hands were shaking too hard to undo the buttons.

"Annie, we need warm towels urgently!" Clara called out.

Annie darted back to the room to see what had occurred since she had been gone.

"Oliver Bankes!" she looked at the shivering man with an expression of horror, then she moved into action.

Disappearing briefly, she returned with large towels, one of which she threw over Oliver's bare shoulders, now his shirt had been removed. She fetched further clean clothes from Tommy's wardrobe as Oliver was stripped of his socks and trousers. With only his underwear to protect his decency, Oliver trembled under his towel and gritted his teeth.

"I think he needs a stiff drink," O'Harris suggested, moving to the Fitzgeralds' drinks cabinet and pouring out a large brandy. "He looks fit to faint."

The drink was pressed into Oliver's hand and he sipped at it, his shivering making it difficult to swallow. They wrapped him in the towels until he was swaddled like a baby and made sure he was sitting as close to the fire as possible. Annie had wasted no time filling a stone hot water bottle from the kettle and put this under Oliver's feet. Warmth started to return to his body and he relaxed. By the time Annie appeared with the cups of cocoa, colour had returned to Oliver's cheeks and he had stopped shivering.

"Well, Oliver Bankes!" Annie said as she pressed the cup of cocoa into his hands. "What have you been up to? You look like a man who has seen a ghost, if truth be told!"

"Not a ghost," Oliver answered, finding enough strength to speak. "But something far worse."

He sipped his cocoa and closed his eyes for a moment.

"Tonight, I have witnessed the impossible and I am sorely in need of Clara's skills as a detective to explain it all to me."

Clara was surprised.

"Where have you been?" she asked him.

"The estate of Lord Howton," Oliver explained. "I was his guest for the evening. He wanted me to take photographic proof of the horror afflicting the family."

Clara was baffled.

"The horror?" she repeated. "Is something wrong with the family?"

"You could say that," Oliver answered. "Clara, if I understood anything I had seen tonight I would be happy, but none of it makes sense. I went to Lord Howton's home utterly sceptical about what I would find or see. Now I come away baffled and very afraid."

"Have you walked all the way from the estate?" Tommy asked, noting the thick layer of mud on the bottom of Oliver's shoes which now sat by the fire, steaming slightly as they dried.

"I ran most of the way," Oliver corrected. "Until I was too exhausted to run anymore. If you had witnessed what I had, you would not have stopped either until you were back among civilisation."

"Old man, has someone been hurt?" O'Harris asked carefully.

"Good question," Oliver nodded. "When this nightmare began, I was in the company of Lord Howton's eldest son, Richard. He ran in one direction, I in the other. I hope he made it back to the house."

"Oliver, what on earth did you witness tonight?" Clara demanded, deciding it was time to get to the bottom of all these riddles. "You speak as if you saw a monster."

"I think I did, Clara," Oliver replied. "I certainly can't explain it any other way. I went to Lord Howton's home to prove that a fraud or hoax was being enacted on the family. I have come away convinced that the supernatural exists and is plaguing them. They are cursed Clara, that is all it can be."

"The supernatural?" Annie said, looking nervous. Out of all of them she was the most convinced that ghosts were a very real thing.

"There is nothing supernatural in this world," Clara said firmly. "Everything has a rational explanation."

"You would not say that if you had seen what I have seen!" Oliver said firmly, almost snapping out the words.

"And what did you see Oliver?" Tommy asked calmly.

Oliver opened his mouth to speak and for a moment no words came out. Then he closed his eyes and resolved himself to talking.

"I saw a corpse rise up from the grave," he said in a

rush. "The corpse of Lord Howton's late brother!"

Chapter Two

There was a long pause.

"You see? This is precisely what I expected. A man is not believed when he is telling the absolute truth!" Oliver snapped, sounding somewhat hysterical. It had been a very long and traumatic night.

"I do believe you, Oliver," Clara said gently. "I believe you saw something inexplicable, at least for the moment, and that it was a terrifying experience. But, there will be a logical reason for it, nonetheless."

"You were not there Clara," Oliver's voice had regained its steadiness. "I saw a man who has been dead these last three weeks! He stood before me smelling of putrefaction, his skin the colour of ashes, his eyes glazed and wild. There were maggots falling off him! I saw a corpse reanimated!"

Clara took a seat opposite Oliver. She was still trying to comprehend how her rational and sensible friend could possibly imagine he had witnessed a dead man come back from the grave that night. Of course, as Oliver had pointed out, she had not been there to witness what had occurred.

"Let's start at the beginning Oliver, what were you doing at Lord Howton's home in the first place?"

Oliver gave a sigh, relaxing somewhat since he was no longer being questioned over what he had seen. He closed his eyes a moment, then lifted them and looked Clara square in the face.

"Lord Howton invited me. This horror is not new to him. The corpse of his late brother has been prowling about the house and terrorising the family ever since the funeral was over and done with," Oliver paused, waiting for a reaction. No one spoke, so he continued. "Lord Howton knew that, just as I have experienced here tonight, he would not be believed if he told people this. He wanted proof that he could show to the world and remove doubt. He knew it was the only way to find help for his family without being laughed at. He wanted the assistance of the Church and the authorities to rid him of this monster. None would help without evidence of his claims."

Oliver gave a wry smile.

"He asked me to come along and bring my camera equipment. He wanted me to take a picture of the monster. I agreed, well, at the time he requested me he did not specify that the person plaguing him was dead. He merely said that someone was trying to intimidate the family and he wished me to take a picture of the culprit for the police," Oliver shrugged his shoulders. "It was one of the stranger commissions I have had, but I saw no reason not to assist him. Lord Howton explained that the family liked to spend the evenings in the drawing room, and the stranger would always appear at the window to this room.

"I did think it somewhat odd that no one had tried to apprehend the intruder. Aside from Lord Howton and his eldest son, there were enough male servants in the house to capture the man. Lord Howton said the fellow was wily and had vanished when attempts had been made to nab him. He wanted to involve the police, but they had been unwilling to post constables at the estate without proof of the man being a real threat. From what Lord Howton had said, it seemed the man was more of a nuisance than anything else. He didn't seem to be causing harm. I assumed he was a tramp or one of those poor souls who lost their minds in the war and don't know what they are doing.

"I never imagined…"

Oliver had to pause. His face had flushed and his body had tensed. Clara leaned forward and gently took his hand.

"You went to take this photograph tonight?"

"Yes," Oliver said, re-emerging from the dark place that had briefly engulfed him. "I took two cameras up there on tripods and placed them before the window where the figure always appears. They were all ready to take a picture the instant the man came into view. I wasn't hopeful of a good shot unless the man stood still. I feared it would be a blurred image and warned Lord Howton, but he said at least it would be something."

Oliver went to take a sip from his mug of cocoa, but it was empty.

"I'll make you some more," Annie sprang forward at once.

Clara guessed that her mildly superstitious housekeeper was beginning to find this tale too worrying and would be glad to get out of the room for a bit. After Annie had departed, Clara nudged Oliver to resume his story.

"What happened?"

"The evening began pleasantly enough. I dined with the family and we retired to the drawing room to have drinks and play cards. The intruder usually appeared after nine o'clock, so as the time approached I stationed myself by the cameras. I was hardly giving it any thought, the family had been quite close-lipped on the subject. It seemed a taboo thing to talk about."

Oliver shook his head.

"If only I had known…" he winced at the memory. "Just after seven o'clock one of the Howton ladies gave a cry and we all looked up at the window. I glimpsed a figure, but was more concerned with triggering my cameras than taking a good look. I managed to use both cameras before the figure seemed to vanish into thin air.

"It seemed improbable for a man to disappear like that, but I had not really been watching the window and I assumed the camera flashes had spooked the intruder. However, the family seemed extremely shaken. I couldn't fathom it at all. Lord Howton, in particular, had gone white as a sheet. No one offered an explanation for his strange demeanour. I started to remove the slides from the cameras, ready to pack them away and develop them when Richard, Lord Howton's eldest son, sprang from his chair yelling that the man was back. 'This time I will have him!' he shouted at his father and raced for the door, his father yelling at him to stop the whole time. 'Please go with him!' Richard's mother cried at me, and I just started to move without thinking. I put down the glass plates and ran after Richard.

"It was raining and dark. We had no light other than the moon when it appeared from behind the clouds. Richard seemed to know where the man had gone, so I followed him. I don't know how long we ran, but we were fools for going outside in that weather without coats or hats. I suppose neither of us was thinking straight. Richard was determined and we soon lost sight of the main house as we ran further into the park. Then we came to this square stone structure placed out in the open, it was the oddest thing, and Richard came to a halt right beside it as if he had been running to this place all along.

"I came up beside him. 'What is this?' I asked. Richard gave this unpleasant laugh. We were both out of breath and I rested my hand on the stone. 'This,' Richard smiled at me, 'is the mausoleum built for my uncle Harvey.'

"I pulled my hand away at once and looked at the structure and realised it was indeed a stone mausoleum, with carved pillars and an arched roof. 'Why here?' I asked, the building being randomly placed in the middle of the grounds, nowhere near a path or trees which might explain the choice. 'It was uncle Harvey's wishes,' Richard explained. 'He insisted. Even wanted it built during his lifetime so he could make sure it was exactly as he liked. My father felt unable to deny him.'"

Oliver pulled a face.

"You have never seen a stranger building. I think I can call it ugly, it was monstrous, a mishmash of styles. Even though I could only see glimpses of it in the dark, I knew it was hideous. 'Why did you come here?' I asked Richard, because I was sure he had made his way to the mausoleum on purpose. He pulled an awful smile. 'This is where he comes from,' he said. 'He rises from his tomb each night and stalks my family.' I was confused. 'Has a tramp invaded the mausoleum?' I asked. 'Nothing so normal,' Richard grimaced. 'The man you saw at the window tonight and took a picture of is my uncle risen from the dead.'

"I was as stunned and disbelieving as you, Clara. I almost laughed aloud, thinking that Richard was joking, but the look on his face told me he was deadly serious. I found myself hesitating. 'No one believes us,' Richard scowled. 'It's impossible, isn't it? But you took photographs tonight of a dead man. They will prove our claim.' 'The man at the window was your late uncle?' I asked in astonishment. 'Yes,' Richard answered. 'But he has eluded me once again. He has a knack for disappearing.'

"Richard started to move back from the mausoleum and I went to follow, only too glad to be returning to the house and the warmth of the fire. I was not convinced by the story I had been told. It was too impossible. I thought the family were victims of a cruel hoax. It was only as we turned away that I sensed someone behind us. I turned my head, even though I didn't want to, but I could not bear to ignore the sensation. And then I saw him, perched on top of the mausoleum. A man, crouching and watching us."

Oliver shook his head again. He was still struggling with what he had seen. He paused to look around him at the faces of his friends.

"What did I see?" he asked them without expecting an answer. "I was as disbelieving as you are right now. Then that man jumped from the top of the mausoleum and walked right up to me. Only, he didn't quite walk, he more shuffled and stumbled as if his limbs were not entirely connected to his body. And then he was before me and I could see this… this monster of a man!"

Oliver had started to shake again, this time from fear.

"There was nothing alive about him. I could smell his rotting flesh. I could see the maggots falling off him! I seemed frozen, unable to move, even when the fiend raised a knife in his hand I couldn't budge!"

"Wait," Clara said sharply. "He had a knife? He was trying to kill you?"

"I suppose," Oliver frowned. "Maybe he just wanted to scare me, and he certainly did that! Fortunately, Richard grabbed my arm and he yelled to run. He had lost his nerve too and we both fled and in the dark we became separated. I panicked and when I realised I was nearer to the road than to the house I raced in that direction and my one thought was to get back to Brighton and to find you Clara. I knew you would be able to put this all into perspective for me."

"That is a long walk from the Howton estate," O'Harris whistled through his teeth.

"Once I started, I couldn't stop. I still feel as though that monster is right behind me breathing on my neck!" Oliver shuddered. "You cannot imagine what I saw. The evil of that creature was like a powerful force radiating off it!"

"Men don't come back from the dead," Tommy said grimly. "I should know. I saw enough dead men in the war."

"I don't say it is common," Oliver replied to him. "But I cannot deny what I saw. That man was a corpse and yet he was walking about!"

"It has been a long night," Clara told him sympathetically. "Everything seems worse in the dark and in the midst of a rain storm. I agree with Tommy that it goes against everything science tells us for a man to rise from the dead."

"I don't expect to convince you, Clara. In a way it was knowing you would be so sceptical that drove me to find you. If anyone can explain what I saw tonight it must be you!"

Oliver fell silent as Annie returned with his fresh cocoa. Clara was relieved that Annie had missed the worst of the revelations. She would not find it so easy to be sceptical. She was convinced that there was more to this world than what met the eye. Annie would be the one to believe that Oliver had had the misfortune of meeting a revived corpse that evening.

"You shall stay here tonight and rest," Clara instructed Oliver, changing the subject. "Tomorrow we can go to the Howton's home and retrieve your cameras and the glass plates. If nothing else, developing the photographs you took will prove someone is stalking the family."

Oliver was now exhausted and had no strength to argue. He just nodded. Annie went into action again, ushering him out of the chair and to the spare bedroom where she had already made up the bed with plenty of extra blankets and another hot water bottle on standby. Clara said nothing as the pair headed up the stairs, only when they were safely out of the way did she glance at her brother and O'Harris.

"Someone is playing a terrible fraud on the Howtons," she declared.

"Trying to scare them out of their minds, by the sounds of it," Tommy nodded. "To do it using the late Harvey Howton's memory is a cruel ploy."

"And probably done for a reason," Clara added. "It is a shame the police are not prepared to take a greater interest."

"It will be due to a shortage of manpower," Tommy shrugged. "They can't spare the men unless it is truly serious."

"Strangers wielding knives and pretending to be dead men seems pretty serious to me," O'Harris pointed out.

"Something very sinister is occurring," Clara agreed. "Though, as yet I don't see the purpose of it all. One thing I am certain of, however, a dead man has not risen from his grave to torment his relatives."

"I suppose we have to ask ourselves the question, why would Harvey Howton want to harm his family? Because it seems plain the family were quick to imagine ill-will from the dead man. Guilty consciences, perhaps?" O'Harris postulated.

"I don't care to speculate until I know more," Clara replied. "And tomorrow will be soon enough for that."

"I think this business could turn quite nasty," Tommy frowned. "There is something about it, something so... evil."

"But not supernatural," Clara pointed out firmly. "No, we shall find out soon enough. Poor Oliver, it was clearly a terrible experience."

"Let's just hope that when he lost Richard Howton, the man made it back to his house safely," Tommy pointed out darkly.

"You don't think...?" Clara shook her head. "No. Let's not go looking for murder just yet."

Chapter Three

Morning brought a return to his senses for Oliver. The pale autumn sunshine streaming through the window seemed to deny the possibility of anything strange and supernatural occurring. There was no room in the stark light of day for talk of the living dead. Oliver looked abashed when he joined Tommy and Clara for breakfast.

"Last night…" he started.

"Was last night," Clara interrupted him. "Don't think on it Oliver, come have some tea and toast."

"I really thought I saw a dead man walking," Oliver said as he sat down, not quite as ready as Clara to give up on the notion. "I would have sworn to it. Did swear to it. Now… now it seems so impossible."

"There are two things I am certain of in all this," Clara told him, putting down her own tea cup. "Firstly, someone attacked you last night, for what end I don't know and whether they would really have used that knife they brandished I can't say, but they attacked you. Second, some sort of terrible mischief is being enacted on the Howtons and I don't think it will simply end with just frightening the living daylights out of them."

Oliver relaxed his shoulders.

"At least I am not completely crazy, there was

someone there last night."

"Absolutely," Clara reassured him. "And I think it very important we find out this person's intentions. So, drink up your tea and we shall go pay a call on Lord Howton. You have to retrieve your cameras, after all."

An hour and a half later, Oliver and Clara were making their way up the driveway of Howton Hall. The parkland looked calm, if rather wet after the night's downpour. The trees were still dripping fat drops of water onto the grass and the ground was patterned with deep puddles.

"Where is this mausoleum?" Clara asked as they walked.

Oliver pointed to her left.

"You won't see it from here, it is just behind that rise in the ground. Who ever heard of someone building such a thing in the middle of a park?"

"People do odd things," Clara shrugged. "Without knowing more about the late Harvey Howton, I wouldn't like to hazard a guess at his motives."

A gardener was raking up leaves next to the path and paused briefly to stare at the new arrivals. To Clara's mind he looked rather surly, as if this was his land and he didn't like people walking on it uninvited. She gave him a nod and a smile, and he quickly turned away. Clara took no more notice, people's servants could be very odd.

At the door of the house they were welcomed in by a butler, who showed them through to the drawing room and asked them to wait while he fetched Lord Howton.

"I am relieved to see you well, Mr Bankes," he remarked as he went to leave the room. "We were very concerned when you did not reappear at the house last night."

He shut the doors and Clara and Oliver were left alone. Clara took the opportunity to survey the room. It was well appointed, facing south and able to catch the smallest amount of sun through tall windows. A terrace ran outside and two sets of the windows opened straight out onto it.

The furniture in the room consisted of large comfy sofas in a striped fabric and several occasional tables, all sitting on a thick pile rug before the fireplace. There was a sizeable drinks cabinet next to an equally grand sideboard and either side of them stood tall house plants in ornate basins. The walls displayed old works of art, mainly hunting scenes or landscapes. There were no portraits of the family in the room, which somewhat surprised Clara. Usually noble families liked to display their ancestors for all to see. There were, however, a series of black and white photographs in silver frames on the mantelpiece. They seemed quite modern and portrayed the current residents of the house. The modest fashion of the pictures, almost easy to overlook, suggested the family were not the sort of people who went in for ostentatious displays.

"That is the late Harvey," Oliver pointed out a picture on the far right.

The man in the image was handsome in a brooding fashion. The sort of gentleman who would be described as moody and difficult. He seemed to scowl out at the photographer and had not bothered to smile for the picture. If ever you could take a dislike to a person just from their photograph, here was the proof.

"He is a lot younger than his brother," Clara noted.

"Their father married twice. Harvey is from the second marriage when the previous Lord Howton was quite elderly. His mother still lives in the house."

"That must make for interesting times," Clara mused. "Why, Harvey looks about the same age as Richard Howton."

"He was."

The voice came from behind them and they both jumped and turned around. In their curiosity about Harvey Howton, they had failed to notice that the drawing room doors had been opened and Lord Howton had joined them.

"I was most relieved to hear from Crawley that you were well Mr Bankes," Lord Howton said, entering the room and closing the doors behind him.

"I apologise for my hasty departure last night. Events overcame me," Oliver flushed a little, still embarrassed by the panic that had come over him. "May I introduce Clara Fitzgerald, an acquaintance who kindly provided me with assistance last night."

Clara held out her hand to Lord Howton, who looked at it with some reserve.

"A modern girl," he muttered, refusing to take his hands from behind his back.

"Clara was kind enough to agree to help me remove my camera equipment from your property. I am sorry for the inconvenience I have caused you," Oliver was mumbling, Clara wanted to nudge him and remind him that he had no reason to feel foolish. He had, after all, been placed in this position by the very man before them.

"Your cameras are quite safe. Crawley removed them to the dining room after the events of last night," Lord Howton was talking to Oliver, but his eyes were firmly on Clara. "Miss Fitzgerald, your name sounds familiar, might we have met before?"

"I do not think so," Clara replied, certain she would have remembered Lord Howton had they met before. "You may have come across my name in the newspapers."

"And why is that?" Lord Howton asked, his curiosity tempered by his natural reserve.

"I am a private detective," Clara elaborated. "I have helped to solve a number of high profile cases that have been reported in the press."

"Oh," Lord Howton seemed to look at her even more sharply. "That is an unusual occupation for a woman."

Clara felt no need to reply to that statement.

"I suppose Mr Bankes has told you something of what occurred here last night?" Lord Howton asked, looking displeased.

"I wouldn't have..." Oliver began, but Clara

interrupted him.

"Oliver was in a state of shock last night, what he said or did not say is hardly relevant. I am not here on business, just as a friend to help him with the camera equipment."

Lord Howton tilted his head, seeming somewhat reassured by her answer.

"Are you good at your profession?" he asked, rather impertinently.

"My clients seem satisfied," Clara responded. "I always have work."

"You solve all manner of mysteries, then?"

"Yes," Clara agreed. "Everything from lost pets to murder. I aim to help my clients in whatever way I can."

Lord Howton paced slowly towards one of the tall house plants and fondled a green leaf. He seemed to be coming to a decision.

"Miss Fitzgerald, terrible things have been happening at my home and the police seem disinterested. It is hard to convince people that you are being plagued by the walking corpse of your deceased brother," he paused, waiting for Clara's response.

She remained mute. She had already heard everything from Oliver and saw no need to act shocked or astonished for the sake of Lord Howton. He seemed to appreciate her calm.

"In truth, I would greatly value an explanation of this strange occurrence," Howton continued. "I am not a normally superstitious man, religious yes, but not inclined towards ghosts and ghoulies. But I can't deny the evidence of my eyes. Out there, at night, walks a dead man and God only knows what his intentions in doing so are."

"Lord Howton, I should state that I do not believe in the supernatural," Clara said carefully. "I believe in there being a rational explanation for everything that occurs on this earth. Whoever is tormenting your family, I am certain of one thing; dead men do not rise from their graves."

"You would not be so sceptical if you had seen the things we have," Lord Howton said with a touch of sadness.

"Maybe so," Clara replied, "In fact, I would like to be here to see things for myself and to learn the secrets behind this rather nasty game that is being played upon you. I might not believe in the supernatural, but I do take this matter seriously, as the police should. Someone is intent on disturbing your family, what their goal in doing so is, I really cannot say. But I can't help but think they have evil in mind."

"Now, on that we can agree," Lord Howton almost smiled, his old and weary face briefly seemed to spark with hope. Here he was, a man in his sixth decade, trying to live a quiet and uneventful life and having all that spoiled by some monster out of a bad novel. It was all too much, he felt it eating away at him.

"This whole affair has left me confused and, I will admit, frightened," Lord Howton continued. "I have felt a fool from the very first, tormented by this creature and yet unable to ask for help for fear that in doing so I will reveal myself to be losing my mind. I am not losing my mind, but I know the sorts of things people who have not seen what I have would say. Asking for help has been nearly impossible, which is why I asked Mr Bankes to take a photograph of the monster."

"That is certainly wise," Clara nodded. "But, anyone with an ounce of intelligence should realise that something sinister is happening here, whether they believe in the supernatural or not. I think there is a rational explanation for everything that has occurred, but that does not take away the fact that someone appears to wish your family ill."

"You are very astute, Miss Fitzgerald," Lord Howton smiled faintly. "It seems fate has brought you to me. I need someone like you to solve this riddle. You seem to be the only other person in Brighton prepared to listen to my story. Even though you are a woman, I would appreciate your help."

Clara did not like his implication, she felt a pang of anger jump inside her. She could turn him down, of course, tell him that as she was a 'woman' she could not possibly take the case. But she wasn't so petty, besides, what better way to prove just what a woman could do then to solve this mystery?

"Are you saying you wish to hire me?" Clara asked.

"I suppose I am," Lord Howton smiled, his grey eyes crinkling into his face as he smiled. "Will you accept?"

"Yes, if we shake on it," Clara offered her hand once again.

Lord Howton hesitated, looking as if her hand might be poisonous to the touch. Then he relented and took it. They shook on the agreement.

"I suppose you will want the full story?" he said.

"Every detail," Clara answered. "But let us start with Harvey Howton, your half-brother. What was he like?"

Lord Howton became sombre, he walked to the mantelpiece and picked up the photograph of his brother. He stared at it for a moment.

"Harvey was troubled," he said at last. "He had his share of demons and was a little too keen on having a drink to keep them at bay. I feared he would die young, he seemed destined for it."

"He lived at the house?"

"Yes. I had no issue with his presence about the place, I might add. We were not close in the sense of brothers, but more like an uncle and nephew. As you noticed earlier, Miss Fitzgerald, Harvey was the same age as my son Richard. They grew up together, went to school together. I always considered Harvey part of the family."

"And what did Harvey think?" Clara asked.

Lord Howton glanced back at the photograph.

"Harvey thought the world owed him something," he said at last. "He got that from his mother. She thought Harvey should have inherited half the estate when my father died. She is not an aristocrat and doesn't seem to grasp that is not the way things work. Harvey was granted a sizeable allowance and could remain in the house for as long as he wished, but he could never inherit the title. It will pass from me to my son and hopefully to his sons. That is how it is."

"But Harvey wanted more?"

Lord Howton shrugged his shoulders.

"Our father died when Harvey was ten. The title went to me, as had always been intended. What more can I say?"

Clara could understand a little better now why Harvey Howton scowled in his photograph. There was nothing worse for souring the soul than bitterness, especially bitterness that is wholly unfounded. As the younger brother Harvey could never inherit the estate, unless Lord Howton's son were to die.

"I heard he had a mausoleum built?" Clara queried.

Lord Howton gave another sigh.

"That horrible thing. It was an obsession of his. He wanted it built in his lifetime, so he could oversee its construction. As for its location, that was controversial, but I conceded because I have always felt a little guilty over Harvey. I feel bad that I am the eldest son," Lord Howton found bitter amusement in this. "He wanted it even nearer to the house, but we were able to settle on its current location. I never imagined it would be used so soon, however."

"What happened to Harvey?" Clara asked.

Lord Howton smiled sadly to himself.

"Life caught up with Harvey," he muttered. "He drowned, in the lake. He swam every day, but on that final day something happened. He was rescued by two of the gardeners, but they dragged him out too late.

"My poor brother, Harvey Howton, drowned. And there was not a thing I could do about it."

Chapter Four

"Were I to hire you to solve my mystery, would you be agreeable Miss Fitzgerald?" Lord Howton asked, escorting his guests as he talked towards the ill-placed mausoleum.

"I would certainly try my best. As long as you do not require me to prove the supernatural, that is."

Lord Howton laughed, but it was with little humour.

"I would much rather you prove otherwise, it would ease my mind considerably. Did you know that the Howtons are supposedly cursed?"

Clara admitted she did not.

"My family can trace its origins back to the Norman period. Back then the original Howton was a knight of distinction who was granted a gift of land for his loyal service to the king. Over the centuries, the Howtons have courted power, not always wisely. Our worst hour came during the English Civil War. As a member of the nobility, it was expected we would side with the king, but my ancestor, Theodore Howton, chose a different path and sided with Cromwell.

"At first this might have appeared a wise decision, after all the Parliamentarians were triumphant and many a loyal nobleman had to flee for the Continent when the king lost his head. The Howtons would appear to have picked the winning side but, as any student of schoolboy history will tell you, the Cromwellian age died with its namesake. Too many powerful people wanted the monarchy restored, and so it was. Suddenly, the Howtons were viewed as traitors.

"Theodore survived the turmoil, losing some of his estates and influence, but at least not his head. However, not all were satisfied with the retribution the Howtons had received. Some of the nobles thought we had, to put it in modern parlance, gotten off lightly. A conspiracy was formed and a small society of Royalists chose to condemn the Howtons for all time using black magic.

"Clearly it was not a secret society, the word spread of what they had done; invoking demons and consulting an aged witch to work their curse. A note was sent to Theodore telling him he was cursed. It is still preserved in the library. Supposedly Theodore laughed at it."

"Sensible man," Clara replied. "He was not going to give in to petty taunts made by his enemies."

"No," Lord Howton agreed carefully. "And many might argue that, considering the fortune and power the Howtons still preside over, the curse was not very successful. But it was meant to strike at something more personal, more private than land and money. It did not seek to remove these things from the Howtons, for if the Howton line died out then there would be no one to suffer under the curse. No, it was meant to be much more cruel. The curse states that no male descendent of the Howton line shall die in his bed, and each will know terrible personal tragedy, so that their days are marred with misery."

"Certainly a very cynical revenge," Clara agreed. "I hope you do not take it too seriously?"

Lord Howton chuckled, amused by Clara's simple scepticism.

"My dear, you come from the standpoint of only just hearing of this silly curse and thinking it all nonsense. I come from a long line of men who have watched the curse unfold upon themselves and those they love. Theodore Howton was the first. Shortly after the Restoration, his beloved daughter stabbed herself with a rose thorn and died of blood poisoning. Theodore, himself, fell from his horse while out hunting and died in a ditch before he was found. Each generation has seen tragedy and no male Howton has died in his bed."

"Do you mean to say that Harvey Howton's death is the work of this curse?" Oliver said in a breathless tone.

Clara cast him a look, but he was not paying attention to her.

"It would seem so," Lord Howton tipped his head, his expression grim. "Miss Fitzgerald looks aghast, I can only say, my dear, that if you lived in this family and knew all the old stories of what has happened in the past, you would not be so stunned."

"I think stories can be twisted to suit a given set of facts," Clara said carefully. "I think most lives are touched by tragedy, depending on how you look at it. And I think many people do not die in their own beds. For instance, I lost both parents in the war during a bombardment. Truly a case of ill luck, neither died in their own bed."

"But you have stated the fault in your own case," Lord Howton said with a satisfied tone. "Many people do not die in their own bed, but not every person. Every male Howton has had the misfortune of dying in strange circumstances, no other family can claim such a thing. Were there even just one or two Howtons who had passed away peacefully in their sleep in their own beds, then I would laugh at this curse. But there is not even that. And the tragedies that have occurred to the family are more than the norm. The things that have occurred to this family were once described by a historian unaware of the curse as 'the most chronic case of appalling bad luck he had ever come across in his research'."

"No Howton man has ever died in his bed?" Clara pressed.

"None," Lord Howton assured her. "Even the late Jonathan Howton, who was bed-ridden the last three years of his life, died outside of his own bed. There was a fire in the house and Jonathan was carried outside to save his life. Unfortunately, it was a terribly cold day, and the shock of events, coupled with the chill temperature brought on a heart attack. He died on the gravel drive, on a couch the servants had brought out for him. Even he could not escape the curse."

"Poor man," Clara said with genuine sympathy. "You must forgive my cynicism, I just find it hard to comprehend anything so... occult."

"On the contrary, your cynicism will be most welcome in this case," Lord Howton smiled. "I need a cynic to see what is real and what is not. I would be delighted if you could find a rational explanation for all this. The Howton curse is bad enough, but it has never taken on such a dramatic form."

They had arrived at the mausoleum. It was a ghastly looking thing. Grecian columns were adorned with winged women from Egyptian mythology, while grinning gargoyles growled from the pediments and arches of the curved roof. The walls were engraved with long passages of script in Arabic, of which Clara could not read a word.

"Peculiar thing, isn't it?" Lord Howton mused. "Ugly as sin. My wife detests it."

"Your brother seems to have been influenced by eastern cultures," Clara ran her hand across the feathers of the wings of the strange Egyptian women. The whole tomb was a hotch-potch and poorly designed at that, but the actual craftsmanship seemed of high quality.

"I don't know what he was influenced by," Lord Howton said with a huff. "He was never a student of Arabic or Ancient Egypt. He was not a learned man in any shape or form, quite the opposite. My wife is convinced he made the thing as hideous as possible, so we would suffer looking upon it each day."

"Did your wife not care for Harvey?" Clara asked.

"They rarely saw eye-to-eye," Lord Howton hefted his shoulders in a shrug. "You have to understand the great age difference between myself and Harvey. My wife and I watched him grow up along with our own children. My wife still perceives him as a naughty schoolboy."

Lord Howton caught himself.

"She did still perceive him," he corrected himself. "I still forget myself sometimes. And with all this... strangeness, I find it hard to consider him gone."

Clara said no more, but rubbed her fingers over the Arabic script which had been highlighted with gold paint. She glanced at Howton.

"What does it say?"

"Knowing my brother, it will either be gibberish or something crude. I don't much care to pay the expense of having it translated."

Clara walked around the mausoleum, assessing its size. It was not huge, but big enough to accommodate one, if not two, individuals if they were laid out side-by-side. It was rectangular in shape, the short ends aligned with the Howton house, the longer sides facing opposite ways across the rolling grounds. The place looked wholly substantial. There were no signs of cracks or secret passages. If a tunnel had been created from the tomb to somewhere else in the estate, it would take some effort to find it. Tracking down the men who worked on the construction might provide some insight into that as a possibility. She returned to the front of the mausoleum.

"What is it made of?" she asked Lord Howton.

"Brick, largely. Just one layer thick, faced with sandstone. It will weather down nicely enough, perhaps, eventually, it will not seem so awful."

Clara tapped a wall and there was a distinctly hollow sound.

"And the entrance?"

"Between the two winged women," Lord Howton explained. "My son says they are harpies, you know, but I don't think the Egyptians had such a thing in their mythology."

He showed Clara the outline of the door, which had been carefully concealed by the cut of the sandstone to avoid it appearing unsightly.

"Before Harvey's death, this side of the tomb was completely open. We had the odd tramp take a liking to sheltering in it during the winter," Lord Howton explained. "After his passing, Harvey was placed inside and the opening was bricked up and the final sandstone slabs put into place. It is still just possible to see where the doorway was."

Clara traced her fingers along the very fine line that showed where the door had been. The workmanship had been extremely precise and she would not have noticed the gap at all had it not been pointed out to her. It seemed unlikely that anyone was somehow opening and closing this entrance every night.

"Might I see up on the roof?"

Clara's request required the finding of a gardener and the borrowing of a ladder. The mausoleum was only just over seven foot in height at its tallest point, but since its occupants did not intend to stand up inside it that hardly mattered. Even so, Clara required a ladder to be able to reach the roof and look over it for potential signs of a hidden entrance. The arched roof, covered smoothly in grey concrete, looked impeccable. Any theory Clara had briefly entertained of Harvey faking his death, emerging from his coffin in the mausoleum and exiting the tomb via a secret door was rapidly becoming implausible. The vault was sealed shut, as far as she could see.

"This was where you came across the man last night?" Clara asked Oliver.

"Yes," Oliver gave a shudder, memories flitting back across his mind. "It was the most horrible sight."

"What do you make of all this so far Miss Fitzgerald?" Lord Howton asked.

Clara was still gazing at the sandstone facing of the tomb.

"So far, I cannot see how a man, living or dead, could be climbing out of his mausoleum night after night, which makes me think this is a red herring to distract us."

"Ghosts hardly need worry about a thing like walls," Lord Howton pointed out.

"Ghosts don't decompose, as far as I am aware," Clara countered. "In any case, all witnesses have suggested that they have encountered a flesh and blood man, not a spectre. No, I think the mausoleum is exactly what you stated, Lord Howton, an eyesore designed to remind you all of Harvey's presence long after he was gone."

Lord Howton sighed to himself.

"I think you ought to meet the rest of the family now. More eyewitnesses to this drama, perhaps their testimony will offer up a solution?" Lord Howton turned away from the mausoleum.

They walked back to the house across the damp grass.

"Does this spectre appear every night?" Clara asked.

"He has not missed a single evening," Lord Howton nodded. "More is the pity."

"And he has not offered a reason for his appearance?"

"Other than to disrupt the family and make us feel as though we are going mad? No. I sometimes think he stands there to make us feel guilty."

"For what?" Clara asked.

"I don't know precisely. For his death, perhaps? Harvey liked to play the misused younger brother, he maintained a tragic air about him which, oddly enough, certain women found hugely attractive. Of course, he had a lot of grievances towards my father, not least that he had failed to make arrangements for the estate to be split between us. Harvey was convinced that before my father died he had promised to change his will to divide the land between us."

"And what do you think?"

Lord Howton twitched his lips into a wry smile.

"My father was a traditionalist, Miss Fitzgerald, he would no more have divided this estate than he would have bestowed it on his favourite gardener. He wanted to see the Howton line and name continue for many generations to come, that would hardly be achieved by splitting the estate in half," Lord Howton paused. "However, he was a mean old goat and he may well have implied to Harvey that the estate would be divided to keep him quiet. He liked an easy life in his final years."

"Harvey would certainly feel betrayed if that was the case," Clara suggested.

"Hardly my fault, Miss Fitzgerald, though Harvey could find a way to twist everything into being my fault," this seemed to amuse Lord Howton. "Harvey knew our father as well as I did. Still, I cannot be held responsible for things that were out of my power to control."

"No, indeed."

They were back at the doors of the drawing room. Clara paused.

"Which window does Harvey always appear at?" she asked.

Lord Howton pointed out the window next to her.

"There," he said. "My daughters are much relieved he has never attempted to appear at the window which opens into the room. The one we left by. The catch on those is loose, you know, it would take no effort to break it."

Lord Howton ushered them back through this set of tall windows, that served as doors to the terrace.

"You will stay for luncheon, Miss Fitzgerald?" Lord Howton enquired.

"Thank you," Clara responded. "I would be delighted."

"Then you may speak with the rest of the family," Lord Howton nodded.

"In the meantime," Clara said. "I would be most intrigued to see what you captured on your photographic plates last night Oliver?"

"Me too," Oliver agreed. "Perhaps that will prove to you, Clara, that the dead are up and walking."

"Perhaps," Clara replied noncommittally.

Chapter Five

The Howton family consisted of Lord Howton, his wife, his three children and his stepmother. When they all came together for luncheon, it was apparent this was not a family who enjoyed each other's company. There were grim faces all around and Clara did not think that was just because of the 'resurrection' of Harvey Howton. The glances that the members of the Howton clan gave each other as they entered and sat down, suggested they would much rather not be all together in the same room.

The luncheon had been organised at the instigation of Lord Howton. He was the patriarch of the family and what he said was what was done, no arguments or excuses. Lord Howton was old-fashioned and conservative. He believed that a lord should hold himself to a higher standard than the rest of society. He was above the rest of the English population because of a fluke of birth, but that did not mean he should squander the privilege he had been given. He had to conduct himself with dignity and grace. He must display only worthy qualities and, when every other man was struck down by fear, or despair, so a lord must be the one to stand apart and to keep his head.

These ideals he instilled in his children forcibly; from

childhood they had been expected to behave perfectly at public occasions, to treat the servants appropriately and respectfully, and to live a life worthy of the great honours and advantages bestowed on them. It was an exacting and exhausting regime. The children, as they grew, bridled at the restraints placed on them by their stoic father. They saw how their contemporaries lived their lives, even the offspring of other lords were allowed more freedoms than them. They saw the world changing, becoming more modern, the young behaving in a fashion their parents would have considered impossible at their age, and all the Howton children could do was watch this new exciting world slip by.

Lord Howton was immoveable on the subject. He was the typical, Victorian stiff-upper-lip, sort of father. His word was gospel, and there was to be no debate once a decision was made. In another man this determination to control his children and keep them to some out-of-date set of rules and preconceptions would appear pompous. Not so in Lord Howton. Clara found him quietly dignified and stern not out of unkindness, but because he felt the Howton title required him and his children to rise above the rest of the world and to hold themselves to greater account. He felt it as both privilege and burden, not something to be cast off lightly, or to be besmirched by carefree antics, as he witnessed among his fellow lords' children. It was rare to see a holder of such an ancient title still gracious about the honour.

Of course, all this great wealth of patriotic and constricting emotion fell most heavily on Richard, Lord Howton's eldest son. Richard was twenty-three, a handsome, slightly aloof, bachelor, who carried himself with a certain degree of arrogance – but then Clara was not seeing him at his most relaxed, he was on edge around her and his family. Richard was 'heir to the throne', so to speak. The idea both delighted and irritated him. There would be changes when he took over the title, something that his father realised and feared. Lord

Howton, therefore, did everything in his power to mould his son into his own form, and had decided to live for as long as was humanly possible, in the hopes that age would dim Richard's rebelliousness.

Richard had a worldly air, as Clara learned over lunch, this came from his time served in the Great War. Richard, as the son of a lord, had been granted the rank of captain at the tender age of 19. No prior military experience was considered necessary, he was heir to a title and thus he was naturally officer material. Richard had served through the last two gory years of the war. He had seen enough blood and mud to last a hundred men's lifetimes. He had come back home hardened and scarred in ways no doctor or surgeon could heal.

Richard Howton seemed the last person likely to believe in corpses rising from the grave, and yet he was as convinced as his father that his uncle Harvey was not resting easy in his tomb.

"I've seen things, Miss Fitzgerald," he explained to Clara, "men who should be dead who still live. There were parts of the trenches in France you never went alone for fear of what, or rather who, you might meet. I'll never simply dismiss such strange things out of hand, not after that."

Richard was as convinced as his father. His sisters were another story. Genevieve Howton was older than her brother. Her slender features belied an iron will and a strong constitution. Genevieve was a countrywoman through and through; she went out shooting and was quietly considered the best shot in the neighbourhood. She rode with the local hunt and was a renowned fisherwoman. There was a stuffed carp of enormous proportions mounted on the wall of the billiards room which Genevieve had caught with her own fair hands.

Genevieve loved dogs and horses, and also pigs, of which she had three named Bubble, Squeak and Bacon. They were pets who she had taught a variety of amusing tricks and they could be routinely found wandering the house with the dogs, Genevieve proudly stating that they were better house-trained than most small children.

This passion for the outdoors contrasted with a complete disgust for the thought of a domesticated existence. Genevieve had revolted against all her parents' plans to marry her off to some eligible bachelor. Now, at the age of twenty-six, she was rapidly becoming too old for the marriage market (suitable candidates largely looking for youth over substance) and this suited her just fine. Genevieve was confident, vivacious and a great talker. She had soon informed Clara of her own views on the 'living corpse'.

"It's all rot, you know. Someone dressing up as poor uncle Harvey to give us a fright. It is a horrible thing, quite ghastly. If father would allow I would go out with my shotgun and wing the fellow, then we would see what this 'corpse' was made of!"

Lord Howton point-blank refused this request of his daughter's. No Howton girl was going to race outside after the supernatural, with or without a shotgun. This, he made it plain, was men's business and the women were to stay inside.

Genevieve rolled her eyes at all this, but her sister, Diana, was more amenable to the suggestion. She did believe in ghosts and, as she told Clara, she thought the 'thing' tormenting the family meant them all harm, and she deemed it wiser to stay inside.

Diana was seventeen, a slightly naïve, innocent creature who had been shielded by her family from most of the ills of the world. She had been a sickly child, unexpected to live long, but had blossomed into a beautiful, if somewhat delicate, young woman. She was shy compared to her siblings, and prone to ducking her head if anyone asked her a question directly. Diana was rather an unknown quantity, as she kept her thoughts to herself and was difficult to draw on any subject into a definite opinion. Next to her two older siblings she was over-shadowed. She said very little during lunch and offered no insights into the drama affecting the family.

Diana's reticence was not helped by her mother's constant interruptions and attempts to talk for her when Diana was addressed directly. It seemed a habit on the part of Lady Howton, rather than an effort to prevent her daughter from speaking. Diana's shyness clearly irritated her mother, who, lacking patience for the slow, thoughtful way her daughter answered any question, had taken to answering for her.

Lady Howton was much like her daughter Genevieve; strong, determined, resilient. She could stand up before a room of working class men and address them on any subject without any hesitation. If she was heckled, she heckled back, if someone was rude to her, she would swear at them like a trooper and (on one memorable occasion) had knocked a man's lights out who had drunkenly insinuated her husband had a mistress.

Despite this force of character, Lady Howton was more inclined to her husband's way of thinking when it came to the late Harvey Howton.

"Harvey was a great traveller, he went all over the world. Well, he could have picked up a trick or two from somewhere," Lady Howton told Clara. "He always resented being the younger brother. I believe he found some sort of spell in one of those foreign places he visited, a spell that would resurrect him after death to enact revenge upon us."

"He could not have known he was to drown, though?" Clara pointed out carefully.

"I don't say he expected to die young, the spell would have acted at any time in his life. He was just the sort to want to carry on being a nuisance after his death. You know, he once told me during the war that if he were to die on the battlefield, he would most certainly come back and haunt us!"

It was plain Lady Howton had had no time for Harvey, despite him effectively growing up with her son. She saw him as a nuisance, best ignored. She held the same opinion now he was dead.

"Ignore him, he will go away," was her final word on the matter.

That only left Angelica Howton, the previous Lord Howton's second wife and mother to Harvey. She had sat and listened to the rest of the family's opinions of her son in silence, her eyes cast down at her plate and her face giving away nothing of her emotions. Obviously, she had to be upset by what was being said. Her son was being painted as a vindictive rascal. Worse, she was listening to all this talk of his corpse walking, which had to be distressing to any mother. She remained stoical all the same, a habit she had long ago learned was best to safeguard her sanity and position among the Howtons.

Angelica had married the late Lord Howton when he was an old man. She was of an age more suitable for marrying his son, but she had accepted the old man's marriage proposal without hesitation. Angelica did not come from money. She was the daughter of a station master on the Brighton to London line. Lord Howton had, one day, been travelling in the train and become unwell. Falling unconscious, he had been carried from the train at the station supervised by Angelica's father. He was taken into the nearby station master's house, where he was laid on a couch and a doctor summoned.

The verdict was that his heart had temporarily stopped. Fortunately for Angelica his heart had restarted itself. The old boy opened his eyes to see a divine angel nursing him, or so he put it in a letter to a friend. Lord Howton was deemed too delicate to be moved and remained at the house for a week. All that time he was looked after by Angelica and grew besotted with her. When he was well enough to be moved home, he swore to her he would be back. Within a month he was, bending creakily down on one knee and asking for her hand in marriage. Angelica accepted, apparently without hesitation. A cruel observer might have pointed out that it was a canny move on her part; his lordship was old and clearly suffering from heart troubles, how long would Angelica have to suffer him before nature would take its course and she would be left financially secure for life? It was certainly the view Lord Howton's son and his wife took.

But the deal was done. Angelica moved into the great house and, within a year, the unimaginable happened – she gave birth to a son. Harvey had the potential to become the future Lord Howton, should his elder brother fail to produce an heir. There was a time of terribleness, the family was divided by the tension this birth had caused, until the following spring Richard Howton was born, and Harvey was once more cast into a secondary role.

All through their childhood the boys knew their respective places and developed a natural rivalry. They competed in everything, from party games to school exams. When war came, and both men went to serve, there had been an uneasy atmosphere in the house; what if Richard was to die? Harvey would become the next heir to the title once more. The tension between Lady Howton and Angelica became almost unbearable, the slightest hint of disaster for one was jumped upon by the other. As it happened, both boys survived the war, only for Harvey to perish in a completely ordinary and somewhat unfathomable accident.

Whatever reason had driven Angelica to marry Lord Howton – a desire for wealth, security or genuine affection – she could not have foreseen how miserable her life would become. At least while Harvey had been alive she had an ally, someone who was on her side, now she had no one.

Clara felt sorry for her. She looked an outsider. She now saw that most of the unhappiness that had surrounded the luncheon had been due to Angelica's presence. She was hated by the others in a way that seemed unreasonable. But then Clara had not been witness to the many years of turmoil that had led up to this point.

Angelica could not be drawn on the subject of her son's supernatural return, even a direct question was pointedly ignored. Whether she was party to this game, or whether she was just dumb-struck by grief Clara could not say for the moment. It would be better to catch Angelica alone.

The luncheon concluded with no fresh clues to the problem at hand, though Clara felt she now had a fuller understanding of the family and their situation. Everyone was eager to depart the table as soon as they could, Lord Howton held them there a moment longer.

"I have decided to ask Miss Fitzgerald to investigate our problem," he announced. "You will all give her your fullest cooperation. I expect nothing less."

No one answered. As Clara rose from the table, Oliver appeared in the doorway of the room. He had been absent from the meal, excusing himself to develop the photographs he took the previous night. Now he came up to Clara and whispered in her ear.

"I've finished processing the pictures," he said. "You best come look at them. You won't be able to deny all this after you have seen them."

Clara was not so sure about that.

Chapter Six

Oliver had created a makeshift developing room out of a closet in the servants' quarters. The space was small and tight, not really enough room to turn around, and not room for two people. He asked Clara to wait outside while he retrieved the photograph.

"It was still drying," he explained as he reappeared. "The edges are still a little wet."

He presented the picture to Clara, clasping it with a pair of steel tongs from the kitchen. She carefully took the tongs so she could study the photograph closely. Clara moved under the main light in the hall.

The image was grainy, owing to the low light in the drawing room at the time it was taken. The flash had illuminated the darkened room so brightly that the edges of the photo had been lost in a foggy white haze. In the centre, framed by the burned-out sides of the picture, were the tall terrace windows. As Lord Howton had mentioned, they were not the ones that could be opened to act as doors. Clara found that interesting, why was the mysterious Harvey avoiding such an easy means of entry and exit? He could walk into the drawing room, if he chose, and come right up to the family rather than stand somewhat pathetically in the dark outside. Unless that was the whole point; perhaps if Harvey came too close, at least one of the family would see through his disguise? Or Genevieve might try to shoot him, or wrestle him to the ground. In either case, his real 'substance' would be revealed. And if he was an imposter, and the real Harvey truly was dead, then getting too close would risk a high chance of being discovered.

Clara held the photograph at an angle, where the light from the overhead bulb would not glare on it, and drew it closer to her nose. The camera had caught the man at the window well-enough, considering the conditions. Oliver was a good photographer and had judged the powder for the flash correctly to illuminate the figure by the window, even if it meant causing the rest of the room to be dramatically over-lit. Even so, the figure was vague because he was behind glass and the bars of the window seemed to cut his body into sections. There had been a real risk the flash would reflect off the window glass and obliterate the man altogether, so the cameras had been set back. All told, the photograph really only hinted at the person in the dark.

Maybe he was Harvey Howton, or maybe he was someone else playing a cruel trick. Either way, the photograph did not convince Clara that the man was dead.

"Fine proof of an intruder," Clara said as she handed back the picture. "You did well to capture that image at night."

Oliver grinned at her, amused by her compliment.

"You still won't admit this is Harvey Howton back from the dead," he smiled.

"I can't tell who it is from this," Clara replied. "He has hidden himself against the far side of the window, concealing half of his face. I don't suppose he caught wind of you coming?"

"That depends," Oliver said darkly, "if you believe him a live man playing a hoax, or a dead man under some sort of spell."

"I don't go in for spells," Clara almost rolled her eyes, but restrained herself in time. "All that stuff Lady Howton said about Harvey going to exotic places and having a spell cast on him is prime material for a pantomime, but not for real life."

"I must admit that was a little too far-fetched for me as well," Oliver ducked his head as he conceded his own doubts. "However, there are many old legends of things like vampires, or living ghosts."

"All of which, over the course of time, have been scientifically examined and found to be wholly natural in their causes. I recall a story from Ireland where a woman slipped into a coma and was thought dead. She was buried in the family vault and in the night grave robbers attempted to steal the rings off her fingers. In the process she was stirred from her strange slumber and sat up, giving the robbers sufficient fright to put them off their work for good. She then walked home in her burial shroud, convincing any who spotted her that her corpse was walking, and arrived at her front door and rang the bell. Only to scare the butler nearly half-to-death." Clara smiled at the tale. "She lived many years after her 'resurrection' and when she died for the second time, at a happy old age, she did not rise from her grave again."

"Are you suggesting that is the case with Harvey?" Oliver asked slyly. "Is the poor fellow wandering around in a state of delusion?"

"If Harvey was accidentally buried, he would have had to find a way out of his sealed mausoleum," Clara shook her head. "It looks to me to be untouched. Of course, opening it would answer a lot of questions."

"I doubt the family would agree to that!" Oliver laughed at the idea.

"No, probably not at the moment," Clara agreed. "But it will likely come to it, eventually."

Clara glanced about her, looking up and down the corridor.

"This place is enormous," she remarked. "I would like a

tour. There has to be a dozen places a person could hide undetected."

"Or a dead man, assuming the late Harvey is not returning to his tomb every morning," Oliver refused to let go of his supernatural notions.

With a twinkle in her eye Clara replied;

"Let's start with the unused cellars, then."

They found a footman who was prepared to guide them around the servants' quarters. He picked up a torch from the kitchen on the way and took them down, at Clara's request, to the cellars. She was disappointed to find them far less expansive than she had imagined for a large, rambling house. They were also all in use, mainly for storing Lord Howton's decadent collection of wines, but two rooms had been set aside as workshops. The footman explained that the gamekeepers used the space to repair traps and guns, and also to store items such as temporary fencing. There was no room for someone to hide down there.

They next explored the servants' world, passing through kitchens, pantries, bedrooms, parlours and all manner of small, tucked away places that each had a name and a purpose. Here was the preserving room. Here the dairy. Here the boot cupboard. There was no space unused, nowhere for a man to hide. But it did strike Clara that, within such a warren of a place, the potential for a person to move around unseen was highly feasible, as long as they knew the routines of the staff and family. She also noticed how many anonymous servants seemed to dart about. How simple would it be to put on a uniform and 'disappear' among them?

Possibilities were brimming over in Clara's mind, but finding the one that was correct would take a lot more detective work.

Their guide politely departed from them at the door that led from the servants' world to that of the family. He was only permitted to go through that door when summoned by Lord Howton and he was not going to risk his position by slipping through with mere guests. His departure left Clara and Oliver without a guide for their tour of the main house. Clara was frustrated, she did not want to miss anything, which was entirely possible in the sprawling house without help. Together with Oliver she walked through the dividing door and stepped into the great hall of the property.

"I'm quite confused by all those twists and turns we just took," Oliver remarked, scratching at his head. "Jolly glad I am not a servant. I would be lost for days in there."

Clara was looking around the hall, noting a great stag's head glaring down with glassy eyes and stuffed pheasants in display cases. Over the door, which led to the outer hall, a shield and two crossed swords hung proudly.

"What must it be like to grow up in a place like this?" Clara mused to herself, wondering at all the history oozing from the very walls.

"Bloody awful," a small voice spoke from behind her.

Clara spun and for a second could not place where the sound had come from and then she spied someone sitting on the great staircase. The wooden bannisters almost completely obscured the person from view. Clara had to walk to the foot of the stairs to see that the speaker was Diana.

"Is it really so bad?" she asked her.

"Oh, probably not," Diana shrugged her shoulders loosely. "But, there is all this stuff about that belongs to great great auntie what-not or great grandfather so-and-so. You mustn't touch it because it is somehow sacred for being left behind by a dead person. This house collects relics, that's the best I can describe it. Sometimes it feels claustrophobic to be surrounded by the belongings of dead people."

"I can imagine," Clara nodded sympathetically. "The weight of history bearing down on you all the time."

"Exactly," Diana groaned. "You know, if you asked my father he could tell you precisely who shot each of these poor beasts and when. Aren't they ghastly? I hate dead things. I much prefer to look at them when they are alive."

Clara glanced around the hall again and could see Diana's point. From every wall the dead eyes of something turned on you, it wasn't hard to feel that their gazes were accusatory. Clara decided to move away from such a morbid subject.

"I don't suppose you could give us a tour of the house Diana?"

Diana tilted her head.

"Why do you want to look around the house?" she asked.

"Just to get a feel for the place and to maybe give me a clue as to what is happening here," Clara answered.

Diana considered this for a moment.

"All right," she said, rising and indicating that Clara should follow her upstairs.

The tour of the house took nearly two hours; there were a lot of rooms and some roused Clara's curiosity enough that she stopped to look inside. One was the Shell Room, apparently a creation of Elizabeth Howton in the late eighteenth century. Diana wrinkled her nose just at the sight of it. The walls had been decorated with thousands of shells and glass cabinets about the room contained miniature houses and picturesque scenes also made completely from shell. There was something obsessive about it all that drew Clara in.

The second floor housed the family bedrooms, they all had names too – the Blue Room, the King's Room, the Rose Room – Diana waved a hand dismissively at the Print Room which was her private space. The room, as its name suggested, had old prints stuck to the walls. A project by another eighteenth century resident.

"I want to paint it all white," Diana pouted. "Father says I cannot, that the pictures are historic. I think they are bloody awful."

There were a lot of things Diana considered 'bloody awful'; the great chandeliers over the staircase, the paintings on the walls (many incredibly valuable), the faded furniture from another century. Just everything, really. Diana's hatred for her home seemed as much due to the restraints placed upon her while she resided in it by her father, as much as a dislike for old things.

"This was Harvey's room," she stopped abruptly by a door. She had happily swung open every other door she had come across, but outside this one she hesitated. "Harvey was all right, really."

Diana scuffed her foot on the worn rug beneath their feet.

"Shame he went and died," with a sigh she opened the door and revealed a room staged for the return of a living person, not a dead one.

Considering the way the rest of the house was presented as a museum to deceased ancestors, it did not surprise Clara that this room remained just as if Harvey had recently left it. The bedroom contained all his old things, placed ready for use. A scent of soap and a male perfume lingered in the air. A clean shirt still awaited Harvey as it hung on the front of his wardrobe. It was as if at any moment Harvey was expected to waltz back in.

Clara found the room more disturbing than the others that had been left to the memory of late relatives. She retreated back to the corridor and they carried on with the tour, going through the nursery and upper servants' rooms on the third floor, before a brief glance in the attic space. They eventually returned to the great hall and to the eyes of the stags and pheasants.

"You would think in a house as big as this you could at least have a room of your own," Diana sniffed, her eyes wandering to the glassy eyes above her. "No such luck."

Clara was about to say something when there was a sharp series of knocks on the front door.

"At least I shall get out of this place when I marry," Diana was muttering as the butler went to answer it. "I can't think why Genevieve absolutely refuses to take a husband. Seems a fine idea to me."

Clara had one eye on the front door out of curiosity. The butler had opened it to reveal a small woman in a fur coat and hat. She was probably no older than Diana. She had an oval face and a look of grim determination on her features.

"May I help, madam?" the butler asked, though there was a hint of disapproval in his tone towards the inferior creature who had appeared on the doorstep. She looked like a shopkeeper's daughter, not the sort you would expect to call on the Howtons.

"I want to see my husband," the woman demanded loudly, aiming her words as much at Clara and Diana (who she had spotted through the door to the great hall) as to the butler.

"Your husband?" the butler asked in bemusement.

"Yes," the woman said in that same loud tone. "My husband. Harvey Howton. I want to see him at once."

The words spilled out and clearly affected even the stoic nature of the butler. Behind Clara, Diana gave a stifled gasp.

"I never knew…" she mumbled. "He never said."

Mrs Harvey Howton strode into the outer hall, casting her eyes over it with a proprietorial gaze. The butler was still mute from her declaration, trying to think of what to do or say. Mrs Howton turned her fierce eyes on him.

"Well?" she demanded. "Where is he?"

Chapter Seven

The butler, Mr Crawley, had a momentary shudder of uncertainty. The shock of this strange woman on the doorstep of Howton Hall demanding to see the late Harvey Howton had rather upset his usual calm sense of protocol. But the lapse was only brief, for he was, after all, a professional, and had been butlering for longer than the new arrival had been alive.

"If madam would follow me to the guard room, I shall summon his Lordship."

Clara was not about to miss this new development, not while she was on a case. The great hallmark of a private detective is the ability to shove one's nose where it is not wanted. It was apparent that Harvey had not mentioned a wife to any of his family. Diana had gasped when the woman had declared herself and was clearly stunned. The woman's arrival was unexpected, that was for certain. If Harvey had confided his new marital status with anyone, it might have been his mother. Clara had a feeling it was not the sort of thing he would tell his brother.

Clara hurried after the retreating butler and Mrs Howton. Oliver decided not to join them, but Diana only paused for a second before following Clara with a clattering of heels.

The butler deposited the visitor in the guard room, so named because at one time it would have housed a porter and perhaps a guardsman, in the days when the family were caught up in the English Civil War. Now it was barely used and housed the Howtons' large collection of historic armaments. Most had been wielded at some point by a Howton; everything from old swords to flintlock pistols. The newest cabinet housed the Webley service revolvers that Richard and Harvey had been issued in the last war. They sat side-by-side, seeming to suggest a unity between nephew and uncle that had never existed in reality.

Mr Crawley had picked the guard room because it was not one of the personal family rooms, like the drawing room or library. It was the space ordinary guests were deposited when visiting, or rather those guests who were not deemed wealthy or worthy enough to be taken into the main rooms. Mr Crawley clearly felt this was the safest place for the disturbing stranger, at least until his lordship was summoned.

Mrs Howton twirled on the spot and admired the room, whistling through her teeth.

"Damn! Are you ready, or what, for the next war?" she chuckled.

"Madam, the family dearly hopes there will never be another war. These arms are largely antiques. Please feel free to look at them while I fetch his lordship."

Mr Crawley hurried out of the guard room, briefly casting a look at Clara and Diana that suggested he disapproved of their presence. Mrs Howton, however, was ignoring them. Instead she walked about the room and peered into cabinets. She came to the one containing the Webley revolvers and gave a small sigh.

"My Harvey, the hero," she purred to herself.

Diana could take the suspense no longer.

"Who are you?" she demanded, striding toward Mrs Howton.

Mrs Howton pulled herself up straight. She was still a

head shorter than Diana, but she did have presence, a confidence to her that Diana could only hope to muster. Diana was currently being driven on by the wings of indignation, Clara reckoned these would shortly depart before the other girl's cockiness.

"I am Harvey's wife," the girl declared. She fluffed the fur collar of her coat up around her neck, as if this was proof. "Who are you?"

"Uncle Harvey's niece, Diana," Diana responded. "He never mentioned a wife to any of us."

The snide tone she gave this statement was bound to rankle the other girl. Clara discreetly moved forward in the hopes of preventing a disastrous argument. Closer, she could see that Mrs Howton had a hard face, one used to difficult times, but she was pretty. Maybe not so much without the make-up which she had slapped on, but she no doubt made up for any lack of aristocratic beauty with a vivacious and striking personality. She had the look of someone full of energy and capable of whirling any man she wanted up into her world.

Clara, who saw no reason a lord's son should not marry a working-class girl in this day and age, decided it was time to intercede before Diana caused the situation to boil over.

"Clara Fitzgerald," she introduced herself to Mrs Howton. "I didn't catch your first name?"

Mrs Howton turned her feisty gaze on Clara. She was a woman who took no prisoners and she had very little time for others of her sex.

"Elizabeth. But everyone calls me Betty," she said proudly. "Posh name, ain't it? Harvey says so. Name of a queen too."

Diana closed her eyes as if she was about to explode. Clara kept talking.

"I am only a visitor to the family myself. I arrived a little earlier today. Have you come down from London?"

Betty tilted her head.

"How did you guess? I've been working on my accent."

"Not enough," Diana hissed through her teeth.

Clara pretended not to hear her.

"I thought it the most likely place to come through, as the trains are so convenient, and you are carrying a suitcase, so clearly you have come from some distance away."

Betty glanced at the battered suitcase she was holding in her right hand. She was clutching it like it contained the crown jewels.

"You don't miss much," she said. "Yes, I came from London this morning."

"Might I ask what brought on this visit? Or was it pre-arranged?" Clara smiled politely.

"It's not really your business," Betty snapped, her friendliness evaporating.

"I was merely curious, as your arrival is clearly unexpected," Clara paused before adding. "Do you like to read the papers?"

"You ask some damn random questions," Betty snorted. "And no, I don't bother with the news rags."

Clearly tiring of her interrogators, Betty stalked off across the hall to look at a set of swords mounted on the wall. Diana started to follow, but Clara caught her arm and took her to the far corner opposite Betty. The room was large enough that it was possible to hold a quiet conversation without Betty hearing them.

"If she has not read the newspapers, she won't know about her husband's accident," Clara whispered to Diana. "I suspect she has come to the hall because she has not heard from him in a while and she wants to know why. Maybe she even fears he has lost interest in her, you know how it is, out of sight, out of mind."

Diana pouted.

"Harvey had no call to go just marrying anyone," she complained peevishly. "Especially someone so, so..."

"Common?" Clara filled in the blank.

"Yes!" Diana declared, not realising Clara was being sarcastic. "Yes! She is not worthy of being a Howton!"

Clara didn't know whether to laugh at the absurdity of the statement, or to be angry on Betty Howton's behalf. She didn't get a chance to be either as Lord Howton now appeared in the guard room. He spotted the intruder first off, then he caught sight of his daughter and Clara.

"Diana, please leave us," he commanded at once.

"But father…" Diana protested.

"Now, Diana," Lord Howton said firmly.

Diana groaned and sulked as she left the room.

"Miss Fitzgerald…" Lord Howton began.

"I would like to request to remain," Clara said quickly. "I cannot say at the moment whether this affair has a bearing on the mystery you have set me to solve, but I would not think it wise to overlook the possibility."

Lord Howton stared at her for a while, making up his mind. He slowly let out a sigh.

"Very well, Miss Fitzgerald, but I must insist that whatever you learn in this room you keep to yourself. This is a private matter."

"Rest assured, I do not divulge the details of my case to anyone not directly involved. Whatever goes on here will remain secret, if you so wish."

Lord Howton gave a nod of his head, then glanced back over to the late Harvey's wife. Betty was still absorbed in examining swords. Clara got the impression she was deliberately ignoring the arrival of Lord Howton.

"Best we get this over with," Lord Howton declared.

Together they walked over to where Betty stood and Lord Howton coughed politely. Betty turned and took a good look at her brother-in-law.

"Are you Lord Howton?" she asked. "I'm fed up talking to all these random people with their questions."

She gave Clara a sharp look.

"I am Lord Howton," his lordship declared. "And you, so Crawley tells me, are the wife of my half-brother Harvey?"

"I am. Been married over a year now. He bought me this coat for our anniversary," Betty fingered the coat again, it was clearly a mark of pride for her. "Look, where is he? I want to speak to him."

"Might I offer you a seat?" Lord Howton ignored her question and instead pulled out a wooden chair with a hessian seat cushion from the wall. "You must have been on your feet a considerable time."

Betty shuffled her feet. Her shoes were a little muddy from the long walk from the train station to the hall, but they were otherwise immaculately polished. She took the chair offered. Lord Howton then drew out two more for himself and Clara. Once they were all seated, he leaned forward and cleared his throat.

"This is a very awkward situation," he said.

"I know you don't want me here. Harvey said you were all very conservative," Betty folded her arms and glared at Lord Howton.

She obviously had a very clear idea in her mind of what her reception would be like, no doubt enhanced by Harvey's own dislike of his brother.

"You misunderstand me, Mrs Howton. I have never made pretensions as to who my brother should choose to share his life with. He has always been a free man on that regard," Lord Howton protested.

Clara imagined it would be a different story should they be talking about Richard Howton, but Harvey was out of the running for heir to the estate. He could do as he pleased, within reason. Truth be told, if Lord Howton had banned his brother from doing something, they both knew it would only make him more determined to do it.

"That is not why I call this an awkward situation. I assume you have not heard from my brother for a few weeks?" Lord Howton continued.

"He writes every day, normally," Betty answered, starting to look worried. "But he hasn't written for several days. I thought perhaps he had took ill?"

Or lost interest in her, Clara thought to herself. That would be Betty's biggest fear – being forgotten when Harvey went home. As soon as he was out of her clutches, and with their marriage a secret, he could turn his attentions elsewhere if he wished. Clara wondered how much Betty actually trusted her husband?

"Harvey suffered a grave misfortune three weeks ago," Lord Howton was working himself up to the declaration of his brother's death.

Betty interrupted him before he could carry on.

"Has he been badly hurt?" she gasped, pressing a hand to her lips.

Lord Howton closed his eyes for a moment, then pressed on with dogged determination. It was better it was said and done with, rather than beat about the bushes.

"Harvey went for his usual swim in the lake. Something happened. He called out for help, but it arrived too late. I am afraid that Harvey drowned."

Betty jerked upright, the colour draining from her face.

"Impossible," she cried. "After he survived all the war, how could he die just like that?"

Then she burst into despairing tears.

"My poor, poor Harvey."

"I am sorry you were not told sooner, but we had no way of knowing about you," Lord Howton apologised, uncomfortable at being faced by such unabashed emotion. "It was mentioned in the papers."

"Why would I be looking in the papers for news of him?" Betty wailed. "This can't be, it really can't be."

Lord Howton had no reply. He had not explained the half of things. Clara wished she could assist him, but how did one go about breaking the news to a recently bereaved widow that her husband had returned from the dead?

"Has there been a funeral?" Betty asked miserably.

"Yes," Lord Howton could answer that. "Harvey is buried in a mausoleum in the grounds. I can show it to you."

Betty nodded, but did not move. Clara suspected she

was too shaken to rise.

"Perhaps Mrs Howton would benefit from a cup of tea?" Clara suggested, his lordship neglecting this vital resource of comfort.

"Of course, I shall ring for Crawley," Lord Howton seemed relieved by Clara's proposal and rose to order tea. The delay while Crawley was summoned and the direction for tea given allowed them all to compose themselves. Lord Howton returned to his seat.

"There is something else I must tell you about," he said.

Betty was fudging in her coat, looking for a handkerchief. Lord Howton dipped a hand into his own pocket and handed her a clean one. She wiped her eyes, staining the cloth with black mascara, and then blew her nose loudly.

"What else is there?" she said, her cockiness gone. "All my happiness, my future, is just smashed into pieces without Harvey. What have I now?"

Not a lot, Clara mused. Harvey could not have left a will with details of his wife, else Lord Howton and the rest of the family would already know of her existence. It would have been read out shortly after the funeral and Betty's name and status mentioned. Either there had been no will, or Harvey had not written one that included his wife. Of course, she would still receive any monies from his personal estate as his direct heir, unless he had already willed it to someone else.

"What I have to say will sound very peculiar," Lord Howton said uneasily. "It has been very unsettling for the family and will no doubt affect you deeply."

Howton flicked a glance at Clara, but this was his story to tell, not hers.

"I don't see how there can be more. He's dead, ain't he?" Betty almost shrieked at him.

"It's all rather complicated. I don't know how to even say it," Lord Howton was twiddling his thumbs unconsciously. "Ever since Harvey passed away and was buried the house has been disturbed by a presence. It is not the easiest thing to describe and I do not wish to frighten you…"

"Will you please spit it out," Betty snapped. "All this dithering is driving me mad!"

"Very well," Lord Howton became firm. "It is as simple as this. It would appear that your husband has come back from the dead, as a walking corpse."

Betty Howton gave a strange gurgle. Then she fell to the floor in a dead faint.

Chapter Eight

Betty Howton was carried through to the drawing room and deposited on a large blue sofa so she might recover her senses in peace. Lord Howton took Clara to one side the moment his guest was made comfortable.

"It does not shock me Harvey secretly married, but his choice does surprise me," they had wandered back into the great hall, better to speak without Betty overhearing them. "He was callous about it too. No provision for her in his will at all."

"He had made a will then?" Clara asked.

"Oh yes, and everything left to his mother. Not a peep about a wife. As far as I can see, he has not left her a penny."

It certainly looked that way. Unless there was another financial arrangement they didn't know of, it would seem Harvey had left his new wife as impoverished as when he found her. She was perhaps even worse off, having expected to be a wealthy woman and moved on from her old life, she was now unceremoniously cast back into it.

"I don't suppose Harvey thought he was going to die any time soon," Clara said, trying to redeem the man. "He probably meant to get around to changing the will."

"He had over a year, according to the girl," Lord

Howton was less inclined to be sympathetic to his brother. "No, a man must take his responsibilities seriously. That was Harvey's problem, he never sorted out his affairs. Now this poor girl suffers."

Lord Howton looked downcast. As a man who felt his responsibilities deeply it clearly troubled him to imagine Harvey being so careless.

"I'll have to arrange something for her," he added finally. "I shall think on it, but I can't see her brought low by my brother's shoddy actions."

Clara had to smile at Lord Howton's overwhelming sense of honour. Many a lord would have gladly been rid of such a woman and could have cared less about her wellbeing. Not Lord Howton.

"What did you mean about his choice surprising you?" Clara asked.

Lord Howton rubbed at his chin.

"I suppose I always thought Harvey was dismissive of the lower classes," he said, his tone apologetic. "He treated the servants derisively and seemed to have no time for anyone who was not of his station. I could imagine him briefly dallying with a working girl for his own selfish amusement, but committing himself to her takes me aback. It seems the last thing Harvey would do."

"Love is a funny thing," Clara suggested.

"Maybe," Lord Howton was unconvinced. "But Harvey had always made it plain he intended to marry well, using all the weight the family name carried to secure a wealthy bride. He had his eye on a couple of extravagantly rich American heiresses. Right up until his death he was set on the idea, which means he was fully prepared to practice bigamy."

"If the marriage to Betty is genuine," Clara pointed out.

"A sham marriage, you mean? To appease the girl but not to legally bind him?" Lord Howton winced as the full extent of that notion swept over him. "Yes, that is just the sort of underhand thing he would do."

They were distracted from discussing Harvey's motives by footsteps on the stairs behind them. Genevieve and Richard appeared at the top landing and glanced down at them.

"Is it true what Diana says? Harvey had a wife?" Genevieve called down.

"Please do not shout, Genie," Lord Howton sighed. "And yes, it is true."

The siblings clattered down the remainder of the stairs.

"Where is she?" Genevieve asked.

Lord Howton was looking more and more fraught.

"She is resting in the drawing room. She did not know Harvey was dead and explaining to her that he was a troubled soul rising from his grave was rather too much. She fainted."

Genevieve and Richard turned and headed to the drawing room. It seemed prudent to both Clara and Lord Howton to follow them. When they arrived in the drawing room, Betty was sitting upright on the sofa, still a little pale but apparently in no danger of fainting again. Crawley had brought the tea she had been promised to the room and was just finished serving her a cup.

"Thank you, Crawley," Lord Howton nodded to the butler.

Mr Crawley bowed to his lordship and departed the room as solemnly as he had arrived. Betty glanced up at the new arrivals. Defensive, she went on the attack first.

"Who are you?" she demanded of Genevieve and Richard.

"What a question from such a person!" Genevieve declared with a laugh.

"Genie!" her father reprimanded. "Manners!"

Genevieve sighed indignantly, but the scolding had reminded her of herself.

"I am Genevieve. Harvey's older niece. This is my brother Richard."

Richard had been strangely silent throughout this

whole affair. Now he moved forward to stand by his sister.

"Harvey never said he was married," he mumbled. "I hope he treated you well."

"You speak of him like he was a devil!" Betty snapped, annoyed by both the rudeness and sympathy displayed by the siblings in turn. "Harvey was a kind, loving husband! I can't believe he is gone."

Betty's last word tailed off into a wail of misery. She looked around her at the Howtons and Clara, and tears streamed down her face.

"What will become of me?" she asked no one in particular.

"Whilst my brother has left no provision for you, as a Howton I cannot see you destitute, and so, I shall make arrangements for an allowance to be made to you," Lord Howton announced instantly.

"Father!" Richard yelped in astonished outrage.

"She is a Howton," his lordship told his son firmly. "Harvey should have made sure of her future wellbeing himself. Since he did not, it is up to me to rectify affairs."

"Stop talking about me like I ain't here," Betty wept. "I don't want your money. I didn't marry Harvey for his wealth. What do you think I am?"

No one answered that. Lord Howton merely took a pace closer to Betty and dipped his head.

"This is a difficult situation for us all, but don't turn down my offer without thinking it over carefully. You are owed this money, it is not a gift or charity. It is your rightful share of Harvey's part of the estate."

"Rightful share!" Richard huffed, storming off to the far side of the room, where the windows looked out into the grounds. He could not see Harvey's mausoleum from there, as a rise in the land hid it from view, but Clara was convinced he was glaring in his uncle's direction.

"This is all too much to take in," Betty was still weeping. "And then you tell me that my Harvey is risen from his grave and is a walking dead man?"

Betty stared at his lordship incredulously.

"Not all of us believe such twaddle," Genevieve jumped in. "I personally think someone is pretending to be my late uncle risen from his tomb to upset the family."

"Why would anyone do such a thing?" Betty asked in horror.

"There are some nasty beggars about," Genevieve shrugged. "If father would just let me go out with the shotgun one night..."

"No," Lord Howton told her firmly. "We have no way of knowing what sort of creature that man is who appears at the window."

"He is no 'creature'," Genevieve groaned. "He is just a man."

"That is your view and I have my own on the subject," Lord Howton persisted. "I am sorry Mrs Howton that you have been dragged into this matter before it could be resolved."

"Can you call me Betty," Betty said. "Everyone calls me Betty. I can't get my head around being called Mrs Howton."

Genevieve pulled a face at this declaration, as if it explained everything she had been puttering about. Lord Howton merely nodded.

"Betty, it is. Now, you will stay here until we can organise things? You have yet to meet your mother-in-law."

Betty's face became stricken with horror by the suggestion. It was slowly dawning on her how difficult her integration into the family was going to be without Harvey for support. Having seen the reactions of his nephew and nieces, she could only wonder at what his mother would make of her presence.

"You might meet your husband yet," Genevieve said darkly.

Her father scowled at her and she stalked off to join her brother.

"I shall have a room prepared for you," Lord Howton

continued. "We dine at seven usually, so you have several hours as yet to rest and recuperate. I understand this has been a terrible shock."

"That hardly sums it up," Betty shook her head. "I came here thinking Harvey was ill, or maybe he had grown tired of me, or forgetful. I'm not daft, I knew what might happen when he was no longer with me. I never thought to find him dead. And now all this 'not being dead' stuff too."

"If you remain tonight, you will see for yourself what I mean," Lord Howton continued. "That goes for you too, Miss Fitzgerald."

Clara had hoped for an invitation. She wanted to see for herself this man who appeared at the windows and pretended to be a reanimated corpse.

"I don't know if I could see my Harvey like that," Betty shuddered.

"Then you need not, but at least do stay here for the time being," Lord Howton insisted.

Betty finally conceded.

"All right, I guess I ought to. I want to see Harvey's grave, anyway."

Lord Howton promised that she would, once she was sufficiently recovered from the shock. Then he said he would leave her in peace and see that Crawley had a room prepared. He ushered Richard and Genevieve from the room, leaving Clara behind. She waited until they were all gone, then went towards the fireplace and sat down on a sofa near Betty.

Betty watched her suspiciously, but for the moment Clara said nothing. She was being patient.

"Are you a family friend?" Betty broke the silence at last, unable to resist speaking.

Clara smiled as she looked over.

"Not really. I am a private detective. I have been asked to solve the mystery of this man who keeps appearing at the drawing room windows."

Betty gave another shudder and looked over her

shoulder as if the man might be stood there already.

"Do you think it is my husband?" she asked Clara.

"I don't know," Clara admitted. "However, whoever stands by that window, I think they are very much alive."

Betty seemed relieved to hear this, though did not grasp at once the implication that that might mean her husband was alive.

"How did you meet Harvey?" Clara asked her. "You seem to have a very different opinion of him to the rest of the family."

Betty gave a sad smile.

"I was a waitress in a nightclub where Harvey liked to go. I used to go around with a big tray of cigarettes sometimes. We got talking once, it just happened so naturally. Next thing he asked me to go to a dance with him," Betty became thoughtful. "We went out a while, maybe six months. Then he asked me to marry him, but it had to be a secret because his family would never understand. I knew by then who he was and who his family were. I understood the need for secrecy."

"Where did you marry?" Clara asked.

"St Martin's church. It was a proper wedding, we had witnesses and everything."

That scuppered Clara's theory that the marriage had been a sham.

"Did Harvey always intend to keep it a secret, your marriage?" Clara wondered.

"I guess," Betty shrugged, she had not looked that far forward or considered the complications of such a long-term secret. "He was a good man."

Clara felt that a 'good man' would have tried harder to find a way to get his family to accept his plans and his wife, and would not have carried on courting American heiresses.

"You loved him a lot," Clara noted. "He was a lucky man."

Betty sniffed as fresh tears blossomed in her eyes.

"Do you think? I know I am common and I ain't a

lord's daughter or anything, but I am a decent girl. I went to my wedding untouched, I told Harvey that. In fact, I refused to let even him have his way with me until we were wed," Betty said this with an air of pride.

Clara thought she was an honest girl who had been badly treated by life. Harvey owed her a lot more than he had ever given her. A fur coat was no compensation for the lack of a secure future.

"Why do the family dislike him so much?" Betty now questioned Clara.

Clara was uncertain how to answer. She had only just stumbled into this complicated family herself and did not have a full understanding of them as yet.

"I think it is partly because of the late Lord Howton's unexpected second marriage and the anger that caused. My impression is that he was perceived to be betraying his first wife's memory. There was also concern that his new wife was a fortune hunter," Clara was careful over her words, knowing that Betty herself might be considered a fortune hunter. "I can only say that if that was the case, Harvey's mother has paid a heavy emotional price that must surely outweigh the inheritance she received from her late husband.

"The other part is that Harvey was a potential rival heir, both to the current Lord Howton and to Richard. This tension only rose during the war when both Howton boys were serving. If Richard had been killed, Harvey would have been the next heir. Harvey was not so much resented for himself, but for the way he had come into the family."

Betty seemed to understand this.

"What do you think Harvey's mother will make of me?" she turned big, worried eyes on Clara.

"That is a good question," Clara admitted. "I'm afraid I don't know the woman well enough to be able to say."

Though, silently inside her mind, Clara feared Angelica would not be pleased. Clara imagined her wanting her son to marry well and to someone who's family could boast financial stability. An American heiress would suit her, she might even be able to leave Howton Hall and live with her son. She could not possibly do that with Betty as her daughter-in-law.

Betty fell quiet, much of her bravado had been blown away by the devastating news of Harvey's loss. Now she looked her age, and she also looked very scared. Clara felt for her and wished she could do more to comfort her, but what words could she say to make this thing better? There were none. And the mystery of the grave walker was only going to make matters worse. The sooner Clara solved that problem, the better.

Chapter Nine

Evening drew around again. Clara had spent the intervening hours making arrangements for her 'ghost' vigil. She had sent a message home to let Annie and Tommy know she would not be back that night, and she had helped Oliver put up his cameras in a position that would make it possible to get a better picture of the man at the window. This involved placing one camera outside, hidden in a tall shrub where it would not be readily seen in the dark. The operation was done in the strictest secrecy, even the family were not informed.

"I still can't fathom why we are not telling anyone about this," Oliver puttered as they struggled to push the camera's tripod into the branches.

"Harvey Howton, or his imposter, is most likely receiving help from someone within the household," Clara explained. "That would be how the man at the window knew your cameras were there and stayed hidden at the edge. Even if I am wrong, I think it prudent to avoid people knowing what we are up to. Whatever is going on, I can't help but feel it is too complicated to be the work of one person alone."

"Unless Harvey really is risen from the dead," Oliver pointed out stubbornly.

Clara resisted sighing aloud.

"You will be able to run a wire through the drawing room doors so you can activate this remotely?" she asked.

"I should be able to fit it through the keyhole and keep it hidden until the time is ready. I'll probably only get the man's profile, though."

"A profile is a start. This close, such a picture will surely enable us to recognise whoever is calling on the family," Clara gave the camera an affectionate pat. "I'll have this mystery unravelled before you know it!"

"Does it never worry you that there might be more to this world than meets the eye?" Oliver asked her as they walked back inside.

Clara gave the question due thought.

"I have reached the conclusion, through experience, that nearly every mystery has its solution if you know where to look, and that includes the supernatural ones too."

"Nearly every mystery?" Oliver picked up on her phraseology.

Clara simply smiled.

"It would be conceited arrogance to state otherwise. There are some mysteries that defy the greatest minds. I only hope to never come across one of those myself."

They went their separate ways to prepare for dinner. Clara had sent a message home, via a footman, to explain she was staying at the hall and would need Annie to select a suitable evening outfit for her and have the footman bring it back. She now went to the spare room she had been placed in and changed from her day clothes to her evening attire.

Clara did not have the currently fashionable waif-like appearance, she was more Victorian in her proportions, with suitable curves. However, in a black dress with silver detail and a long string of pearls, she looked quite attractive and felt satisfied with herself. She combed her hair as she took in the room she had been offered.

Like all the rooms in the house it was a relic from the

past, this time from the late seventeenth century, when the hall was extended. In latter years the hall had suffered a devastating fire that had destroyed much of the earlier architecture, but this room was a survivor. It was called the Prince's Room, because the family legends held that one of the Georges, before ascending the throne, had stayed in this room. No one could quite remember which one, or what the room was called before that. Everything was panelled, even the door to the adjoining bathroom looked like part of the oak panel walls. Clara found the room oppressive, but it was only a temporary living quarters and she doubted she was going to be doing much sleeping in it anyway.

She still had a couple of hours before she was required for dinner. Clara decided to carry on with her investigating. She wanted to take a better look at Harvey's bedroom, this time without an escort.

The house was something of a warren, but the uniquely named rooms acted as landmarks, of a sort, and Clara was able to navigate by them. She was careful to avoid the family, even though she heard their voices coming from rooms she passed, once or twice. She didn't want anyone guiding her or trying to prevent her from examining Harvey's room. If someone in the household was helping the stranger in the park – and she was convinced someone inside the house was – then she did not want that person interfering with her investigation too. And as she did not currently know who that person might be, she felt it best to avoid everyone.

Harvey's room was unlocked – why would it be otherwise? Clara slipped inside and shut the door behind her. Now she had the room to herself and any clues it might reveal.

Harvey Howton had been a typical young man from a wealthy family. His room revealed a love for sport; Clara found two tennis rackets and a cricket bat, all deposited rather carelessly, propped up corners or by a chest of drawers. There were also several cricket balls perched on the window sill. Clara picked one up and found it had been carefully written on. According to the faded ink, this particular ball had been used to score the winning over for Harvey's school team in 1912. The other balls were similarly inscribed. Harvey was clearly keen to commemorate his sporting achievements.

On a set of shelves by the window there were a couple of trophies and a perpetual shield from Harvey's school for the best sportsman of the year. The shield was awarded to one student annually. From the gaps on the shield it looked as though there was room for several more names, but Harvey had kept it rather than handing it back at the end of the year to be awarded to the next lad. Probably the family paid for a new one. Harvey seemed to have a great desire to keep trophies of his successes. Was this a sign of his feelings of inferiority when compared to his older brother?

Clara turned her attention to the many cupboards and drawers in the room, hoping one contained a secret or clue that would reveal what Harvey was about. Unsurprisingly, most contained clothes. She searched through pockets on his jackets and trousers in his wardrobe, but found them empty. The drawers contained socks or underwear, one was full of carefully arranged ties.

The room was beginning to feel like a stage set, something that had been prepared by another hand. Clara feared someone had been here before her, someone who had seen fit to remove anything that might hint at what Harvey was thinking or feeling before his accident. Her last hope was the upright writing bureau that sat against the wall at the foot of the bed. Clara pulled down the front and was confronted with the usual array of small drawers, alcoves and racks these things contained. Pale blue writing paper was stacked upright in a slot set aside for the purpose. Clara pulled a sheet out and saw that it was headed with Howton Hall's address and, more significantly, with Harvey's own name. It was a surprising thing to find in the writing desk of a lord's younger son. Normally such conceits were the preserve of the titled member of the family. Harvey seemed unable to concede anything to his older brother, he resented everything.

There were envelopes to match the stationary, a drawer full of pens, and another full of spare nibs. One contained a glass inkwell full of black Indian ink. Another was specially designed to perfectly house the blotter that came with the desk. Clara moved on from the middle drawers which seemed only to contain the paraphernalia for writing, to the larger outer drawers. These were arranged either side of the bureau, with the smaller equipment drawers and paper rack set in the middle. The outer drawers were large enough to contain flat sheets of paper, perhaps even a small notebook. Clara went through them systematically.

She found letters, mostly from the current year – 1921 – but some were older and had clearly been kept for sentimental reasons. Harvey presumably stored the rest of his older correspondence elsewhere, there would not be room for it all in the bureau. The oldest letter was dated 1907. Clara quickly did some calculations in her head and realised Harvey would have been nine or ten when he received this letter. It had been sent to him by his father just before Christmas. Harvey was in his first year at boarding school and would have been counting the days to the holidays and a chance to get home. This letter must have therefore come as a shock; Lord Howton was gravely ill and had been forced to take to his bed. He was writing to his son to let him know he was alright and would be back on his feet by Christmas Eve, in time to greet his youngest son on the doorstep of the hall. The letter was full of promises of plum pudding and a fat goose for Christmas dinner. The way the letter was rumpled and stained at the edges, suggested it had been read and re-read a great number of times. Underneath it was a letter with black edges. Clara had a sense of foreboding about this second letter as she took it out to read. It was dated two days after the previous letter, and the black edges plainly indicated it was sent from a house in mourning. Clara jumped to the signature first and saw that this letter had been written by Angelica Howton.

Angelica's writing was scrawled and taxing to read, but her words were plain. Lord Howton had died, it would be best if Harvey stayed on at school as the house was preparing for a funeral. There was to be no plum pudding and plump goose in the family dining room that year.

The significance of the two letters was not lost on Clara. One was the very last letter Harvey received from his father and the second was the one that must have brought his boyhood world crashing down about his ears. No child can confront the death of an immediate family member and remain the same after. Harvey had kept these letters near to him, on top of the piles of his more recent correspondence. He would have seen them and been reminded of their contents every time he went to write a letter. It seemed this one event had overshadowed the rest of Harvey's life.

Clara put the letters back carefully. Would anyone come for them? Or would this room and these letters become another museum set-piece within the great house? Would a future Howton find him or herself sharing this room with the memories of Harvey?

Clara started going through Harvey's more recent correspondence. His letters were mainly to friends, though some were to distant relatives. The replies gave more evidence of Harvey's love for sport. He was arranging informal cricket matches right up until his death. If Harvey had planned his passing, faking it so he could play some ghoulish prank on his family, he had certainly not revealed this in his letters. Clara found one absence interesting; there was not a single letter from Betty. The obvious answer, the one the family would happily believe, was that Betty could not write. But Clara doubted that. Children from all backgrounds had to go to school these days. Betty would have learned her letters and, though she might not be a great writer, she would most certainly be able to compose a letter.

Either Betty did not write to Harvey, presumably at his behest, or he had destroyed her letters to him. The omission suggested Harvey was keen to keep Betty's existence secret, he had even gone so far as to avoid having letters in his bureau from her. Did he think someone might search his bureau? Or did he fear that letters arriving in an unknown but feminine hand would attract the attention of his relatives?

Clara had searched all the drawers on the left of the bureau, now she turned her attention to the right. The drawers here were also filled with letters, but she now realised there was a pattern. The drawers contained the correspondence from one individual or set of individuals. Occasionally there was over-spill when the number of letters from a given person no longer fitted into a single drawer and had to be moved into the next drawer, but the system was there. Drawers on the left contained personal correspondence, drawers on the right contained important correspondence. Clara found letters and bills in these drawers, the occupations of the senders were another window into Harvey's life. Here was one from his dentist, another from his doctor (Harvey was in rude health, the doctor confirmed), here was one from his tailor accompanied by a bill. This one was from a jeweller (Betty's wedding ring perhaps?), another was from the garage that serviced Harvey's car. But the letters that caught Clara's attention were those from his solicitor.

These letters had been written in the last few weeks before Harvey had drowned, and they were all about Harvey's intention to change his will. The letters confirmed appointments and the final one, dated just a few days before the accident, implied that a new will had been drawn up and was ready for Harvey to sign. There was no letter to state whether that had happened or not, but Clara could find that out from the solicitor. It raised one unhappy thought; presuming the will that had been read out was this new one, why had Harvey not included his wife in it? Even in death was he determined to keep her an absolute secret?

It seemed a callous thing to do. Leaving her nothing, just so his family would not know of her. But that seemed to be exactly what Harvey had done.

Clara put the letters back and pulled out the final drawer on the desk. This one did not contain letters but a red leather-bound book. Clara removed it and saw she was looking at a diary. It bore no date on the cover, inside the pages were hand-dated and ran through a number of years. Harvey was not a regular diarist, he filled in pages as and when he thought of it or had the time. There were, however, several entries from the weeks before he went for his swim in the lake. Here, after all, might be a clue. But Clara had no time to read it, for the clock in the hall was chiming a quarter to seven. She would just have time to take this find back to her room before she would be expected for dinner.

Clara closed the diary. She would have to wait until later to find out the secrets it contained and whether they had any bearing on her latest case.

Chapter Ten

If Clara had supposed the Howtons had looked glum at luncheon, they looked even more sullen at dinner. Angelica Howton, in particular, had a look on her face that suggested her world had disintegrated about her. She had been introduced to Betty that afternoon, a private interview away from the rest of the family. Clearly it had not been a happy occasion.

As for Betty Howton, she looked equally miserable. Having arrived at the hall in a state of righteous fury and determined to confront the husband she had thought had abandoned her, she had instead found him dead and herself facing hostility from most of his remaining family members. She had red eyes from crying and looked utterly devastated by the whole affair. Clara carefully placed herself beside her and gave her a friendly smile, hoping she would understand that at least one person here would support her.

They entered the dining room for dinner. The Howtons were old-fashioned in their ways, and while many noble families had dispensed with lengthy dinners and the large number of servants to cook and serve them, Lord Howton had not. The table shone beneath a candle-lit chandelier. There were no electric or gas lights in this room for a reason; Lord Howton felt dining by candlelight was the only way to behave. In winter fires might be lit in the large hearths that faced each other across the rooms, but dinner was always illuminated solely by the candles overhead.

The room had a timeless feel; constructed after the fire that had stripped the hall, it was Georgian in style and much of the furniture was from the same period. The table could seat twenty-two (including the chairs at the head and foot) and was of a well-polished mahogany. The chairs were a little worn from decades of use, but to replace the upholstery would be to remove a part of the family – this was the very chair uncle Rothsburgh used to sit in, this the very fabric his backside rubbed upon, and so on – and was therefore forbidden until the seat was practically beyond use. The silverware and plates were of similar great age and there was a feeling of being about to sit down in a little piece of the past. You could almost imagine some stately Howton ancestor, in white powdered wig and breeches, wandering into the dining room and being quite at home.

Clara found all this homage to the long dead somewhat disturbing. It seemed to be the overriding power in the household, an obsession that was stifling the living and making the hall less of a home and more of a museum. Or mausoleum. How had a stationmaster's daughter fitted into this historic stage set? Not very well, she imagined. Angelica was an outsider, much like Betty. What a pity the two seemed to have failed to realise this.

Clara had been sat next to Oliver, near the foot of the table and away from the top seat where Lord Howton presided, flanked on either side by his wife and son respectively. The younger siblings were next, facing each other, and then came Betty sitting opposite her mother-in-law. Clara and Oliver were consigned to seats beside them. The seating arrangement probably followed some sort of old-time protocol, but Clara was mildly annoyed to have been placed so far down, in fact, as the last person sitting on the left side of the table, she was the furthest away of all of them, and felt this was a reflection of the importance (or lack of it), that Lord Howton placed upon her presence.

No one seemed inclined to speak as the meal began. Clara had hoped to listen in on the conversation of the family, but as no one was uttering a word that was impossible. She also felt uncomfortable trying to start a conversation herself. She had to confine herself to quietly eating her soup.

"I can't bear it!" Genevieve declared as the soup tureen was removed from the table to be replaced by a whole poached salmon.

"I thought you liked fish, dear?" her mother said mildly.

"The silence, I can't bear the silence!" Genevieve expanded. "Why are we acting so ridiculously because it turns out uncle Harvey found himself a wife? What difference does it make?"

No one felt like pointing out the significant difference it made to her; for instance, it meant that any marriage plans Angelica might have had for her son went out the window and, because of Lord Howton's deep sense of honour, an allowance must now be maintained for Harvey's widow. There were other things, more personal – the fact Harvey had done this all so underhandedly, even keeping the secret of his wife in death. Angelica, more than the others, had a right to feel hurt and spurned. Her son had deliberately deceived her. He had still been courting a wealthy American heiress while all the time he was married. It was a bitter pill for his mother to swallow. Perhaps she had hoped her son would treat her better and certainly not keep secrets from her.

"This is not just about Mrs Howton's arrival," Genevieve's mother spoke placidly. "We are all still feeling the shock of recent events. These mysterious night-time visits have unsettled everyone."

"I would soon deal with the fellow," Genevieve

grumbled. "He does not unsettle me."

"That is beside the point," Lady Howton persisted. "The affair is a nasty business that is bound to upset people."

Genevieve seemed unconvinced, but there was no more she could add. She got down to her salmon without another word.

"I take it you are staying the night, Miss Fitzgerald?" Angelica spoke to Clara.

Clara had not heard her speak before and it was somewhat of a shock to have this silent creature suddenly make a sound in her direction. Her voice was frail for her age, wispy and soft, easily blow away by a sharp blast of air. Clara glanced up.

"I am. I hope to resolve this puzzle swiftly."

Angelica pulled her lips into an amused smile.

"You think it so simple?" she asked.

"Why should it be complicated?" Clara replied. "Mysteries like this must have a human agent behind them, find that person and the mystery will unravel."

"And what if there is no human agent?" Angelica pressed. "What if my son really has returned from the dead?"

"Then, I suppose you will need a priest rather than a private detective," Clara shrugged, hoping her answer sounded carefree without seeming rude. "I don't think that will be necessary, however."

"Glad to see another woman with her head screwed on!" Genevieve responded, almost slamming her fist down on the table with her delight. "Far too many people have their heads in the clouds about such things!"

"Genie, you should not scorn what other people believe," Lord Howton said, though it was a half-hearted rebuke, he was too intent on his salmon.

"Father, people are far too sensitive," Genevieve rolled her eyes.

"You would not speak like that if you had been in the war," Richard said darkly.

"I would have gladly served and you know it, Dickie, had they only allowed women to join the army!"

"Thank heavens they did not!" Lady Howton said adamantly. "Now, might we eat our dinner in peace?"

Genevieve was silenced and the meal continued with barely a mutter. Clara was disappointed that everyone obeyed Lady Howton's request.

When dinner was finished, the family made their usual retreat to the drawing room. As Lord Howton had a male guest, Oliver, at his table, he might have suggested the menfolk remain for an after-dinner drink. But he was far more interested in getting to the drawing room and seeing what mischief awaited them there to raise the point, so, for once, he broke with tradition and followed the women straight through to the other room.

Here at least there was electric light and the room seemed bright against the backdrop of the night outside. The tall windows seemed to be rectangles of black space, an empty void created by the brightness of the lights in the room. The main lights were soon turned off, leaving only the lights either side of the mantelpiece. The room at once became cosy as its corners drifted into shadow and the pool of light seemed only to fall on the family.

The family's evening had a set routine to which they abided almost religiously, it seemed much like the rest of the house, a tradition that had become ingrained and immutable. Lord Howton took out his pipe and made a great fuss of preparing it and then settling to smoke. He liked to smoke standing and would pace occasionally, sometimes looking out of the darkened windows, at other times staring into the fire and reflecting on his day.

His wife took up a work of embroidery, a white piece of linen she was detailing with pale roses as a present for her sister at Christmas. She sat as near to the lights as possible and worked bent over, thoughtful in her stitching. Beside her Diana sat and took up some knitting with a slight sigh. She worked her project without referring to a pattern and with the easy mindlessness of an experienced knitter.

Diana and her mother sat on the sofa with its back to the windows which formed the far side of the three-sided square of sofas. On the sofa at right angles to this, the one that faced the fire, Genevieve and Richard sat with a comfortable distance between them. Genevieve subscribed to a countryside magazine, along with Shooting Weekly and The English Gamekeeper, and was kept busy reading the latest articles by her favourite huntsmen. At her feet sprawled her dogs, two large white and liver spaniels.

Next to her Richard was reading a book on English history. Clara had not spotted the title, but it looked to be a lengthy volume. He hardly acknowledged his family as he read steadily.

On the remaining sofa, the one that faced both Diana and Lady Howton and the windows onto the garden, Angelica sat bolt upright, looking like a stiff doll that had been posed awkwardly on the furniture. Unlike the others, she had nothing about her that suggested where her interests might lie, or what hobbies might distract her. She seemed uncomfortable in the room. Clara could not blame her for wishing to not be a part of this family setting. She was out-of-place and she knew it. Even so, Clara wished she would make the best of it and read or distract herself with a project like the others. Her unease seemed infectious and could hardly be healthy. It would be better if she learned to relax.

Betty had found herself sitting next to her mother-in-law and this clearly made her as tense as Angelica. She was desperate for someone to talk or do something, anything, that might take her mind off things. But no one was taking any notice of her.

Clara would have come to her assistance if she was not already helping Oliver, who was inspecting his camera and ensuring it was ready to work. He was perturbed that, with the electric lights on, there was a glint of light in the windows that he had not noticed during the day. With his camera in a different position to the one it was in the night before, the reflection of light was very apparent and at risk of spoiling any picture he took. There was nothing for it but to try to reposition the camera.

Clara would have liked to have slipped outside and checked the camera in the bushes, but there was no time for that. The hour Harvey usually arrived was nearly upon them and the anxiety within the room was becoming distinctly palpable. Clara could only surreptitiously check the length of cord they had slipped through the keyhole and which could be pulled to activate the camera outside. It seemed in place.

The clock ticked on. Lord Howton was now staring constantly at the windows. Lady Howton was struggling to keep her stitches neat and Diana had stopped knitting altogether. Everyone was waiting.

Outside the night was still. There was no rain, nor wind. Clara watched the panes of glass, braced for what she might see. Now, with darkness upon them and the added tension of the others, she was feeling less sanguine about her previous assessments. Oh, she still thought the man at the window was a hoax! But she could not help but feel a knot in her stomach as she waited for him to appear. Surely this man's intentions were sinister, else why play this horrible prank even in the midst of a storm?

She readjusted her fingers on the cord through the keyhole. Oliver would take his picture first, acting as a distraction for the actions of the second camera. They only had to hope the man did not turn his head away.

Clara tensed. Was that a footstep she heard? Outside the windows was a terrace and steps onto the lawn. Even the most careful of treads would make a sound. Had Clara heard the approach of the man? She glanced at Oliver, then her head slipped to the others. In that split-second Oliver gave a gasp and exploded the flash of his camera. Clara was momentarily blinded, but did not hesitate to pull the cord and activate the second camera. She turned her head back to the window. A moment ago there had been nothing there, now she saw a face, close enough to the panes that it was visible to the room. Backlit by the night stars, the face seemed a horrible mask. It was difficult to see colours, but the eyes were ringed with black and the mouth was pulled into a rictus of... what? Horror? Anger? Hatred? It could have been any of those emotions or none of them.

The eyes of the man in the window were wild and the whites plainly visible. He seemed to be looking at the family though the camera flash had to have blinded him.

Betty jumped up from the sofa, astounded too much to be shocked by what she was seeing. She ran towards the window.

"Harvey!"

Her appearance, Clara was certain, startled the man and he started to pull away. Betty flew to the glass, pressing both hands against it and staring into the dark.

"Harvey!" she wailed.

But Clara had no time to worry about Betty. She had opened the French windows and was now dashing out into the darkness to intercept the intruder.

Chapter Eleven

Clara raced across the grass behind the fast disappearing figure. She had wasted time fussing with the door onto the terrace, pulling loose the cord that had operated the camera and stumbling outside a fraction too late. Already the man had a head start and was vanishing into the shadows of the night. She ran on anyway, hoping to keep pace at least and to spot where he went. She was not surprised when she found herself alongside the mausoleum. The stranger was nowhere to be seen.

Frustrated with herself, Clara headed back to the hall and returned to the drawing room. The scene inside was one of respectable chaos. Betty Howton was weeping, but no one was doing much to comfort her. She was wailing over and over that the man at the window had been her Harvey and she could not possibly have been mistaken. Clara had to admit the girl had been close enough to get a good look at the man. It seemed likely she would have recognised her husband.

Lady Howton was making a majestic effort of not allowing the trembling of her hands to be noticeable. The revelation of Betty recognising her husband had clearly upset her. Lord Howton was stoic and still smoking his pipe, but he too looked unsettled. As for Genevieve, she was being prevented from fetching her shotgun by her brother Richard. She was angrier than ever before and determined to hunt down the culprit behind the prank. She was arguing with her brother, while her parents watched on, apparently unable to do anything.

Diana had jumped to her feet when the figure had appeared and, in her panic and confusion, had spun around and knocked a glass flying from a side table. It lay smashed on the floor and she was trying to get someone's attention to ask if she should ring for a maid to clear it up. Her mother, however, was almost catatonic in her determination to not show emotion and her father just huffed when she tried to ask him. Diana seemed unable to act on her own initiative and stood looking at the glass on the floor in a state of complete hopelessness.

Clara took a moment to catch sight of Angelica. She was collapsed on the sofa where she had been sitting. She was not in a faint, but was clearly dazed. Since no one appeared to be attending to her, Clara pushed her way between the unhappy Howtons and knelt beside her.

"Are you all right?" she asked Angelica.

The woman had gone very grey in the face. She looked at Clara with a wan smile.

"I had almost convinced myself it was a hoax, until she confirmed my worst fears," Angelica said.

Clara frowned.

"Your worst fears?"

"I don't want to talk here," Angelica cast her eyes around her at the assorted Howtons. "Would you be good enough to help me to my room."

Clara hesitated a moment: she had intended to see to Betty and offer her some comfort once she had assured herself Angelica Howton was well. But that now seemed impossible and, as much as Clara wanted to be a Good Samaritan, she could not miss following the potential lead Angelica was offering. If she refused to help her, would Angelica be so willing to talk to her another time? She was vulnerable at the moment, her guard was down, and she wanted to confide in someone. Clara had to take the opportunity and neglect Betty.

Clara offered Angelica her arm and the woman rose weakly. She seemed frail for her age. Clara supposed she was only in her forties, but she acted like an old woman. There was no strength in Angelica as Clara assisted her from the drawing room and they made the precarious ascent of the stairs. Angelica's room was on the second floor. She actually had a small suite of rooms set aside for her private use.

"Courtesy of my dear late husband," she explained to Clara as they approached them.

It seemed the former Lord Howton had not been oblivious to his family's distaste for his wife and had made arrangements that she should have a private space where she might escape them. Angelica spent most of her time in these rooms, only meeting with the family at meal times. It was family custom to always dine together in the evenings and no protest Angelica could suggest would stop that. She had to dine with the Howtons, even if they were acrimonious towards her and she towards them. Howton tradition, once again, overrode emotions.

Angelica had no friends in the district, so she rarely left the hall except to walk in the grounds. She was an anomaly in the neighbourhood. Too working class to be considered a fitting acquaintance for the other well-to-do families in the district, and risen too far above her station to make comfortable friendships with the ordinary folk. Angelica felt isolated; her son had been her only consolation and now he was gone too.

Clara was tempted to point out to her that Betty was in exactly the same situation and it might be worthwhile the two women banding together, but she did not want to risk Angelica taking offence and refusing to talk to her. Instead she helped her into her sitting room and drew the curtains at the tall windows.

Angelica's rooms were in the older part of the hall, above Clara's bedroom. They were decorated with the dark panelling the Howtons of the seventeenth century had preferred. However, her sitting room was heavily personalised, unlike many of the other family rooms Clara had seen. There was no sign of the Howton ancestors here. No old paintings or furniture, no random memorabilia from the past. Angelica had fitted the room out with new furniture at the time of her wedding. It was now over twenty years old, but looked fresh among the old world setting of panelled walls, and was certainly more up-to-date than anything else in the hall. She had chosen her own paintings for the walls and they were mainly watercolours in liquid hues of blues and reds. She liked floral images and landscapes. Even the rug on the floor was of English wool rather than an old Persian rug as was found everywhere else.

Angelica sat in a sagging but comfortable blue armchair by the fire. She let out a sigh of relief.

"Thank you," she said.

Clara sat also, not waiting to be invited.

"You were going to tell me about your worst fears," Clara reminded her.

Angelica gave another sigh and flicked away a tendril of hair that had fallen across her brow. She knitted her fingers together in her lap.

"I was hopeful it was not the case," Angelica murmured. "But a terrible thing befell my son during the war."

Clara tried not to appear too keen.

"I assume this was an especially terrible thing, considering the circumstances?"

"Yes, you might say that. Certainly lots of terrible things were happening during the war to a lot of poor young men. No, this was something else, something extraordinary," Angelica gave a sad smile. "My sister-in-law talks a lot of rot, but she was correct about one thing. Harvey did travel extensively and was very curious about anything exotic, particularly anything involving the occult."

Angelica frowned. She clearly didn't like talking about such things.

"Harvey was always very concerned about death. I believe it was due to the sudden passing of his father when he was a little boy. It left him deeply unsettled and with this terror that people would suddenly disappear from his life. It was a terror that even as an adult he could not rid himself of. Harvey struggled with traditional religion. He was not so much interested in life after death, but rather how to prevent death altogether. His obsession with this notion took him to far flung places, talking to shamans and magicians from many cultures. Seeking the impossible, a cure for death," Angelica's expression was cautious, she was worried she was going to be laughed at. Clara said nothing. She wanted to know about this mysterious side of Harvey.

"When war came, Harvey's obsession became almost impossible to control. Death was all around him and filled his waking thoughts. He confided in me his passion. I was shocked, naturally," Angelica groaned to herself. "I tried to console him with words from the Bible, but he would have none of it. Harvey was determined to find a way to prevent death, effectively he was seeking immortality, but at that precise moment he was just trying to survive the war. How many old school friends had he seen die on the battlefield? Too many. I dare say he was also driven by a desire to outlive Richard. There was a strange atmosphere in the house during those years. We were all on tenterhooks for news, but there was this terrible competition between myself and Lady Howton. It was unspoken, but we were both waiting for the other's son to die.

"Horrible, I know. I speak of it now and feel sick to my stomach over it. Maybe she does too. But it was how the war took us. Of course, if Richard died Harvey would become heir to the title. I suppose that was why I hoped he would be killed and why she hoped Harvey would die. In any case, they both survived. Just as well, I think, because if one of us had won that awful competition it would have eaten away at us forever."

Angelica paused.

"My dear, there is some sherry in that cupboard. Might you pour me a glass? And please help yourself."

Clara obeyed the request, though she declined a glass for herself. Once Angelica was suitably equipped with a drink, she continued her story.

"Harvey was fascinated by the commonwealth troops from Indian who served in the war, or rather he was fascinated by their various spiritual practices. He spent more and more time among them, learning about their gods and their folk magic. Eventually, he found someone who could offer him what he was looking for, a way to stop death," Angelica almost hissed the last sentence, it seemed to take effort to spit it out. "The man was a Fakir, a religious teacher, but he knew a lot of old magic. Some of it forbidden. He told Harvey that he knew a spell that would prevent a man dying. It was dark magic, but it had an attraction to Harvey difficult to describe to any rational person. He could not resist."

Angelica drained her sherry, she looked in need of the fortification.

"Harvey insisted the man cast his spell upon him. I don't know the details, for Harvey did not care to describe them to me. I think he only told me about the spell because I was so concerned about the possibility of him dying and he wanted to reassure me. He was so pleased with himself for finding a way to defy death," Angelica shook her head, still struggling to believe her son had been so foolish. "What he had to do to work that spell I dare not think. But work it they did. Harvey was ecstatic when he told me. He would never die! The Fakir had sworn it!

"Well, he was right, wasn't he? He cannot die. His poor tormented soul shall never know peace because of that dark spell. I had hoped I was wrong, that it was some imposter at the window. I was not brave enough to get close enough to look for myself, but Betty had the courage, and now she has confirmed that it is my son standing in the garden night after night. My son, unable to die, and yet also dead. He has defied death, but at what cost?"

Angelica sunk her head into her hands and sobbed. Clara could not blame her for feeling so beaten. To imagine one's loved one forever kept from the peace of the grave was a horrid vision. But Clara did not believe there was a magic powerful enough to stop death itself. If Harvey had defied death, it was by practical devices, not by witchcraft. She was careful when she spoke to Angelica not to make her disbelief too obvious.

"I would imagine there was a lot of talk about charms and spells that might prevent death during the Great War," she said. "Death was very much on everyone's minds. Harvey no doubt believed in that spell very strongly, maybe just by believing in his invulnerability he was kept safe?"

"You don't think the spell was real? Even after what you saw downstairs?" Angelica persisted.

"I saw a man at the window," Clara spoke plainly. "He resembled Harvey, but he was not dead. He sprinted across the garden far too well for a corpse. Besides, I saw the surprise on his face when he recognised Betty."

Angelica stopped crying abruptly.

"He was surprised?"

"Yes. It was quite obvious. I don't think a dead man would care that his secret wife had turned up at the house. Actually, I am going to persuade the Howtons to leave the terrace doors open tomorrow and invite the fellow inside. I would stake a shilling he won't set foot through the door and risk standing in the glare of artificial light," Clara was pleased with her idea. "I shall find out who is playing this terrible hoax on you all and defiling the memory of your son. Rest assured on that."

"That is most comforting," Angelica bleated. "Oh dear, but I am so tired. Might I kindly ask you to leave now so

I might rest?"

"Of course," Clara rose from her chair. "Thank you for your honesty. I see now how someone might have concocted this whole scheme, basing it on your son's interests in the occult to make it seem more authentic."

"That would be a very wicked thing to do," Angelica said miserably.

"Very wicked," Clara agreed. "And, as yet, our culprit has not demonstrated what possible motive could have inspired such callousness. I suppose we shall find out soon enough."

Clara let herself out of Angelica's rooms and checked her watch. She doubted the family would have remained in the drawing room, in any case, she had no need to return. Not with the stranger in the dark long gone. She decided it was time to get some rest, to refresh her mind ready for the day ahead. There would be lots to be done come the morning. For a start, she had to set a suitable trap for this intruder. Once she had him ensnared, he would be revealed for what he was.

Of that, Clara was confident.

Chapter Twelve

Clara lay in her bed in the guest room and turned the pages of Harvey Howton's diary. She had yet to find any stark revelations within it that might explain his, or someone else's, reasons for pretending he had returned from the dead. It was filled with a great deal of bitterness and vitriol directed towards his half-brother and his family.

Harvey felt cheated by life and by his father. It wasn't so much that he was the younger son of a lord and therefore unable to inherit the title. It was the fact that he was from a second marriage, a marriage viewed with derision and hate by those members of the family who felt they had the better pedigree and therefore a better claim to the Howton name. His brother was not so much the problem as was his wife. Lady Howton had resented the arrival of Angelica into the household. She had felt her place threatened.

The late Lord Howton had been a widower for many years and his daughter-in-law had stepped into the role of 'lady of the house' early on; taking charge of household affairs and running her father-in-law's life. It had made her feel important and purposeful, especially when her first child had proved to be a girl and she realised she had failed to produce an heir.

Then Angelica had walked into the house unexpectedly. This woman of working class stock. She was presentable enough, but what did she know about running a lord's household or the correct protocols for treating servants? None! She stumbled into the lives of them all and made a pig's ear of nearly everything until she was corrected.

It was absurd! It was disgraceful! And all the future Lady Howton could do was bite her tongue and endure it all. She had felt thrust out, and the longer it went on without her producing a son, the more she felt threatened by this imposter who, at any moment, might produce an heir and compound her own failure.

There were dark days when both ladies fell pregnant within weeks of each other. For Angelica, her desperation to produce a baby boy was driven by her need to consolidate her position within the family. She still felt second class and needed to prove her worthiness to be there, to exist even.

For her rival the pressure was even worse. If Angelica produced a son where did that leave her? She had to produce an heir for her husband, a future Lord Howton. If Angelica succeeded where she could not, the shame would crush her.

Such unnecessary pressures governed the two women. As the weeks passed and their times grew near they were almost paralysed with anticipation and dread. Many years later, it was hard to imagine that terrible time, since the outcome was known and the fears seemed unfounded. But back then they were very real and were felt throughout the household. It was all there in Harvey's diary. His mother had told him of that time and he had recorded her memories. According to Harvey, even the servants were brought to a state of despair over the drama, which only ended with the birth of Richard.

That should have been the end of it all, but, of course, Angelica gave birth to Harvey and so the rivalry remained. Anything that threatened the life of Richard instantly put Harvey into the spotlight. The slightest childhood cough put Richard's parents into paroxysms of anxiety. Should Richard die, then Harvey would be the next heir to the title. It was unthinkable, and yet it was entirely possible, especially when Diana was born and hopes of a second direct heir were dashed. There were to be no more pregnancies after Diana. Harvey hinted that the birth had been so difficult that the doctors had told his brother his wife would never have any other children. Now all hope was placed on Richard.

What a burden to shoulder! And the rivalry of the parents now seeped into the children. Two boys so close in age they could be brothers, and yet divided by the impossible prejudices and hate of their parents. All through Harvey's life there had been one overriding theme – should Richard die he would be heir. It had infected the boy with a morbid fascination for sickness and death. He had been trained to relish every illness Richard contracted, to anticipate his death with a disturbing excitement. Harvey confessed all this to the pages of his diary. He also confessed that it was only during the Great War, when death became an inevitable daily comrade, that he realised how sickening his preoccupations with Richard's demise had been. He now came to resent his mother for instilling these dark horrors in him.

The realisation might have brought the two men together, brothers-in-arms as they were, but the deep strife between them ran too deep. It was a gulf impossible to overcome. They would be rivals, enemies even, until their dying days. There would be no compromise.

The diary contained Harvey's gripes concerning the family. Some were genuine, others he had constructed from random events that were probably meaningless. He was so paranoid that anything someone said became an attack upon him, even when it was not. He heard whispers and assumed they were about him. He saw servants laughing and thought they laughed at him. Harvey's entire life was driven by this deep-seated sense of inadequacy, of being the son of a stationmaster's daughter. His mother might have married a lord, but even Harvey could not resist the idea that she had done so motivated purely by money.

What an unhappy man. Clara mused to herself. She closed the diary, having read through all but the final pages, and placed the book on the cabinet beside the bed. The clock on the wall stated that it was now past one o'clock in the morning. She was meant to be sleeping. Clara lay back on the pillow and wondered what life must have been really like for Harvey in this hall. Here he was, surrounded by a history that stemmed back centuries and of which he was a part, yet he was still an outsider, an anomaly. He could never quite place himself into the family's shared history because he believed that all his ancestors would have resented him as much as his living relatives did. Driven by a mix of hate and insecurity, he had drifted to London for long spells to escape the claustrophobia of his family. His diary recorded those trips; he mainly went to night clubs, the newest craze to hit the city. He enjoyed the opportunity to disappear and become a nobody in such places. In one of them he met his wife, yet she too was absent from his diary. Strange that even his most private thoughts, when placed onto paper, appeared censored.

Had Harvey feared people getting hold of his diary?

Clara shut her eyes and tried to drift off, but her mind was racing. Why does anyone decide to fake their death? If, indeed, Harvey had faked his drowning that could only mean he wanted to finally escape this life and this world. He wanted to disappear for good, with no one to pursue him.

Then why come back and act as a living corpse? Revenge? To get back at the family who had spurned him so? Clara felt she was missing a piece of the puzzle. Something much more sinister was going on here, she had just stumbled in too early, before the real drama took place.

Clara was just about to turn over and try to go to sleep, when someone knocked on her bedroom door.

"Miss Fitzgerald?"

She recognised Richard's voice.

"Just a moment," Clara quickly rose and pulled on her slippers and donned her dressing gown. She knew before she opened the door that something had happened. That the next stage of the drama had begun.

"I am sorry to disturb you so late," Richard apologised hastily as Clara appeared before him. "I think there is something you ought to see."

He led her back downstairs, through the great hall and into the drawing room. The room was dark. Richard turned on the wall lights.

"We all went to bed not long after the commotion," Richard explained. "None of us felt like staying up. The wind had been knocked out of us. I was having trouble sleeping, so I came back down here for my book. That was when I spotted those."

His arm pointed to a spot behind the sofa. Clara's eyes had already been drawn in that direction because the door to the terrace was open. She could not recall if she had shut it behind her when she raced back in, but surely the family would have closed it before going to bed? The open door suggested someone had come in later on.

Clara walked across the room so she could see behind the sofa. On the floor, tracking the path of the person who had opened the door, was a line of footprints. They appeared wet and muddy. They stopped in the middle of the room.

"He came in," Richard said, his voice husky.

Clara glanced up at him and saw the shadow of fear in his eyes.

"He could still be in the house!" Richard added in a hiss.

Clara bent down and examined the footprints. They

were very clear, as if they had been carefully arranged. Anyone who had walked into their house with muddy boots would know that prints were not normally left so even on the floor. Dirty shoes leave crude marks, the dirt quickly falling off. Prints are usually partial, whereas these were well defined. Clara had the impression these prints had been strategically placed, the shoes used to make them had been evenly coated in something dark and sticky to make sure the prints were easy to read. Whether that meant the person was still in the house or not was another matter.

Clara rose and closed the window to the terrace. She examined the handle and lock. As Genevieve had stated the lock was broken and the doors could not be fastened. Anyone could open the door from the outside and wander in.

"I suggest we take a look about the house," Clara said. "Just to be on the safe side."

Richard nodded, he looked white as a sheet. Clara had forgotten that the young man took the possibility of his uncle's return from the dead very seriously.

They made a circuit of the hall, going floor-by-floor. They left the servants' quarters alone in the hopes that, firstly, there were enough eyes and ears down there to spot an intruder, and secondly, because it was unlikely the trespasser would go that way. He was after the family, by all accounts.

The ground floor proved empty, however, on the first step of the staircase in the great hall, Clara pointed at something. They were lighting their search by a torch Richard had taken from an old cupboard in the guard room. Now, as its beam stretched across the staircase, Clara noticed something. She moved forward and crouched down. Here was more mud, but this time a clump of it, fallen perhaps from clothing rather than placed there. The intruder had left a trace of himself by accident instead of design.

"He went upstairs," Richard was beginning to look like

a man about to face his executioner.

Clara tried to reassure him.

"Someone went upstairs. I don't think it was a spectre, but a very real man. A burglar perhaps."

This did not console Richard. He would not be dissuaded from the idea that his uncle had crawled out of his grave to hunt the family. Clara felt it was best they just press on. She went up the stairs and they conducted a careful search of the first floor as they had the ground floor. Signs of the interloper had disappeared again. They crept past the family bedrooms trying not to make a sound and disturb anyone. They came to the corridor outside Angelica's room and Clara put a hand out to stop Richard walking any further forward. She directed him to shine the torchlight on the floor and there, on the runner outside Angelica's door, were more of those extremely careful footprints.

The footprints came down the corridor as if headed from the stairs and then turned and stopped outside the door. There were only five of them, but each was carefully defined and the last two were side-by-side indicating that the culprit behind them had stood outside the door.

Richard was dumbstruck. Clara was worried. Since she did not believe in the supernatural, it seemed plain to her that the person behind these footprints was intending to leave a message. That the footprints were only in two locations, remote from one another, told her that they had been put down for a purpose and were not caused by someone carelessly walking into the house with muddy feet. She crouched by the footprints and took another look. They were very dark and the details smooth. When a person walks mud into a house, as Annie would quickly tell her, they don't just traipse in a stain, but also dirt, bits of grass or fine gravel. The result is that the stains are gritty, you can see grains of soil or sand in them.

These had none of that. They were a very dark brown, but there was no trace of grit or dirt or gravel. Clara guessed someone had used ink to create these footprints.

Which meant someone had very deliberately walked up here, covered their shoes in ink and made these marks. She guessed that if she returned to the footprints downstairs she would see exactly the same.

"We ought to check Angelica is safe," Clara stated to Richard, who was still pulling a face.

Clara knocked lightly on Angelica's door.

"Mrs Howton?" she paused and then rapped again. "Mrs Howton, sorry to disturb you but there may have been a break-in."

Angelica pulled back her bedroom door sharply, she glowered at them both.

"No one has broken into my rooms!" she snapped and slammed the door in their faces.

"Well, at least she is unhurt," Clara shrugged her shoulders. "I don't think the intruder is still in the hall. I suggest we go back to our beds and try to get some sleep before unravelling this puzzle further in the morning."

Richard seemed unconvinced that the puzzle was possible to unravel, but he was glad enough to retreat to his bedroom where there was a stout lock on the door. He was so upset by the night's events, he did not even offer to escort Clara back to her room, only gave her the torch as he locked himself in.

Clara wandered the long corridors back to her room. She was in no rush as her mind was whirring with fresh thoughts. Why were the footsteps outside Angelica's door? What was the significance? What message was their man from the dead trying to express? If Angelica was a target, why?

Clara reached her room and locked herself in, despite having reassured Richard that the intruder was long gone. She lay down in bed and pondered over everything. Mysterious midnight footsteps were all well and good, but how did they fit into this curious game?

She could only hope morning would bring new answers.

Chapter Thirteen

"It makes my blood run cold!" Lady Howton stared at the now closed door to the drawing room terrace and the footprints leading away from it. "To think, my home invaded by a monster!"

"Mother!" Genevieve scowled. "This man is a tramp or a nuisance maker, not a monster! If you would just let me get…"

"Not the shotgun, Genie," Lord Howton said rapidly.

Genevieve placed her hands on her hips and pulled a face.

"What do we do now?" Diana whispered in a trembling tone.

"Get the lock changed," Clara said, feeling there was a desperate need for someone to be practical. "Anyone could try the door and come in with the lock broken. Any burglar, for instance. Get the lock changed and you can sleep peacefully in your beds."

"What if the new lock won't stop him? What if he can pass through locks?" Lady Howton looked wide-eyed at those around her.

Clara felt like giving a loud sigh of frustration.

"Locks are locks. And the man outside is just a man. Change the lock and he won't get back in."

"You think we are all fools," Richard Howton turned to Clara. "You think we are spouting nonsense, that we have taken leave of our senses."

Clara said nothing, even a denial would sound false right at that moment. She was growing impatient with the whole affair. Had the family taken the man for what he was, a prankster, they would have already changed the lock on the door and no one could have walked in to leave footprints. Instead, they were so immobilised by this notion of a man back from the dead that they could do nothing but lie shaking in their beds.

"Does no one even care that the footprints stopped outside my bedroom door?" Angelica spoke up.

It was unusual for her to say anything, and certainly to complain. She was usually as mute as a nun, quietly getting on with her unhappy existence. But the night's events had taken their toll.

"My son came back to me last night," she said, her voice taut with unshed tears. "He stood outside my door, and it was locked so he could not enter."

"You would not have wanted him to," Lady Howton said rapidly. "You would not want to see him like that."

"How do you know?" Angelica snapped at her. Her sharp tone was such a surprise that nearly everyone jumped. "How do you know what I want?"

Betty was standing to one side and she gave a low moan. Clara glanced at her, sensing that she was imagining her dead husband returning to her and it was enough to nearly have her drop down into a faint.

"My son came back to me, and he will come again!" Angelica now rose from her chair and confronted the family. "You will not change the lock on that door! My son must be able to enter this house and come to me! I shall welcome him with open arms! He wants to speak to me, impart a final message for me, I shall not allow you to prevent that!"

Clara felt like screaming. Yes, someone had come into the house, but whether that person was Harvey or not, they were certainly not dead or trying to impart some final message. She feared they were up to something sinister, but what would Harvey or an imposter gain from scaring Angelica?

"I can't have a dead man wandering about my home!" Lady Howton protested.

"And what about my home?" Angelica squawked back. "This is my house as much as yours! I was the lady here before you!"

Clara had had enough. She left the two women rowing and went to find Oliver. He was in his makeshift dark room again, processing the photographs from the previous evening. Clara was not expecting any great revelations from the pictures, but she hoped they might prove to the family that the 'monster' was actually a living, breathing person.

Clara knocked on the dark room door.

"Just a moment."

There was a clatter inside and Oliver muttered under his breath. As much as Clara was fond of the man, his sheer clumsiness, accompanied by a pathological ability for untidiness, drove her mildly crazy. Oliver opened the door and thrust out a dirty plate. Clara glanced at it, then raised an eyebrow at him.

"Oh, sorry, I thought you were the maid come to collect my breakfast plate. They were good enough to bring my food to me," Oliver smiled at Clara and brushed a strand of loose hair off his face. "I expect you want to see my photographs?"

"I do," Clara agreed.

Oliver pushed the door to the cupboard wide open, so Clara could see what he was doing. There was not really room enough for her to climb in, so she hovered in the doorway. Oliver took two large pieces of paper off a washing line strung across the room. He passed them to Clara.

"This is the picture I took from inside, and this the one from outside."

Clara examined the two images. The first had been taken from an angle, to try and prevent the flash of the camera glaring off the glass of the window and obliterating the image. The photo showed the man at the window. He was looking directly into the room and Clara felt his face would be recognisable to anyone who happened to know him well. If this was really Harvey Howton, she could ask the family to identify him.

The second picture had been taken from outside, by the camera in the bushes. It had captured a clear profile image of the man. He had been distracted by the flash of the camera inside and had not noticed that another flash had come from the bushes beside him. In this photo there was no doubting the appearance of the man. To Clara the individual looked hale and hearty, he did not appear to be a walking corpse.

"I am going to take these to the family," Clara said. "Well done Oliver, looks like Lord Howton finally has his proof."

Oliver beamed with delight at the praise.

"What is your verdict on the condition of the man?" he asked, his eyes twinkling mischievously.

"He looks alive to me," Clara said plainly. "And you?"

"From the photographs he looks pretty alive," Oliver admitted, slightly shamefaced by his earlier convictions. "I've photographed quite a few corpses for the police. You can always tell from the picture they are dead, even the ones who are in their beds seemingly asleep. But, you have to believe me Clara when I say the man I saw that night was something else. The maggots, the smell, the way he moved!"

"All props to make you believe," Clara said gently.

Oliver shrugged his shoulders.

"I would like you to be right. It was dark that night and I was already on edge, expecting to be confronted by a monster."

"Exactly," Clara reached out and touched his arm, trying to alleviate his embarrassment at being so fooled.

"You saw what you had been primed to see. Like a magic trick in the theatre. Nothing to be ashamed about."

"Only, you were not fooled," Oliver pointed out.

"The difference being I don't believe in the supernatural, or even the possibility of it, so I could not be fooled. If you know a man cannot make a dove appear out of thin air except by trickery then, no matter how clever the act, you will not be made to believe in magic."

Oliver nodded.

"I see your point."

"I am going to take these to the family and see what they make of them," Clara said. "In the meantime, might you do me a favour and take a few photographs of the footprints outside Angelica Howton's room? Some from a distance and some close up. They seem odd to me, rather like more set-dressing, and I would like a record of them."

Oliver agreed to do that. Clara left him to his work. She wandered back to the drawing room where she was not surprised to find the family still arguing over the best thing to do. Angelica was still stubbornly refusing to have the lock on the door changed, in case it prevented her son from coming to her. Lady Howton seemed appalled at the idea that she might wish to see her son risen from the grave. Clara had to admit the idea seemed rather ghoulish to her too, but Angelica would not be swayed.

Betty was huddled in a chair to one side, looking pale and frightened. She seemed more like a child than a married woman in that moment. Clara guessed she was regretting coming to the hall. Clara knelt beside her and passed over the photographs.

"Is that Harvey?" she asked her.

Betty examined the two pictures.

"These were taken last night?" Betty asked. She fingered the photographs, tracing Harvey's face as if caressing it. "That is Harvey."

"If I was to see these pictures without knowing the context, I would say that Harvey looks pretty alive,"

Clara said bluntly. She pointed to the second picture, the one taken from the bushes. "He doesn't look like someone who has been dead several weeks."

"Who is to say how these things work?" Betty whispered breathlessly. Some colour had come back to her cheeks. "I was struggling to believe it, now here he is in black and white. Harvey, come back from the grave!"

Clara was stunned. She had meant the photographs to prove her conviction that the man outside was a living person playing a stunt, not to convince Betty that Harvey was a dead man walking!

Clara ran a hand over her face, feeling despondent. Could people really be so incredulous?

"Surely it makes better sense that he is actually alive?" she tried again.

"Why?" Betty asked her innocently.

"Because..." Clara found the simplicity of the question unsettling, "because it is more likely that a person is alive and has pretended to die, than for a man to come back from the dead."

"So you say, but Harvey believed in dark magic. He had this spell cast over him."

"I heard about that," Clara nodded. "An Indian Fakir worked magic to prevent him from dying."

Clara spoke in a dull, disbelieving tone. Betty didn't seem to notice.

"He was triumphant about it," Betty said. "He told me how the spell had worked. How a bullet had whistled passed his ear, he heard it! How he had just avoided being blown up by a shell! How every man around him had died but he remained!"

"Then why did he drown?" Clara pointed out.

Betty blinked fast, her mind working faster.

"But, but he didn't drown. He is out there still."

"But not alive," Clara indicated, playing on Betty's logic.

"The spell prevented death, that's all. I suppose making a bullet miss is one thing, preventing a man from drowning is a lot harder. So, the spell worked another way. It resurrected him."

Clara tried not to groan. Betty was twisting and turning ideas to suit her preconceptions. None of it made sense, but Clara saw that arguing this was not going to work. Betty had convinced herself of the reality of this fantasy, of a man rising from his tomb, and she was not going to be dissuaded easily.

Clara took the photographs back off her and rose to her feet. She thought about showing them to the others, but what would be the point? If Betty could see hard evidence of the supernatural in the pictures, rather than realising they actually demonstrated the opposite, what were the chances the others could be swayed in their opinions? Clara had hoped to demonstrate that Harvey was alive, now she saw that certain members of the family were too far gone in their delusions to see anything but what they expected. The dove would appear from thin air and they would think it magic.

Still, she had proof for herself and potentially for the police if matters became more complicated. Fortunately, so far, no crime had been committed. Perhaps there was no intention of a crime occurring at all. Perhaps this was just a great joke designed to make the Howtons examine their consciences and to regret their failures towards Harvey. Perhaps... Perhaps...

Genevieve approached Clara.

"What do you have there?"

Clara handed over the pictures. Genevieve examined them both carefully, her brow wrinkling into a frown.

"That is Harvey, for certain," she said, giving back the photographs. "It seems it is him behind this."

Genevieve pressed her lips together into a thin line.

"That means we have to assume he faked his own death."

Her statement jerked Clara back to reality. She had become so obsessed about proving Harvey was alive and not a spectre that she had forgotten that there was a real mystery at the bottom of all this. Harvey had died and been buried in the mausoleum. If none of that was true, which must be the case because he was lurking outside the house, then there had to have been a conspiracy to fool the family. It meant that what Clara had suspected early on, that Harvey had accomplices, was correct.

"Remind me, Genevieve, about the way Harvey died?"

Genevieve shrugged.

"He drowned in the lake," she said.

"But who told you that?"

Genevieve's frown deepened.

"The two under-gardeners. Jimmy and Charlie. They saw him struggling and tried to save him. Jimmy swam out, but it was too late."

"And he was brought back to the house already dead?"

"Yes," Genevieve was looking confused.

"No doctors were called?"

"Why would they be? He was pale and soaking wet. Jimmy said he was not breathing."

"And no one checked?" Clara nodded to herself. "No, no one would because they would all be so upset. It would be possible, just possible…"

Clara headed towards the terrace doors, squeezing through the family and heading outside.

"Where are you going?" Genevieve called from behind.

"I need to speak with your under-gardeners," Clara replied.

Genevieve pursed her lips again and said nothing.

Chapter Fourteen

Clara walked out into the garden. The morning was bright with autumn sunshine, but there was a nip in the air. She wished she had put a cardigan on.

Clara walked directly to the mausoleum and stood before it. It was truly a monstrosity. Someone had slapped together a grotesque mixture of styles without any thought for how the whole construction would look. Like a child picking up random objects and lumping them together to make a hotchpotch. Clara wrinkled her nose in distaste.

Clara walked around the tomb. It was tall but not very wide. She had estimated before that it could contain two full coffins if laid side-by-side. There would be plenty of room for Harvey's single coffin. Now she was returning to the idea of a possible escape route from the structure. Harvey had designed the thing, after all, he could have engineered a way out, so cunningly disguised it could not be seen. Meaning he really could rise from his own grave.

The sides of the mausoleum looked very solid. They had been sealed together with a thin line of cement. There did not appear to be a way to circumvent them. Clara had already examined the tomb once, but decided the roof needed a second look, just in case there was some sort of hatch she had missed. She braced her foot on the bottom of a pillar and used the outstretched head of a grimacing gargoyle to haul herself up. The mausoleum was considerably taller than her and the roof ran to a high peak like that of a cathedral. From her perch Clara could see two sides of this peaked roof. There seemed nothing suspicious. The roof was made of stone too and you can hardly make a hatch out of stone, at least not one that is easy to open.

She dropped back to the ground and walked to the opposite corner. She repeated the procedure of bracing her foot on a pillar and pushing herself up to view the roof. This side was just as unremarkable as the other.

"Oi! What you doing?"

Clara glanced to her right to see a man glowering at her. From his outfit she surmised he was a gardener, that and the spade he was carrying.

"Just looking," Clara said with a smile, hopping down off the base of the pillar and brushing dust off her hands.

"That's someone's resting place. Show some respect!" the gardener growled.

Clara was surprised by his ferocity, considering he was a servant and she was a guest of the family. She continued to smile at him.

"Harvey Howton is buried inside," she said. "Died in a tragic accident, I hear?"

"Tragic is not the half of it," the gardener grumbled.

"Might you be Jimmy or Charlie?" Clara asked him.

"Neither," the man almost coughed at the suggestion. "I am Samuel Blake, head gardener."

Clara now realised her mistake. Samuel was an older man in his fifties and his stern sense of propriety over the gardens would only come from having the responsibility of looking after them. He was like the butler indoors, except his territory was the grounds about the house, and he would guard them diligently. He was the sort of servant who has been in his role so long that he sees the place as his own, and has no concern about accosting guests who appear to be misusing his gardens. His abrupt nature would be tolerated because he was such a long-standing feature of the hall.

"I apologise for my error," Clara said politely, hoping to appease the man and get him talking. He might be able to provide her some clue as to how all this mischief began. "I ought to have realised you were more than an under-gardener."

Samuel was slightly mollified.

"Maybe you could show me the lake?" Clara enquired, trying to win him over. "I have heard it is rather beautiful."

"It is," Samuel admitted grudgingly. He moved the spade from one hand to the other. "I take a personal pride in keeping the banks well-groomed so the view across the lake is not obscured."

"Then you would be the perfect person to show it to me," Clara persisted. "I imagine you know more about it than the family do."

Samuel ducked his head at the compliment, somewhat abashed, but also pleased to have his expertise recognised.

"I do know a lot about it," he mumbled.

"Then, would you take a moment out of your busy day to show me it?"

Samuel kept toying with the spade, indecision fighting against a delight in his work being recognised. In the end his personal pride won.

"I can't spend all morning over it," he warned Clara as he motioned for her to follow him.

Clara gave him another broad smile.

They walked to the lake which was set back from the house and surrounded by tall willow trees that draped their drooping branches of leaves down to the water's edge. The leaves were turning and there were great scatterings of fallen ones across the grass. Samuel cast an irritated eye over them, as if they had done this on purpose to spoil his moment. He muttered under his breath about getting his rake out.

As they drew closer, the lake became visible through the gently dipping branches of the trees. The water glistened in the sun, sparkling as though diamonds bobbed across its surface. Samuel came to a halt on the bank. A water bird gave a call and then fluttered up into the sky some distance from them. Clara watched it disappear.

"The lake is manmade," Samuel told her, his eyes trained across the water. "Took two years to dig out the basin. The then Lord Howton employed men from the estate on the work. He wanted the lake fed by a natural spring he had discovered in the grounds."

"What year was this?" Clara asked.

"1652," Samuel answered.

"Just after the civil war," Clara watched the lake ripple. "When the Howtons were on the winning side."

"Yes," Samuel looked uncomfortable with the statement. "The family is very patriotic these days. The old Lord Howton met Queen Victoria more than once."

"Are there fish?"

"Yes, trout and carp," Samuel said. "The lake was always meant for fishing. I have seen carp caught from this lake the size of which you would not believe!"

"I think I have seen them, stuffed in the great hall."

"That you would. I dare say there are a few monsters lurking down at the bottom of this lake."

The trees rustled in the wind and the place seemed to take on an otherworldly air. Clara could turn around and see the house, yet as she looked across the water, she seemed alone, as if nothing else existed. She could understand why such a place would draw a man like Harvey, who was forever denied peace in his home. This place would be a sanctuary for him.

"Harvey was fond of the lake," she said. It was a statement, not a question.

"He swam here most days when he was home," Samuel had not taken his eyes off the water, as if he expected to see Harvey swimming across to them at any moment. "He was a good swimmer, but even good swimmers can get their foot tangled in weeds."

"Was that what happened?" Clara asked.

Samuel nodded.

"He tangled his foot and was pulled under. He fought for as long as his strength held out, calling for help as he did. But even strong men grow tired and he could not resist the pull any longer. The weed drowned him," Samuel pulled a face. "This was Harvey's place, the place he was happiest and most at peace with himself. He was a troubled soul, no one can deny that, but this lake was his haven."

"You said tragic was only the half of it."

"And I meant it. Accidents are one thing, but to be taken in this place which was his sanctuary seems the cruellest twist of fate. After surviving the war, too."

"Were you here when it happened?"

"No. The two under-gardeners were," Samuel paused. "You mentioned them by name."

Clara had been caught out, but she did not show it.

"I was told the names of two gardeners in the grounds who I might speak to about looking at the lake," Clara lied. "I wanted to ask about the plants around the banks."

Samuel did not seem entirely convinced, however, he took her at her word and started to show her around the lake, pointing out the plants and shrubs that grew there. Clara let the names wash over her, she was more interested in earning his trust.

"Have the willows always been here?" she asked when there was a pause in the list.

"Yes, they were planted the year the lake was completed. Personally, I would like to thin them out. I think they obscure the view. But I am just the gardener and his lordship will hear none of it," Samuel sighed. "I liked to talk about my ideas with Harvey. He always said that if he ever became lord of the estate he would let me have free rein over the gardens."

Samuel glared at the water of the lake.

"That was never going to happen, though."

"Was no one near enough to reach him in time?" Clara asked, noting how, from the point where they had stopped, the lake looked enormous.

Samuel shook his head.

"Jimmy and Charlie were working on the rhododendrons over that way," Samuel flung out an arm and indicated a large swathe of rhododendrons. "They heard him calling and came running, but they were too late. Charlie can't swim anyway, and Jimmy is only just able. They pulled him out, of course."

"Terrible, terrible," Clara sighed. "They were the only witnesses?"

Samuel gave her a strange look.

"What is this all about?" he demanded.

He was sharper than Clara had given him credit for. She decided it would be better to confess her motives and see if this encouraged him to talk. He was too suspicious of her now to continue the conversation about Harvey otherwise.

"I suppose you have heard the talk from the hall? It's not something that can be kept secret long," Clara said. "Harvey's unhappy soul is said to be still walking the grounds."

Clara glossed over the part where Harvey's corpse was actually said to be on the wander.

"I had heard the odd rumour," Samuel clamped his lips together, a fierce look coming over his face. "I take no heed of such nonsense. It is a wicked thing to say about poor Master Harvey."

"The family have asked me to intercede and put an end to the nonsense," Clara was aiming to get him on her side again, by suggesting they were thinking along the same lines. "I am trying to get proof together to lay Harvey's ghost to rest, so to speak."

"Which is why you were examining the mausoleum?"

"I wanted to see if it was possible for someone to get in and out of it. If it was, then that person would be able to fake Harvey's return from the dead."

"Why would anyone do something so wicked?" Samuel frowned unhappily. "The dead should be allowed to rest in peace."

"I agree. I believe this is an act of maliciousness against the family designed to cause them great distress. I want to lay my hands on the perpetrator."

"Well, no one is getting in or out of Harvey's tomb," Samuel spoke firmly. "I watched the construction myself. That place is solid, even has a concrete floor. And the door was carefully sealed."

"That is reassuring to hear," Clara said, though it was a disingenuous statement. If Harvey was not using his tomb as a hideout, where was he? For that matter, how had he managed to get himself out of the mausoleum in the first place? Was it really just a red herring?

"Would you like me to introduce you to Jimmy and Charlie?" Samuel suddenly asked.

The offer came completely out of the blue and took Clara by surprise.

"Yes, I would."

"They would be the best people to speak to, to put this nasty business to rest. They will tell you they saw Master Harvey drown and that is that," Samuel was still pulling that face at the lake.

Clara rather felt he was holding a personal scorn against the expanse of water, as if it had maliciously taken Harvey's life.

"You liked Harvey Howton?" Clara spoke.

Samuel shuffled his feet.

"It's not my place to like or dislike the family."

"But you were fond of Harvey?"

Samuel gave a long sigh.

"I knew him since he was a boy. He was a good lad, friendly. Master Richard keeps his distance, which is right and proper in the son of a lord. I am just a servant," Samuel added the last in a hasty voice.

"Everyone seems to have a different view of Harvey,"

Clara threw out the statement in the hopes it would draw a response from Samuel. She was not disappointed.

"Harvey was misunderstood by his family. Not their fault, really, it was a difficult situation. The late Lord Howton married his second wife seemingly on a whim. It caused a great deal of hurt," Samuel was being careful with his words. "Harvey rather took the brunt of that emotion. He never did quite fit in. He seemed happier talking with the gardeners than he did with his family. I did hear some nasty talk about that being because his mother was the daughter of a stationmaster."

"People can be horrid," Clara sympathised.

"They can," Samuel said bleakly. "Harvey was always good to me. I watched him grow up. I looked out for him. I remember warning him when he started to swim in the lake. I said it was a dangerous thing to do. But Harvey laughed at me. After serving in the trenches a lake swim hardly scared him, that's what he said. I wish I could have convinced him otherwise."

"It wasn't your fault," Clara told him.

"Still doesn't stop him from being gone," Samuel shook his head. "I hate this lake now. I would have it filled in, if I could."

Samuel breathed deeply and stood upright, shaking off his sadness as best he could. He took a pace back from the bank of the lake.

"I'll take you to Charlie and Jimmy now."

"Thank you."

They left the lakeside behind, along with its sad memories of Harvey's final swim.

Chapter Fifteen

Jimmy and Charlie were working together to reduce a rather unwieldy laurel bush that had taken liberties over the space it occupied during the summer months. Samuel gave Clara a brief description of the two men as he led her to them.

"Good gardeners. Brothers," he said. "They like to work together, which in the main is not a problem, though sometimes I need them working on different projects at the same time and they can be difficult about it."

"They are close, then?"

"Only a year between them in age," Samuel nodded. "They have been inseparable since they were boys. Local lads from Hove. I knew their father, God rest his soul, he was a fine gardening man. Used to grow all manner of fruit and veg for the London markets. Very clever with strawberries. You've never tasted the like."

Samuel smiled to himself at the fond memory.

"He died last year. Pneumonia. A peril to all us souls who work outside in all weathers."

Clara nodded sympathetically.

"The boys didn't want to go into their father's business?" she asked.

"Oh, they have an older brother who took over that," Samuel shrugged. "Not really enough work for all of them. Its seasonal, largely, and too big a workforce reduces the profits. No, they had to look elsewhere for work. It was rather fortunate I had a space for two under-gardeners at the same time. My last two went off to the war, you see. One vanished in No-Man's-Land, the other lost a leg and couldn't come back to gardening. For Jimmy and Charlie it was most fortunate."

Clara doubted the other men and their families viewed things that way, but she said nothing. Life goes on and one man's bad luck is another's good. For Jimmy and Charlie the war had created an opportunity for them that might otherwise have not existed.

"Did the brothers serve in the war?" she asked.

"Yes. Actually, they were in the same regiment as Harvey and Richard. The estate raised a number of troops and they were two of them. Harvey took great care over the men from Howton, he saw them right. The men were very fond of him."

"What of Richard?"

Samuel wrenched his face into a contortion of shapes as he tried to avoid speaking ill of the man who would eventually be his employer.

"Richard is more aloof," he said in the end. "He is very proper. He looked after the men too."

But not the way Harvey did, Clara surmised. She was garnering a whole new insight into Harvey's character by talking to the servants, the people who perhaps knew him best. It seemed that, at least to them, he was caring and kind. He took an interest and responsibility towards them. Perhaps he also was able to relate to them better than Richard, which made him seem more approachable, more one of the lads.

They were nearing the scene of the laurel's decimation. Samuel raised a hand and pointed.

"That one is Charlie, that one Jimmy. Charlie is the older."

The two men were of equal height and build. Had she not been told, Clara would have been able to judge for herself that they were brothers. Charlie, the older brother, had a slightly longer face than Jimmy, and his nose was narrower. Jimmy's face was broader and fairer in appearance. The two men worked together in silence, each seeming to perfectly understand their role in the project and how to avoid getting in the other's way. The laurel was slowly yielding, yet, despite its heavy pruning, the brothers had managed to keep the bush looking smart. Some would have hacked away at it and left it looking a mess. The brothers pruned with care and an almost artistic eye.

"Jimmy. Charlie," Samuel paused before them. "This is Miss Fitzgerald. She is staying with the family."

The brothers turned, almost in unison. Close up they had a disturbing symmetry, as if they were one man duplicated. Neither spoke, but both stared at Clara with unveiled suspicion. She sensed they distrusted her. Perhaps they had heard about her and her investigations.

"Miss Fitzgerald is trying to lay to rest these foolish rumours about poor Master Harvey," Samuel's face became bleak. "I still can't fathom why anyone would wish to spread such evil nonsense. I feel for his mother, she must be very distressed by it all."

Neither under-gardener spoke. Samuel did not seem to notice the pointed silence they were projecting at him and Clara. He was too engrossed in his own thoughts. Finally, he shook his head, muttered under his breath and glanced at them.

"I've got work to do over by those beds Lady Howton wants filled with winter pansies. I'll leave you to talk."

Samuel turned and, giving another loud sigh, wandered off. Clara sensed a man as much in mourning for Harvey as any of the family. She turned to the two brothers who had still not said a word.

"As Samuel stated, I am trying to find who is behind the troubles at the hall. I suppose you have heard by now that each night someone appears at the window of the drawing room to disturb the family?"

The brothers still remained stony silent. Clara was becoming frustrated.

"That was a question," she pointed out. "You were both present when Harvey drowned, I believe?"

Clara waited. She was about to get cross and remind them that she had just asked another question, when Jimmy opened his mouth.

"We were near the lake working," he said.

Clara waited for more, but it failed to be forthcoming.

"How did you know Harvey was in trouble?" she asked.

Jimmy glanced at his brother. They seemed to be silently judging how much to say. Clara wondered why they were being so cautious. Was it because her suspicions that Harvey had never drowned were correct? If so, the brothers had to be complicit in the cover-up that followed. They were the only witnesses, it was their testimony that convinced the family Harvey had drowned and prevented further action being taken.

"We heard him shouting," Jimmy said at last. "We weren't sure at first what the noise was, then Charlie thought we ought to look."

Clara turned her attention to Charlie. He shrugged his shoulders at her.

"Master Harvey was in some trouble. Weed had tangled round his leg and the more he struggled the more entangled he became," Jimmy continued, he was getting into his stride now. "I swim, but Charlie doesn't. Poor Master Harvey's head was only just out of the water, he had to fight to keep his mouth and nose out. He started to flag and the weed pulled him down. I never got to him in time."

Jimmy cast a sideways look at his brother. Charlie had his lips clamped shut, as if he dare not speak a word. Clara was more convinced than ever that the brothers were hiding something.

"What if I was to say I don't believe you?" she said to them sternly. "I think Harvey left that lake alive and that you conspired with him to fake his death."

Jimmy made a good job of looking shocked. His brother hung his head and concentrated on the ground.

"That is a terrible thing to say!" Jimmy declared.

Clara put her hands on her hips and glared into his eyes.

"I have photographs that prove the man at the window is likely Harvey Howton. If he is an imposter he is most remarkably similar to the late man. The family are convinced Harvey comes to their drawing room window at night and, since I do not believe in the supernatural or dead men rising from their graves, I am left to conclude that Harvey never died at all. That this is all some elaborate hoax, though I cannot see its purpose," Clara took a pace towards Jimmy. "If all that is correct, it means you must be aware of the hoax. You must have known Harvey was alive when he left the lake and lied to the family."

"I'm no doctor!" Jimmy said, almost jumping out of his skin. "How was I to know Harvey were actually still alive? He looked dead."

"Leave us alone," Charlie rumbled, at last finding his tongue. "We told what we saw and that's that."

Clara turned to face him.

"And what did you see?" she demanded of him.

"Master Harvey going under the water. He was still as still could be when Jimmy dragged him out. He looked dead to me."

"And me!" Jimmy agreed.

"What happened when you pulled him onto the bank? Did you send for help?"

Jimmy looked to Charlie again. Clara wanted to shake him and stop the quick glances. Was he taking cues off Charlie? If so, she would be better to get them both alone.

"Well?" she snapped, her patience with them lost.

"We went for help," Jimmy said, taking care over the

words. "We fetched Mr Crawley."

This was news to Clara. Was Crawley in on this drama too?"

"Then what happened?"

"Mr Crawley had us carry Master Harvey to the house. We laid him on his own bed. Everyone was most upset."

Everyone not in on the subterfuge, Clara thought. How many of the servants had Harvey inveigled into his fraud? Perhaps not that many. The two under-gardeners would make excellent witnesses to his 'death' and the butler could have easily been the inside man. Clara needed to know what had gone on after Harvey was brought to the hall. Had there been no undertakers? Had a doctor not been called for the formality of a death certificate? All these hurdles could have produced potentially dangerous witnesses to the truth. How had Harvey circumvented them?

"I don't see why it can't be a ghost," Jimmy filled the pause that had come after his last statement. He looked more confident now. "Ghosts are real. Our mam saw a ghost. It was her grandfather who had been dead three years. He appeared by her bed, did he not Charlie?"

"He did," Charlie backed his brother.

"Looked as real as when he were alive, she said," Jimmy continued. "Master Harvey may have had unfinished business."

"Such as?" Clara asked.

Jimmy was caught out. He had said too much and he knew it.

"Oh, I don't know," Jimmy corrected himself. "When someone passes young there must be a lot of things they haven't quite finished."

Clara narrowed her eyes. She wanted to get cross with the brothers, but doubted that would achieve anything. Instead she decided to try a different approach. Clara thought carrots worked better than sticks in the majority of cases, and badgering the brothers was bringing her up against a brick wall. She acted as if she accepted what Jimmy had just told her.

"I was told you served with Harvey during the war?"

It was Charlie who now spoke, jumping in before Jimmy could open his mouth.

"We did. Harvey was our commanding officer."

"Samuel told me he was a good officer."

"He was," Charlie said firmly and now Clara could see a strong streak of loyalty coming out. Charlie was devoted to Harvey. "He cared about his men, made sure we were treated right. Nearly all of us were from the estate and surrounding villages. We knew each other well. Harvey knew nearly all of us from before the war too. At least for a time. Then we started to lose men and others, strangers, joined our unit."

Charlie winced and Clara realised that while the pain of losing friends was hard enough, the fact they were replaced with strangers hurt more. Charlie and Jimmy were like a lot of men who had grown up in the same village and worked on the same estate. They were insular and guarded with outsiders, even in times of war.

"Harvey joined later in the war?" Clara said.

"He wasn't old enough at the start," Charlie replied quickly, as if he thought Clara was implying Harvey had avoided serving. "Our unit had not seen a lot of action before he arrived, either. We had been serving in quieter sections of the front and we were mostly all the same men as when we first signed up. It wasn't long after Master Harvey arrived that we were finally thrown into the midst of everything. Then we lost people. Harvey took each death personally."

That didn't sound healthy to Clara's way of thinking, but Charlie clearly thought this an indication of Harvey's quality and loyalty to his men.

"He was good to you," Clara said.

"Master Harvey was the finest of captains I served under," Charlie said staunchly. "He saved my life once."

"Really?" Now Clara was truly intrigued. "How?"

"During this one battle, I fell into a shell hole and couldn't get out and it was filling up with water. I'd seen men drown in holes like that. It was horrid. I was shouting for help until I was hoarse and the night came on," Charlie's face hardened as he drifted back to that terrible time. "Jimmy was beside himself when I didn't return after the battle."

"I wanted to go out and search for him myself!" Jimmy said quickly.

"Master Harvey insisted on organising a search party, not just for me but for any men of the platoon who might be out there alive but injured. It was dangerous because we were under enemy scrutiny and his superiors were uncertain it was wise until they could get word from the Germans that rescue parties would not be fired upon, but Master Harvey would not wait," Charlie said proudly. "Master Harvey was not one to tarry. He said he would go out alone if needs be, but there were plenty of volunteers to go with him. He set out and he found me. Just in the nick of time too. It had been raining and I was up to my neck in muddy water."

"You almost drowned then?" Clara said, thinking of the irony of the situation.

Charlie did not appear to notice. He was standing very upright now.

"All you need to know about Master Harvey, is that he was a noble and honourable man," he said, his tone suggesting he would not tolerate any argument on the subject.

Clara smiled at them. They had told her more than they realised, mainly that they had a very good reason for owing Harvey a favour. Their loyalty to him would have made them perfect accomplices to his scheme. The question remained, however, why had Harvey gone to such trouble? Clara doubted she would get that answer from the brothers, they probably did not even know Harvey's motives. Clara suspected she had learned all she could.

She thanked the brothers for speaking to her and wandered back across the garden. She wanted to find Mr Crawley and hear his side of the story. Someone within the house had been helping Harvey and now she knew who that person was.

Chapter Sixteen

Clara had hardly walked into the house when there was a shriek. She ran into the great hall and found Betty in hysterics; a stuffed fox head had just departed company with the wall and fallen down near her. She was shaking as Clara grabbed her shoulders and moved her out of the macabre hall of dead animals and into the lighter front hall.

The moment of terror had passed. Betty began to calm down and her sobbing became less dramatic and more self-pitying.

"It just flew off the wall at me," Betty groaned. "It was like a demon lunging down at me. This damn house is haunted!"

Clara made her sit down in a chair.

"The house isn't haunted," she told Betty. "But it is old, and it creaks and things fall apart…"

"You can't tell me I didn't see my husband last night at that window!" Betty growled and the ferocity of her tone quite took Clara by surprise. "That was Harvey, as I live and breathe!"

"I don't doubt that," Clara responded.

Betty looked at her suspiciously.

"Then how can you say the house ain't haunted?"

"Because I don't think Harvey is actually dead."

Betty stared at Clara blankly for a moment, then she burst out into bitter laughter.

"And you think me believing in ghosts is fanciful?" she looked at Clara incredulously. "If Harvey wasn't dead, why didn't he contact me?"

"He was clearly working on some scheme..." Clara began.

"Scheme?" Betty became even angrier. "You don't know Harvey or what he was like. He would have contacted me. He would have! There was no reason not to as his family knew nothing about me. If this was some... some hoax, then he could have still played it out while letting me know he was ok. Instead, I heard nothing!"

Betty suddenly shrank back in her chair and mournfully rocked herself back and forth.

"He wouldn't have abandoned me," she insisted. "He had to be terribly ill, or... or... When I decided to come here I knew that must be the case. He wouldn't have left me with no word."

Betty closed her eyes and hugged her arms about herself.

"I can't stay here," she said abruptly. "This place scares the living daylights out of me. It is so full of dead people."

Betty reached out and grabbed Clara's hand.

"You should see my room. It's all laid out like something from my grandma's day. There is all this personal stuff left behind by someone else, someone now dead. I keep thinking they are going to walk back in, in the middle of the night. I can't stand it."

"I know what you mean," Clara sympathised. "The house is like a museum."

She paused as an idea came to her.

"Have you seen Harvey's room?"

Betty shook her head.

"Let me show you," Clara wasn't sure why she offered the suggestion, she wasn't even sure if seeing Harvey's room would help Betty, but she felt his wife should see his

126

private space and perhaps feel a last pang of connection with him. Clara had no idea what Harvey's intentions towards his wife were, but she suspected he had lost interest in Betty. She was right, after all, that he had nothing to lose if he had informed her he was alive and well. She need never know anything was wrong if he kept up his letter writing. In fact, it would have made better sense, as then she would not have turned up unexpectedly at the hall looking for him.

Clara guessed Harvey had been swept up in his other schemes and had simply neglected his wife. He had forgotten to write letters, or never found the time, and had become careless. He would not be the first nobleman to lose interest in his secret lover and to discard her callously.

That Betty had proved a little more determined than Harvey had expected was obvious. He had clearly been surprised when she confronted him in the drawing room. If Clara had needed proof that the man at the window was alive, it was abundantly plain when he became startled at the sight of his forgotten wife.

Betty followed Clara upstairs and along the cold passages until they came to Harvey's room. It was the same as when Clara had last looked in it. No one had bothered to lock the door, why would they? The room still held a faint hint of aroma, some sort of cologne perhaps that Harvey liked to wear. Betty walked inside and gazed about as if seeing a room full of treasure. Her eyes were wide with a genuine look of wonder. She reached out a hand and caressed Harvey's old cricket bat as if it was some precious antique.

"I feel like he is still here," she said, her eyes straying to the school trophies. "I knew so little about him."

Betty sat down on Harvey's bed. She had lost her look of wonder.

"Would he ever have brought me here?" she asked the room.

Clara said nothing, she didn't feel it was her place.

"It seemed so exciting at first, being his secret, being special. Now I am not so sure. Was I a secret because he was ashamed of me? Because he didn't want his family to know about me?" Betty shut her eyes tight and fought back tears. "He said he loved me, he wanted me. I said, no matter if I was a poor girl, I weren't no tart and I weren't giving myself to him for free."

"Good for you," Clara said gently.

"He said 'what if we were married?' and I said everything would be alright then. So, he obtained a special license and we were wed with no one knowing, not even my mum," Betty was grimacing now. "I thought I was being canny. I thought once we were wed he could not be rid of me easily, like. I didn't want to be one of them girls who plays around with a gentleman only to be cast aside with nothing but their clothes to their name."

Betty rose restlessly. She went to the writing desk and opened it. Her fingers ran over the leather of the writing surface.

"He wrote some of those letters to me here," she said, and her voice softened again. A smile crept onto her lips. "I can picture him sitting here, thinking what to say, and all the time laughing to himself that no one else knew about us."

Betty opened drawers and took out a fountain pen. She turned it over and over in her hands, smiling at the workmanship, then she replaced it. Next, she started looking through the drawers that contained Harvey's latest correspondence.

"I wrote back, but never to this address. It would have been too risky. I used to address my letters to the local Post Office and Harvey would collect them from there," she pulled out letters and glanced at the handwriting, as she pulled out a selection so a postcard fell from among them. It flopped onto the writing shelf. Betty picked it up and casually flicked it over to read the back, then her smile vanished.

Betty started to sway on her feet. Clara thought she

might faint, so she came up behind her and tried to move her to the bed, but the woman wouldn't budge.

"He lied to me," she whispered.

Clara took the postcard from her unresisting hands. The front showed a picture of the hills of Scotland, on the back in an elegant and clearly feminine hand was scrawled a message;

My Sweetest Harvey, what a wonderful time we had! I have told father about your proposal and he is happy to give his consent! I accept, dear Harvey, I would be delighted to marry you! I shall not whisper a word until all is ready, as I promised. Write soon, dearest. Your ever loving, Elizabeth.

The date on the postcard was from earlier in the year. Since there had been no announcement and the family had made no mention of a fiancé it would seem the engagement was still a secret, or had fallen through. Whatever the case, it was plain Harvey was courting other women, even proposing marriage to them, when he already had a wife.

"I'm sorry," Clara said to Betty, feeling guilty for bringing her up to this room and revealing Harvey's double-dealing.

Betty merely shrugged her shoulders.

"I should have known," she said miserably. "Why would he want a wife like me? What could I offer him? I don't have a fortune or a fancy title. I am the sort of girl more fit to be a servant to the Howtons than part of the family. They have made that plain enough to me."

Betty hung her head.

"Was any of it real? Even the wedding?" Betty started to cry. "Was that all a lie too? I trusted him, but what if the license was fake? What if we are not legally married at all?"

Clara hoped Harvey had not been so cruel.

"That doesn't matter," she told Betty firmly. "Whether you were really married or not, Lord Howton will make sure you are taken care of. He will honour his brother's actions."

"I feel so stupid," Betty wept to herself. "I believed him. I believed every word."

"You had no reason not to," Clara comforted her. "Don't berate yourself."

"I have to leave this house," Betty wiped away her tears. "It's bad enough all this, but I keep thinking about those footprints. Harvey came into the hall last night and I think he will come again. I don't want to be here when my dead husband appears."

Despite it all, Betty was certain Harvey was deceased. He may have betrayed her over their marriage, but she could not imagine him faking his own death. Clara admitted it would have been quite a feat of planning and sheer gall. At any point he could have been discovered. But Harvey was a man who took chances.

"Will you go home?" Clara asked Betty.

"I don't know," Betty gnawed on her thumb agitatedly. "Lord Howton says we must talk about my future and my inheritance from Harvey. And, I can't go home just yet, I need to know what dark magic has resurrected my husband from the dead and who is behind it. I can't go home thinking of him as a walking corpse. I have to see that resolved."

Clara nodded, she understood. Betty had loved Harvey and, although he had treated her badly, she still wanted to know that his soul rested in peace. Clara wished she could convince her that Harvey's soul was not currently in jeopardy as he was very much alive, but she knew when she was faced with a battle she could not win.

"There is an inn a couple of miles away that rents out rooms," Clara told Betty. "You could stay there if you have money?"

Betty shook her head.

"I don't have enough," she looked bleak. "I'm stuck here, aren't I?"

"Not necessarily," Clara smiled. "I'll loan you the money. You can pay me back when you get your inheritance."

Betty narrowed her eyes.

"Why would you do that?"

"To help you," Clara answered honestly. "I can see the distress being in this house causes you and I would like to offer you an alternative."

"That would be most kind, thank you," Betty replied, ducking her head so she didn't have to meet Clara's eyes. "I would like to leave now."

Clara had to return to her bedroom to fetch the money. She gave more than enough to Betty for at least two nights at the inn and extra for meals. She hoped by the time the money was gone she would have solved the case and Lord Howton would have made financial arrangements for Betty, so she could go home knowing she would be provided for.

"That is all I have," Clara told the girl.

"Thank you, it is more than kind," Betty clutched the money to her chest. "It will be good to sleep somewhere without all this stuff hanging over me. Who wants to live in the shadow of the past?"

Who indeed, Clara thought to herself.

Betty went to her room to finish packing and Clara wandered back downstairs to the grand hall. The stuffed fox's head was lying on the floor where it had fallen. The moth-eaten nose had been badly knocked in the fall and the animal looked as though it bore a lop-sided grin rather than the snarl it was meant to have. Clara picked it up and took a good look at the old thing. It certainly would give you a fright with its bared teeth and glass eyes as it hurtled down from the wall. Looking up, Clara could see the space it had forsaken when it plummeted down on Betty. There was a gap between the heads of another fox and a badger mounted quite high. There was a circle of darker colour on the wallpaper where the head had hung and prevented the red flock from fading, unlike the area around it.

Clara turned the fox head over and looked at its

mountings. It had a brass loop at the top which would have hung over a nail in the wall. Clara peered up and could just see the nail protruding from the wall. It was a stout thing and looked solidly embedded. The brass loop had neither perished nor worn away. There seemed no reason for the fox head to have suddenly parted company with the wall.

Clara gazed upwards again, she noticed something sitting just on top of the badger's head. She changed her angle and tried to see what it was. It looked like a hook, similar to a fishing hook but bigger, and it was lodged in the badger's head, a thin slip of twine hung off the end, snapped from a longer piece. Clara pressed her lips together, starting to see the shape of things. The hook would have been slipped under the brass loop of the fox head, raising it up slightly from the nail. Then a length of twine would be tied to the end and run up to somewhere on the staircase which dominated the ground hall. With a sharp enough tug, the hook would jerk the brass loop free from the nail and the fox head would plummet down.

Now Clara could see how the prank was done. Clearly someone wanted Betty out of the hall. Unfortunately, there were a considerable number of suspects for such a desire. Clara sighed. Well they had got their wish.

She propped the fox head up against a cabinet and went in search of Mr Crawley, hoping he might have some answers for her.

Chapter Seventeen

It took over an hour to track down Mr Crawley. He was in the butler's pantry, a rather misnamed room that served as a workspace for Mr Crawley. He was carefully ironing Lord Howton's shirts, which he considered his personal duty. Clara had been directed to the pantry by a disgruntled laundry maid who took Crawley's insistence on ironing his master's shirts as a personal affront. She probably had good reason to feel that way, Clara reflected.

Mr Crawley had taken off his jacket to do the ironing. He was put out when Clara peered around his pantry door.

"Miss Fitzgerald, you are in the servants' quarters," he told her bluntly.

"Indeed, it happens to be where you find the servants," Clara replied with a smile.

"It is not fitting," Mr Crawley grumbled.

He was a middle-aged man of considerable height, so he could tower over nearly everyone in the household, including his lordship. He had a very oval head, made to look somewhat dome-like because of his slicked back dark hair. He never seemed to smile, though Clara thought that was a trait peculiar to butlers. Smiling was something other people did, but not such respected and high-ranking servants. He was really rather typical of a bygone age, but then much the same could be said about Howton Hall in general. There was a sense that everyone was clinging onto the past within the confines of the hall; clinging on for dear life. Crawley was just the same as the rest of them, unable to shed off the prejudices and expectations of the last generation.

Crawley had not stopped ironing. He swept the flat iron around the buttons of a shirt with slick precision.

"I thought the hall had a fully staffed laundry?" Clara could not resist prodding him, though she made the comment sound innocent enough.

"The hall is fully staffed, but I am of the opinion that his lordship deserves something better for the ironing of his shirts than the careless hand of a laundry maid."

The comment was said with pure arrogance and more than a smidge of spite.

"Are the laundry maids so hopeless?" Clara asked, thinking that the ironing of a shirt was not a great art. As long as the creases were all gone, surely that was what mattered? Annie could probably correct her on that.

"The laundry maids are young and they come and go. No sooner has Mrs Reed the housekeeper trained one up, then she goes off and gets married. His lordship cannot have his shirts passing through such a collection of inexperienced hands," Crawley flicked the iron down a sleeve with the lightest of touches. The shirt was done and he held it up to the glare of a bare bulb to examine its appearance. Satisfied he placed it on a metal hangar and fitted it onto a clothing rack where other shirts hung.

"I had hoped to talk to you about Harvey Howton," Clara filled the pause which fell as the shirt was restored to its place, ready to be taken back upstairs to his lordship's wardrobe.

"I doubt I can tell you any more than you have already learned from the family," Mr Crawley said brusquely. He had picked up another shirt and was looking it over.

"There! See what I mean? They have lost a button when washing this one! Utter carelessness!"

"Perhaps his lordship lost the button?" Clara suggested.

"Certainly not!" Mr Crawley looked offended, as if she was questioning his professional abilities. "I personally collect his lordship's washing from his room and check all the items before passing them to the laundry. I make sure each item is in fit condition. I hardly would bother sending a ripped shirt to be cleaned. I also make note of stains, so I can check on the thoroughness of the staff. Naturally, I count the buttons too."

How delightful, Clara thought. No wonder the laundry maid had pulled a face when she had told Clara where the butler was. He must be impossible to work with. She appreciated that such households ran on precision; everything was done to perfection, from the cleaning of the silver, to the sweeping of the floors. But it must be infuriating for the laundry staff to have Mr Crawley glaring over their shoulders and questioning their work all the time.

"Fortunately, I have a full stock of spare buttons," Mr Crawley moved to a cabinet containing a number of small drawers. He opened one and took out a button which he compared to those remaining on the shirt. Satisfied it was a match, he took out a reel of thread and a needle and began work on the replacement.

"I wanted to ask you about the day Harvey died," Clara said.

Mr Crawley appeared to be ignoring her as he worked on the shirt, which was surprisingly bold for the uptight butler, considering she was a household guest and therefore technically to be afforded his full attention.

"What precisely would you care to know?" Mr Crawley asked, still not looking up.

"You were summoned when the under-gardeners pulled Harvey from the lake?"

"I was," Mr Crawley agreed. "The gardeners are not

allowed inside the house unless given explicit permission. One of the under-gardeners came to the kitchen door and said Master Harvey had been in an accident. I went at once."

"He did not state Harvey had drowned?"

"He had enough sense in his head not to upset the kitchen staff that way. He explained as he escorted me to the lake what had occurred."

"And Harvey was truly dead when you came to him?"

Mr Crawley's head shot up and, for just a moment, Clara thought he looked uncertain. The question had startled him and it was hard to startle Mr Crawley.

"That is a very peculiar question," he hedged.

"The situation is most peculiar," Clara pointed out. "It is not every day a notable family claim a deceased member of their lineage is stalking their property."

"On that you have a point," Mr Crawley admitted grudgingly. "Not that I care for this talk of the walking dead. It is most inappropriate."

"The talk, or the walking dead man?"

"Both," Mr Crawley growled. He finished with the button and took the shirt to his ironing board. His flat irons had been sat by the fire and were sufficiently hot again to use.

"But Harvey was dead?" Clara persisted, feeling he was trying to ignore her again.

"Madam, to suggest otherwise would beggar belief!" Mr Crawley snapped. "I personally saw him carried to the house and deposited in his bedroom."

"What happened after that?" Clara asked, guessing she was not going to get a straight answer to her previous question and that it was not worth pushing it.

"I broke the news to the family. It was a most difficult time. Lord Howton wished to see his brother, as did the former Lady Howton. I escorted them to his bedroom and they looked upon him a while, then removed themselves. I did not pursue them, as it was not fitting," Crawley was back to sweeping his iron around the buttons on the shirt.

"What about the funeral arrangements?" Clara asked.

"Master Harvey had given very specific instructions. He did not want a funeral and he was to be buried in his mausoleum. He wanted to be carried there by those among the staff who served with him in the war."

"He had made all these arrangements?" Clara said, surprised that a young man would have taken the time.

"Master Harvey had detailed his desires during his service in the war, when it was feasible he might die at any moment. His requests were honoured even though he had not died on active duty. The family agreed Master Harvey would have wanted it that way."

That was a reasonable explanation. The war had brought death close to many and had made even the young contemplate their mortality.

"Was a doctor called?"

"Only to sign the death certificate," Mr Crawley explained. "It was a mere formality. I summoned the family doctor and explained the situation. He briefly looked at Master Harvey and then signed the certificate."

Another potential hurdle overcome, Clara thought to herself. She was beginning to see how, with Crawley's help, Harvey could have manipulated the situation to make it seem as if he had drowned.

"There were no undertakers?" Clara asked.

"I laid out Master Harvey personally. Every Howton who has died in the hall has been laid out by his butler or, in the case of the ladies, by the housekeeper. It is tradition. I placed Harvey in his coffin myself."

And so no one would have handled Harvey and realised he was alive except those already in on the scheme.

"And then he was entombed in the mausoleum?"

"Yes. It was a private service, just the family and the household staff. I thought it most beautiful."

And completely fraudulent, Clara mused.

"May I ask why you wish to know all this?" Mr Crawley was still not meeting Clara's eyes, but he was observing her nonetheless.

"To understand everything," Clara replied, deciding that she could be vague in her answers too. "You must be aware of the disturbances affecting the family on a nightly basis."

"Of course," Mr Crawley said.

"I wonder what your opinion on the matter might be?" Clara leaned against the frame of the pantry door and waited.

Mr Crawley flicked up the iron from the shirt and placed it by the fire. He took his time checking his work and placing the shirt on a hangar. Clara knew he was buying himself time.

"I do not have an opinion on the subject," he said at last.

Clara almost snorted with laughter at the suggestion, but she maintained a neutral expression.

"Do you believe in the supernatural, Mr Crawley?"

"I have not given the matter much thought," Mr Crawley responded, plucking up another shirt. "I find myself overall too busy with material concerns to spend time contemplating such things. I believe in God, naturally."

"I was just curious," Clara said. "Considering you know the family so well and obviously for so long. What do you say to the other servants when they raise the topic of Harvey's ghost?"

"That they ought to be getting on with their work and minding their tongues," Mr Crawley said sternly.

He at last turned his full attention on Clara.

"I appreciate you have been asked to solve this little conundrum, but you are looking in the wrong place. No one here knows anything and I would rather you do not go about asking too many questions among the servants. They are disturbed enough as it is."

"Disturbed by what?" Clara asked bluntly, trying to draw him out.

"Disturbed by the rumours of ghosts and demons," Mr

Crawley snorted. "Now, I really do not have time to talk further."

This was plain rudeness to a guest and something which, under normal circumstances, Mr Crawley would never have considered. Clara was pleased to see her questions had rattled him enough to cause him to drop his usually impeccable manners.

"I don't think the staff need worry themselves," she said lightly, starting to turn and leave.

"Why would that be?" Mr Crawley asked, unable to stop himself.

"Well, it is quite obvious," Clara smiled.

"Perhaps not to all, might you elaborate on what you are thinking?" Mr Crawley had dropped his head and was assessing her like one of those stains he had mentioned on his lordship's shirts.

"It is simple really," Clara enjoyed stringing him along. "Since ghosts do not exist and the dead cannot rise from their graves, quite plainly the man at the window is a living being."

Mr Crawley said nothing.

"I first thought someone was playing a cruel hoax on the family and masquerading as Harvey," Clara continued. "Now I believe Harvey was never really dead. That he fooled the family into thinking he was so he could play this cruel hoax on them all."

Mr Crawley managed to mask the gasp he was going to give at this explanation with a snort instead.

"I find that most incredible," he said after a moment.

"And yet, it must be the only answer to the problem," Clara was enjoying herself. "The only thing I cannot as yet answer is why Harvey would go to such lengths. My fear is that he has something sinister in mind."

"Master Harvey was a fine man. One of integrity and honesty," Mr Crawley countered. "He would not play such games."

"So, he has your loyalty?" Clara smiled. "I wonder how far you would go for him, Mr Crawley? How far you would go for any member of this family?"

Mr Crawley was silent, he had no response fitting to such a question. Clara had learned enough. His reluctance to speak along with the little information he had given her, explained how the trick had been performed. All it took was three men loyal to Harvey and the rest could be manipulated to suit his needs. Mr Crawley was the key man; with him in charge of the arrangements he could ensure that the doctor did not examine the body and that only he was present when Harvey was placed in his coffin. Whether he then helped him out before the mausoleum was fully sealed up, or made some sort of switch earlier on remained unanswered, and the butler was not likely to reveal his trickery. But Clara could see how it could all be done now. It was risky, but Harvey would have played on the fact that, other than his brother and mother, none of the family would be interested in viewing his body. His family's very disinterest in him would have played to his advantage.

"You clearly have a lot of shirts to iron," Clara smiled, moving back from the pantry doorway. "I shall leave you alone."

Clara left the butler to his work. She had clearly upset him. Throwing out the comment that she thought Harvey was alive was a tactical ploy – she wanted to draw Harvey out. She had no way of knowing if Mr Crawley was in contact with Harvey, but she guessed he was as someone was passing him news from the household. He knew about Oliver's cameras after all. Now she hoped Crawley would reveal this new information to Harvey and he, in turn, would feel the need to push his plan forward. With any luck, this would give her the opportunity to intercept Harvey. Chasing him when he appeared at the drawing room window was clearly not working. She had considered hiding in the bushes and ambushing him, but she could not be sure someone would not warn him.

No, best to play things his way and to use the fact he had a contact inside the house against him. Sooner or later Harvey was going to make a mistake and she would snare him. Then they would find out just what he was playing at.

Chapter Eighteen

They gathered in the drawing room again that evening. Betty was absent. She had departed earlier in the afternoon with her luggage, to head to the inn Clara had mentioned. The family seemed relieved she was gone, there was a distinct leavening of tension in the air. Clara felt sad that Betty's presence had been so despised. She didn't think she deserved such hatred, especially from Angelica who should surely understand the situation the girl was in? It seemed they all, (perhaps except for Lord Howton) thought her a fortune hunter who had latched on to the wrong brother.

Richard was sitting in his usual place working through a heavy volume on Medieval architecture. He didn't seem to be getting very far. He put down the book, his thumb serving as a book mark to keep his place, and glanced towards the windows. The night outside was dark and blustery. Clara could hear the trees rustling and occasionally a sharp gust would rattle the door leading onto the terrace.

"The hour cometh," Richard remarked in sepulchre tones.

"Don't!" Diana begged. She was sitting near the fire trying to read a woman's magazine that featured knitting patterns. Knitting was Diana's passion, but tonight she could not focus on her needles. They remained silent in her work bag. "I hate thinking about it. Why must we all sit here and wait?"

"My thoughts exactly!" Genevieve interjected. "All we need do is place someone outside to grab the fellow when he appears!"

"We ought to respect the dead," Lord Howton said solemnly. "I have grown convinced these last few days that Harvey is trying to impart a message to us."

"He could try harder!" Genevieve snapped. "A letter or a telegram would suffice!"

"I think what father is saying is that Harvey's spirit is burdened, and he is using what little spectral energy he has to try and communicate with us," Richard talked down to his sister, as if what he said was obvious. Clara found it amusing. "He clearly has little strength and is unable to deliver his message as he would like."

"Do you actually listen to yourself when you say such things?" Genevieve spluttered. "Someone is trying to frighten the family. Stand someone outside and nab him."

"I don't think we should dismiss the supernatural so simply," Lord Howton rebuked his daughter gently. "None of us knows what awaits us on the other side. I would hate to do something rash that could condemn Harvey's soul to torment."

"What is this?" Genevieve demanded. "Before you wanted rid of him, you were talking about exorcisms and such nonsense, now you are fretting about Harvey's soul?"

"It was the footprints," Angelica interrupted. The fact she had spoken up at all before the family was enough to silence Genevieve. "Harvey came into the house. He was trying to reach me. He is a lost soul. I think his brother has come to understand that now."

Clara, listening to this conversation at a distance, studied Lord Howton's face during this speech and realised it was true. He had first thought that a demon was tormenting the family, now he was coming to see the man at the window as a messenger. Clara thought this new idea as incredulous as Genevieve did, but it was plain his lordship would not be swayed. He was a very spiritual man and he had convinced himself that Harvey's spirit was walking and wanted to tell them something.

"I can't believe what I am hearing!" Genevieve laughed hollowly, "You are all quite mad!"

She was stopped by the clock in the room chiming. Everyone paused. As Richard had stated so grimly, the hour had come.

Earlier in the afternoon, Clara had asked Lord Howton if she might hide herself outside the drawing room in the bushes and observe the man from there. She was hopeful that, if she was discreet, she might be able to track him back to his hideout and reveal him for what he was. Lord Howton had denied the request for the same reasons he had just given Genevieve. Clara thought it nonsense, but then she recalled that this was a family who believed themselves cursed. It was hardly far-fetched, when you believed in witchcraft, to start believing in the dead returned.

Clara had to abide by his instructions, even if she did think they were foolish.

Oliver was stood near the sideboard watching the windows with his hands in his pockets. He had not set up his cameras again. They had served their purpose already. Clara had examined the pictures he had taken of the mysterious footprints, though it still eluded her what substance had been used to make them. It was certainly not mud, she had wondered about ink as they were so black, but she thought there must be some further component to the mixture. The maids had been hard at work all day removing them. It had been a test of wills between their elbow grease and whatever substance had been used to make the prints. So far, the prints were winning, though they did appear paler than before. Clara moved beside Oliver.

"When I agreed to photograph dead people for the police, this was not what I had in mind," Oliver said to her, his voice hushed. "I've seen my fair share of grisly crime scenes. In none of them did the corpse get up and start wandering around."

"Corpses don't," Clara assured him

"You won't be swayed, will you?" Oliver grinned at her. "I mean, even if you can find a rational explanation for this, can you really say there is no such thing as the supernatural?"

"I am quietly confident," Clara replied.

"Well, I'm not. I like to think there is more to this life than we know," that was Oliver's final word on the subject.

Everyone's attention was now on the terrace. While not all the family were exactly looking at the windows, everyone was waiting, listening in anticipation. Diana was pulling a face rather like one you might wear when about to have a tooth extracted. Angelica was stiff as a rod and had her eyes shut. Lord Howton smoked his pipe in hasty puffs. Only Lady Howton, Genevieve and Richard had their eyes trained on the terrace. Clara turned her attention from the family and to the windows. Oliver had moved to lean against the wall, staring at the carpet rather than look outside. Clara had made the mistake of looking away just before Harvey had appeared last night. Tonight, she would not break her gaze.

She waited. The minutes ticked by.

The wind howled violently, like a banshee in the trees. The world outside seemed in torment. It was the sort of night to draw the curtains and sit close to the fire. The sort of night when all manner of horrible, unnatural things could be imagined to lurk in the dark.

Richard started to tap his fingers on the hard cloth cover of his book. Genevieve folded her arms across her chest. The clock chimed the quarter hour.

"He appears to be late," Clara remarked to no one in particular. "Possibly the weather has delayed him."

No one responded, not even to tell her that it was a crass thing to say. The silence was becoming oppressive. Diana had dropped her head into her hands, trying to pretend none of it was happening.

Clara tapped the toe of her shoe on the carpet. She was impatient at the best of times, but especially when waiting for a prankster pretending to be a dead man. When she did catch hold of Harvey Howton, she was going to give him some stern words.

Another fifteen minutes crept away and still there was no sign of the man. Lord Howton relaxed his shoulders and began to tap out the bowl of his pipe. The tension was easing; it seemed Harvey was not going to come.

Angelica sharply rose from the sofa and walked to the windows. She put her hands either side of her head and pressed her face to the glass to see out better.

"Where is he?" she asked pitifully.

"I don't think he is coming tonight," Lord Howton said gently.

Angelica took a step back from the glass.

"Why not? He has never missed a night before?" she looked around her, trying to discern an answer from the faces in the room. "Is this it?"

"It's over," Diana gave a low moan, akin to a sigh. "He isn't coming. He has gone."

"Gone?" Angelica's voice had narrowed to a squeak as her throat contracted in distress. "Gone where?"

"Perhaps to heaven, my dear," Lady Howton said softly.

"No, no, no!" Angelica turned back to the windows and glowered out into the night. "He mustn't! He has not told me what he wants yet!"

"Maybe I was wrong," Lord Howton said swiftly, trying to placate his stepmother. "Perhaps he wanted nothing. I do recall that in the past the deceased would appear on successive nights to their relatives to let them know they had passed into the next life. I read it somewhere."

"No!" Angelica burst out, her voice shrill before it descended into a sob. "It's my fault! I locked my room last night! I never lock my room door!"

Angelica cupped her hands over her mouth, her distress volatile.

"I was scared in case he came into the house. I was scared of my own son," she cried. "So, I locked my door and look what happened! He came to my room and stood outside, unable to enter. I turned him away, his own mother! I let my fear govern me!"

"I think, my dear, you are being irrational," Lady Howton said, though her words were cold rather than comforting.

"Don't you see? Last night was it, his final attempt! He came to me, to my room, to tell me what it was he wanted and he could not enter! And that was it, the last time!" Angelica was hysterical. "He won't come again. He won't! I missed my last chance!"

Clara stepped forward to the woman, as no one else seemed inclined to help her. She put her arm around her shoulders and tried to comfort her.

"Think of things this way, you are in no worse a position than before. Whatever he intended, it was probably just a message of love, to let you know he was alright," Clara wittered on, wondering where she had conjured such nonsense from. The man at the window had never been dead, any message he wanted to tell them he could do so at any time, and without this play-acting. Harvey ought not to torment his mother like this.

"I suggest we forget things for tonight," Lord Howton interceded. "We are not qualified to understand the ways of the supernatural. Possibly there is another reason Harvey has not appeared tonight. Let us go to bed and sleep on things."

Angelica seemed unconvinced, but Clara also thought sleep would do her good.

"Perhaps he got wind that I was going to shoot him with my shotgun," Genevieve said with more than a hint of pride. "I do hope so. Clearly scared the life out of the fellow."

"Darling, try to be more tactful," Lady Howton reminded her daughter, though not with much force. She seemed to have drifted away from the idea Harvey was a spectre too.

"We shall all retire," Lord Howton insisted. "Tomorrow we can look at this problem afresh."

Angelica did not move, she seemed frozen to the spot. When Clara tried to gently ease her from the window she threw off her arm.

"You changed the lock on the terrace door!" she suddenly declared, pointing a finger at a shiny new lock and handle on the old wood. "We agreed this morning you would not!"

"I did not give instructions to change the lock," Lord Howton said quickly, looking as surprised as Angelica.

"I gave the instruction," Lady Howton said, rising from the sofa where she sat. "I do not want a strange man, dead or alive, wandering my home at night."

"But, Harvey has to be able to get in!" Angelica demanded. "Where is the key? I must unlock this at once."

"You shall do no such thing. I cannot abide the thought of a corpse creeping into the hall while I sleep," Lady Howton was firm.

"My dear," Lord Howton turned to her, "we did agree…"

"You agreed," Lady Howton shot back at him. "No one cared for my thoughts. No, I shall stand firm on this. Look at Diana. The distress this is causing her is dreadful. I shall not have her left in terror to go to sleep because this man in the dark might enter the hall. You are not thinking of the living people in this house, who are far more important than the dead."

"Far more important!" Angelica almost exploded. "My Harvey was the most precious thing in my life! You have your children alive and well! I do not have my child!"

Angelica burst into painful sobs.

"He was the only thing that made this life bearable," she slumped to her knees. "Please! Where is the key for the door?"

Lady Howton looked at her coldly, unmoved by her tears. She did not say a word as she marched to the door of the drawing room and left.

Angelica howled, a terrible, grief-stricken howl.

"Come on, we have to get her to her room. She will make herself ill like this," Genevieve commanded, thumping her brother on the arm to get him to move.

Together they pulled Angelica to her feet. She was unresisting. A broken woman who had been cut into pieces by her suffering. They led her from the drawing room and upstairs.

"I think we must all retire," Lord Howton said in a small voice to those who remained.

Diana jumped up at once and headed for the door. Clara and Oliver were not far behind. Lord Howton lingered a moment to put out the fire and the lights, then he joined them in the dark grand hall.

"I hardly know what to say to the woman," he said, glancing at Clara. "She is so deeply distressed. Her loss is so painful."

"There is nothing you can say," Clara told him. "But we must put this mystery to bed. I do not think Harvey Howton is dead."

Lord Howton, rather than being amazed, laughed at her.

"My dear, you really cannot accept that there is more to this world than logic and reason dictate."

He walked up the stairs still chuckling to himself. Clara decided not to let it offend her.

Chapter Nineteen

Clara fell asleep rapidly enough, unafraid that spectres were roaming the halls of the house. She was tired and the questions that would usually plague her mind and keep her awake were thankfully absent. Her mind was exhausted and could not be bothered to conjure up endless possibilities and problems concerning her case. She rested her head on her pillow and slipped safely into the void of dreamless slumber.

She was rudely awakened sometime in the early hours of the morning. The light in the room was just going from the pitch black of full night, to the hazy grey of pre-dawn. Clara jerked awake and, for a moment, failed to understand what had roused her. Then the scream that had woken her came again.

Clara sat up and glanced over at a small clock that stood on the mantel of the fireplace. She shook her head; too dark to read the time. She dragged her feet from beneath the warm blankets and nestled them in her cold slippers, hauled on her heavy dressing gown and headed for the door. There had been no further screams and, as she stood in the corridor outside her room, she found herself uncertain of which way to head. Perhaps, after all, it had been a dream?

The house seemed cloaked in silence, no one else appeared to be stirring. Clara rubbed at her eyes. It might have been an owl, some species could make the oddest of noises and, in the moment of waking, might seem to be a person crying out. She started to go back into her room when she heard the thumping of feet somewhere deeper in the house, and the exclamation of a man;

"Good lord!"

Clara headed in the same direction, fumbling her way down unlit corridors, her memory poorly raking up a floorplan of the house, so she lost her way before finding where she wanted to be. She was attracted by the light of a torch shining at the end of a hallway. The corridors of the hall were not fitted with artificial lighting, only the main rooms downstairs had that luxury. To navigate at night the family either used candles or torches, or walked blind.

The torchlight was moving, as if someone was examining the floor. Whispering voices were speaking together. Clara hurried to the end of the corridor she was in and turned left to find herself confronted with a wholly unexpected scene. Lord Howton was shining the torch over a person lying on the floor. To his left was Diana, white as a sheet and clutching a hand to her mouth. Next to her, an arm awkwardly placed about her shoulders, was her brother Richard.

Clara stepped closer and looked at the person on the floor. The way no one was bending down to help the figure, suggested the person had not merely fainted or tripped. Lord Howton acknowledged her with a nod of his head, then helpfully moved the light of his torch to illuminate a large puddle of blood on the floorboards. It was spreading out from beneath the fallen person, who Clara could now see was a man lying face down, his legs bent at the knee, his arms splayed out. Clara crouched down and tried to see his face.

"I shall save you the bother, Miss Fitzgerald," Lord Howton spoke. "It is Harvey."

His lordship's face had drained of all colour. Clara rose, her lips pursed together.

"I think we ought to call the police," she said quietly.

Lord Howton nodded.

"I think that would be advisable. Richard, if you would?"

Richard Howton shuffled his sister away downstairs as he went to make the phone call. Clara moved to stand next to his lordship and look down on Harvey. She wished the corridor had proper lights so they could get a clearer picture of the scene, rather than the snatches the torch afforded.

"What happened?" Clara asked Lord Howton.

"I am afraid I hardly know," Lord Howton replied. "I heard a scream and left my room. I heard another and came to this spot where I found Diana stood by the body. She, apparently, had heard a bang from her room and had come out to investigate. She found Harvey. Richard arrived a few moments after me."

Clara had not taken her eyes off the body on the floor.

"Well, I cannot argue Harvey is alive now," she said softly.

"That is a somewhat insensitive comment, don't you think?" his lordship responded sharply.

"I apologise," Clara added hastily. "I spoke without thinking."

She tilted her head, trying to see the face of the victim better. He had fallen with his head down but leaning to the left, so it was possible to see some of his features in profile.

"You are certain this is Harvey?" she asked.

"Yes, my dear," Lord Howton moved the torchlight over the man's face. "I would not mistake him."

Richard reappeared in the corridor.

"I have called the police," he said. "Diana is in the drawing room. I poured her a glass of brandy. What about everyone else?"

"We best rouse them all before the police arrive," Lord

Howton decided. "It would be unkind to keep them in the dark until rudely awakened by the police."

"Someone should stay by the body to see it is not accidentally disturbed," Clara added quickly.

"Then, might I suggest you fulfil that role Miss Fitzgerald?" Lord Howton requested. "I ought to explain this to my wife and stepmother personally. You are not afraid to remain here alone?"

"No, Lord Howton," Clara assured him. "This is not my first body."

Lord Howton grimaced.

"What a strange occupation for a woman," he muttered, then he turned to his son. "Richard, will you wake Genevieve and take her to the drawing room? Then we must summon Crawley and have him briefed on the matter."

"Could someone also awaken Mr Bankes?" Clara quickly added. "He is the police photographer, after all. He could be taking pictures of the scene while we await the police."

Lord Howton agreed, then he and his son departed on their various errands. Clara remained by the now definitely deceased Harvey Howton. What had just occurred? She could not see what had caused the fatal wound, as he had fallen onto his chest and the blood pooled from beneath him. It could have been a knife wound, but it might just as easily be a shot from a gun. The only certainty was that Harvey was now dead. Clara shook her head. Why had he played such games?

She was alone for what seemed like hours, the darkness in the hall not receding as the time fled by. The corridor had no windows and the only natural light it received would come from the rooms that led on to it. As they all had their doors firmly closed, no chink of light crept in. Clara became bored, she tried the door nearest to her and found it was one of the forgotten bedrooms, some timeless space left in memory of a long dead ancestor. The thick burgundy curtains were not drawn, and probably had not been drawn in years. An antique four-poster bed, hung with matching curtains, seemed haunted by the shadow of its former owner. The door opened inwards and Clara pushed it back and placed a chair in front of it to keep it open. The dawn light was now visible and poured into the corridor; a milky glow seemed to reflect over Harvey's body.

Clara went to the next room and opened its door too. This led into an old dressing room, still containing the clothes of a former Howton. More light streamed into the corridor. Carefully stepping around Harvey, Clara opened the two rooms opposite. The four doorways cast triangles of light into the corridor and overlapped one another to provide illumination on the scene. Clara could now get a better look at the victim, not having to rely on the small pools of battery-powered light flashed by the torch.

Harvey was dressed in clothes that had been artistically made to look ragged. She had seen the clothes worn by tramps and others whose rips and tears were caused by endless wear. They did not look like that neat cuts someone had made to Harvey's clothes. It was the work of someone who was wanting to give the impression of the decaying clothes a corpse might be dressed in. The trousers had been torn in various places, but the hems were completely intact, an oversight by someone not aware of how frayed trouser cuffs can become when worn a long time. The shirt was the same; snags torn in it, but the cuffs perfect.

A better job had been done of muddying the clothes and also streaking them with green, as if the person had rubbed against some moss-covered wall. Clara, however, thought it had been rather overdone. Harvey had been buried in a coffin in a stone tomb, he had not had to claw his way up through the ground like some stunt in a horror movie. He should not be so muddy, for that matter, his clothes were too ragged for the brief time he had been dead. Clothes do decay in the ground, but they take a long time, and they do not develop such great tears in the space of a few brief weeks.

Harvey had certainly been trying his hardest to give the impression of being a dead man walking. There were maggots on his clothes. Clara noticed one of his pockets appeared to be moving and when she gingerly poked it, she realised it was full of wriggling maggots. This was how Harvey had fooled Oliver. He had probably hidden behind the mausoleum and quickly sprinkled himself with the maggots he kept in his pocket for such a possibility. Then he sprang out, looking like a rotting corpse. The make-up on his face and hands added to the impression. He appeared to have open sores on his exposed flesh, but closer examination proved them to be rather rough work with rouge and putty. The sort of thing a person would wear on the stage and which would look effective at a distance and in dimmed light. If any further proof was needed, when Clara pulled down his shirt collar she found there was a distinct line where the make-up ended and Harvey's normal skin tone began. Even in death his skin had a tanned appearance.

Clara wrinkled her nose. There was an odour about Harvey. Oliver had mentioned this too, the smell of rotting flesh. Clara poked at the maggoty pocket again and there was an ominous squelch followed by some purplish-red matter oozing through the weave of the cloth. The death-smell suddenly became ten times worse and Clara nearly gagged. Of course! The maggots wanted rotting flesh. Harvey would be farming them on some rancid meat and he was carrying small pieces of it, along with the maggots, in his pockets to give the illusion of decay.

Harvey had certainly gone to a lot of effort to put on this fraud. The really important question was, why? What had he hoped to gain? For that matter, what was he doing in the house? Clara could easily enough guess how he gained entry. Crawley would have unlocked the terrace door when everyone was abed, she was certain the butler was Harvey's man on the inside. But where had Harvey been headed?

Clara took her bearings again. The staircase of the great hall was to her left, but there was a back staircase for the use of the servants to her right. From the way Harvey was laying, it looked as though he had come up by the servants' stairs. Clara pictured the house in her mind. If she carried on along this corridor she would eventually make her way to the part of the hall where Angelica had her suite of rooms away from everyone else. Yes, that made sense. Harvey had made his way to Angelica's room once before, why not again? But what he was hoping to achieve Clara could not say, and he was no longer able to tell her.

She heard footsteps and looked up to see Oliver approaching, lumping his heavy camera and tripod under his arm.

"Oh," he said as he came to the scene. He blushed a little. "It seems Harvey was not a walking corpse then?"

"He put on a fair performance," Clara consoled him. "Do you need a hand?"

She took a case of glass plates from Oliver, which left him free to set up his tripod and arrange his camera.

"Do you think Inspector Park-Coombs will come?" he said as he focused the lens for his first shot.

"I would imagine so," Clara replied.

Clara and the inspector had a good working relationship and rarely stepped on each other's toes. She had come to know the inspector through her first murder case and had earned his respect by her professionalism and practicality. They worked well together, she just wished they did not always have to meet over a body.

"That is a lot of blood," Oliver mused, fitting the first plate into his camera.

"Have the family all been roused?"

"As far as I know. They are all in the drawing room. I suppose one of them did this?"

Clara drew her eyes briefly off the corpse.

"Perhaps. Always the possibility a servant might have

slipped up here after Harvey, of course."

"You have considered that Genevieve was constantly threatening to shoot the fiend?" Oliver said.

"It was my first thought," Clara grimaced. "If it turns out Harvey was shot, then Genevieve will be a prime suspect."

"Do you suppose it makes it murder if she thought she was shooting a ghost?"

"Genevieve never believed the intruder was anything but a living, breathing man," Clara reminded him. "I'm not sure telling a court you thought you were shooting a dead man is any defence anyway, other than if you are suggesting insanity as a plea."

Oliver took his first photograph, the flash blinding Clara temporarily. She blinked her eyes furiously to bring the world back into view.

"Warn me before you do that again," she grumbled.

"Sorry!"

There were more footsteps coming along the corridor now. Clara looked to her left, to the turning in the hallway that would take you to the main staircase. Shadows were visible on the far wall as people approached. A second later Inspector Park-Coombs appeared at the head of the corridor, a police constable just behind him and Lord Howton directing them from the rear. The inspector walked down the hallway and paused at the scene. He looked at the body, then up at Clara. He raised his eyebrows.

"I hear you have been chasing dead men, Clara?"

Chapter Twenty

Clara smiled at the inspector.

"I was chasing not-so-dead men," she answered. "This gentleman, to be precise, who, it seems, someone decided was not authentic enough in his role."

Inspector Park-Coombs looked down at Harvey Howton.

"Nasty mess," he reflected. "We'll take it from here Clara. The family are all in the drawing room, if you would care to join them."

"I would be glad to be away from this," Clara agreed and started to walk towards the main stairs.

Inspector Park-Coombs sniffed the air and scratched his head.

"What is that awful smell?" he wondered aloud.

"I think you will find the dead man has rotten meat in his pockets, along with maggots," Clara called over her shoulder. She could hear Park-Coombs exclaiming in strong terms as he confirmed her statement for himself.

As the inspector had stated, the entire Howton family was gathered in the drawing room. Clara paused at the door before entering; one of these six people was a murderer. She found herself glancing at the scene and wondering who would have the gall and the inclination to murder Harvey?

The natural choice was Richard. Long years of resentment had created a bitterness between uncle and nephew. During the war, both of their mothers had hoped for the death of the other's son. Had a similar morbid preoccupation afflicted Richard and Harvey? Richard had always seemed convinced Harvey was a dead man walking. He seemed afraid of him, but was that really pretence? Had he hidden his true feelings behind a cloud of superstition and terror?

Then there was Diana. She had been stood over the body when everyone else had arrived. Clara could not help thinking that it was extremely brave of the girl who was terrified of the thought of Harvey entering the hall, to leave her room and investigate a bang. It struck her as out-of-character. Surely, if Diana had heard a bang, she would have hidden herself deeper under the bedclothes and hoped whoever was behind it would go away? What had changed to convince her to leave the safety of her room and track down the source of the sound?

A more likely person for getting up in the night to check on a sudden noise was Genevieve. She was sat on a sofa looking grim-faced, her usual bravado gone. The reality of the situation was falling on her. Did that suggest a guilty conscience? Genevieve had threatened time and time again to shoot the man at the window. If Harvey proved to have been killed by a shotgun blast...

The older members of the family seemed less likely to be murderers. Lord Howton felt a responsibility towards his brother, despite his fears that he was turned into a post-death monster. He did not seem to have stocked up the resentments of the rest of the family, perhaps because he was one of the few in the family utterly secure in his position. He would be Lord Howton until he died and that was that. What of Lady Howton? She had confessed to feeling hate towards Harvey, even to wishing him dead during the war. Had she decided to go further than just wishing? She had been in two minds about whether

Harvey was a spectre or not, Clara had sensed that. Did she come to the conclusion a dead man should remain dead?

Angelica seemed the only family member who could not possibly have killed Harvey. Her grief was all too violently palpable. Someone, probably Lord Howton, had clearly explained to her that Harvey had never been dead – that it was all a charade, its purpose unknown. But now he was dead, very dead. There was going to be no further spectral returns, no more glances in the drawing room window. Clara could only guess at what Angelica was now feeling. To know your beloved son had been alive all the time you thought him dead, and yet now he really was deceased, must be so utterly confusing along with tormenting. And it could not have escaped Angelica that her son had deliberately put her through a great deal of emotional torture for some sort of prank. That had to make a person feel angry.

Clara stepped into the drawing room and closed the doors behind her. Lord Howton glanced up.

"The police are here?" he asked.

"They are upstairs," Clara stated. "The inspector will no doubt be down to question you all shortly."

She stood in a spot where she could see all their faces. She was stumped as to what to say.

"This was all a hoax?" Richard spoke and filled the silence. "All along, Harvey was making fools of us?"

"I think it appears that way," Clara said gently.

"Why?" Richard looked at Clara, then at his family. "Why would he do that?"

Clara could not answer him. Harvey would have known the answer, but whether he had confided his plans to any of his co-conspirators was another question. Crawley might provide some answers, if she could persuade him to talk.

"My son wouldn't…" Angelica mumbled, then she was overcome with emotion and pressed a handkerchief to her mouth.

To Clara's — and perhaps to everyone's — surprise, Lady Howton sat down beside her loathed mother-in-law and put her arm around her. Angelica's shoulders shook as she sobbed, her world truly broken into fragments.

"It was a wicked thing to do," Genevieve muttered.

Clara wondered if she was referring to Harvey's prank or to his murder?

They were all distracted by the arrival of Inspector Park-Coombs. He strode into the room with a respectful half bow to Lord Howton. He seemed almost apologetic as he took out his notebook and prepared himself to ask questions. Clara had not pegged him as a man cowed by rank and nobility. She was learning something new about the inspector.

Inspector Park-Coombs cleared his throat.

"I apologise for the necessity, but can I just confirm that the gentleman upstairs has been identified by you, Lord Howton, as your brother Harvey?"

Lord Howton mumbled a confirmation.

"And who was first to discover him?"

Diana raised her hand as if she was in a school classroom facing teacher.

"I did," she whispered.

"May I ask what you were doing in the corridor at that time of night?" Inspector Park-Coombs asked.

Clara was keen to hear Diana's answer to this question.

"I couldn't sleep and then I heard a strange bang. I thought maybe a window had been left open and with all the horrid things that had been happening I couldn't bear to ignore it. I went to investigate. I thought the noise came from the direction of the west wing, I am in the east. I had to walk along the corridor where Harvey was lying..." Diana tailed off, there was no need for further explanation.

Clara thought the answer was reasonable and explained a few things. She still couldn't see Diana as being brave enough to risk stumbling into an intruder, however.

"And who arrived next?" the inspector asked.

"That would have been me," Lord Howton said. "I heard Diana scream and I left my room to see what was wrong. Richard arrived shortly afterwards."

Lord Howton stated this very carefully, almost as if, Clara felt, he was trying to make it plain that Richard could not have been involved as he arrived after hearing his sister cry out.

Inspector Park-Coombs took a moment to write all this down.

"Do we know how Harvey came to be in the hall?" he asked.

"I believe your answer lies there, Inspector," Lord Howton pointed behind him to the terrace door. Its new lock was still intact, but the bolt had been pulled across meaning it was useless. The door could have been opened whenever Harvey pleased. "I locked that door myself before going to bed. It appears someone opened it after I had gone from the room."

The inspector made further notes in his little book.

"And, do any of you have an idea why he came back into the hall?"

"No more than we have an idea why he played this ghastly trick on us all," Lord Howton said. "Why would the fellow wish to fake his own death and then haunts us like that? It is preposterous!"

"There will have been a reason," the inspector said calmly. "I assume Harvey was of sound mind?"

"Absolutely!" Angelica hastily defended her son.

"Then he had a reason," Inspector Park-Coombs concluded. "He went to a lot of effort to look the part."

Inspector Park-Coombs flicked over a page in his notebook then casually asked;

"Do you have a gun room?"

"Naturally," Lord Howton said steadily. "There are two, in fact. The Guard Room contains antique armaments and the Gun Room contains fowling pieces and shotguns used during the pheasant season."

"And these are easy to access?" the inspector persisted.

"Neither are locked," Lord Howton agreed. "Though many of the older pieces are not in working condition."

"But the ones in the Gun Room would be ready to use?"

"Yes Inspector, they are available at all times in case someone wishes to go shooting."

Clara's eyes had fallen on Genevieve. So, Harvey had been shot.

"Those pieces in the Gun Room consist of hunting guns?" the inspector clarified.

"Yes, those are the only sort people would be expected to use on the local wildlife," Lord Howton looked puzzled.

"Was he killed by a shotgun?" Angelica asked, her voice husky with rage, her eyes pinned on Genevieve.

"Don't look at me like that!" Genevieve reacted fast. She had gone pale ever since mention of the Gun Room had been made. She clearly grasped the implications. "I did not shoot Harvey!"

"You threatened to enough times!" Angelica started to rise from her chair. Lady Howton's consoling arm now acted to restrain her mother-in-law. "You said you were going to shoot him!"

"I only said I would wing the fellow who was causing all this bother! Give him something to think about!" Genevieve snapped defensively, her eyes now turned to the inspector. "I had no intention of killing him. I wanted to give the culprit a fright and prove to everyone he was a live person, not some demon from hell. I wanted to make people see things rationally again! Please, Inspector, believe me!"

"You killed my son!" Angelica screamed. "You shot him!"

"I never left my room until I was woken by Richard!" Genevieve countered. "I am not responsible!"

"Who else would have done it?" Angelica cried. "Who else?"

"I believe you are both under the misapprehension that Harvey Howton was killed by a shotgun," Inspector Park-Coombs interjected calmly.

He had allowed the accusations to fly as much as anything to get an insight into the family's mood and who they might consider the murderer. Now he put the argument to rest.

"The wound looks likely to have been caused by a pistol of some description. Do you have such guns in the house?"

Lord Howton took a long moment to speak. He coughed and cleared his throat before words would come. He seemed to be unconsciously avoiding looking at Richard.

"The only guns of that type in the hall are the Webley service revolvers Richard and Harvey retained after the war," he said at last.

"Could I see where they are kept?" Inspector Park-Coombs asked.

Lord Howton escorted him from the room, Clara tagged along since no one had said she could not. The inspector was fairly lenient about her presence at a crime scene as long as she did not interfere with his investigations.

They entered the Gun Room. The morning light was now streaming through the windows and glinting off the metal barrels of old muskets and flintlocks. But what caught the eye at once was the glass cabinet standing against the wall. It caught the eye because it was placed centrally and was clearly newer than the other cabinets. That morning there was another reason it attracted attention – the glass front was smashed.

Inspector Park-Coombs looked into the case where, a few hours ago, the matching revolvers of nephew and uncle had sat side-by-side, only differentiated by neat little typed labels that gave their owners' name and rank. Harvey's Webley remained in its place. Richard's was missing.

"This seems to be where the murder weapon came from," Park-Coombs observed. "Were bullets available for the gun?"

Lord Howton's throat seemed to have shrunk; his words squeaked out.

"Richard's revolver was still loaded. The last bullet in the chamber. He had been about to fire it when he had news of the Armistice. Seems silly, but we were superstitious about unloading it."

"When you say 'we', do you actually mean Richard?" the inspector asked in his placid, even tone that was so disconcerting when he was asking such serious questions.

"No, I agreed with him," Lord Howton quickly said.

"Well, I have a number of things to look into further," Inspector Park-Coombs finally put away his notebook. "I shall have my men comb the grounds for the missing revolver. I'm afraid it will be necessary to search your home too."

Lord Howton cringed, but he did not argue.

"If you must," he said.

"I must," Inspector Park-Coombs assured him. "I shall make the arrangements. Good day Lord Howton, Clara."

The inspector left the Gun Room. Lord Howton did not move. Clara found herself staring at the smashed glass of the case.

"It was a sealed case," Lord Howton said quietly. "We never meant for it to be opened again. That was important. Sealing these guns away for good rather felt like we were shutting away what they represented. Richard always said, if the last bullet was never shot, it was like holding back time. War could never rip this country apart again if we just kept these revolvers frozen in their last moments of violence. A strange notion, but it made sense in those strange first days after the war ended."

Lord Howton picked up a shard of glass.

"Now that moment, maybe that magic, has been broken for good. Peace is so fragile. All it took was the smashing of a sheet of glass to destroy ours," Lord Howton shut his eyes and hung down his head.

"You think Richard did this," Clara stated.

Lord Howton groaned.

"I fear it," he said. "Richard has such darkness raging inside him, and he won't talk to me. I know he hated Harvey."

"Don't condemn him without knowing the truth," Clara told him firmly. "There is still a lot to be discovered."

Lord Howton opened his eyes and fixed them on her.

"You will continue to investigate, won't you Miss Fitzgerald? There are too many questions remaining. Who killed Harvey is the most pressing, but I would also like to know why he played these games with us."

"I shall continue to look into it," Clara promised.

"Thank you, Miss Fitzgerald," Lord Howton sighed. "Harmony must be restored to this family. The truth will save us."

Clara was not so certain about that.

Chapter Twenty-one

Harvey's body was removed from the property. The police were satisfied they had retrieved all they could from the scene of the crime, and the servants were allowed to take charge with buckets of soapy water to clean up the mess. If only the murder could be erased so easily and thoroughly from the minds of the family, Clara mused. Angelica took herself to her room and shut herself away. The rest of the family attempted to get on with the day as normal, but there was a constant reminder, in the form of policemen searching the grounds and rooms of the hall, that the day was far from normal.

Clara had her own investigations to perform. She went in search of Diana, to get to the bottom of this mystery of her sudden desire to confront intruders in the night.

Diana was in her room, or rather, the room that was currently hers as everyone in the house seemed but a passing visitor and had no real place there. Diana's bedroom contained the relics of two prior residents, both female. One was a seventeenth century lady, the sister to the then lady of the house, who had used this bedroom for several decades. A fine collection of needlepoint dotted the room, including a footstool and the bed curtains. They had been a labour of love for the woman in question.

The second woman had been one of the lord's daughters in the early nineteenth century. The poor girl had died in her eighteenth year of consumption. The evidence for her existence came in the form of several pretty watercolours hanging on the wall, all floral arrangements hand painted by the tragic consumptive. Also, there were several large porcelain dolls stacked on top of a wardrobe, mementoes of a lost childhood. Even the furniture had once belonged to the young lady before Diana had taken her place in the room, aside from the bed which harked back to the days of the seventeenth century lady. It was not hard to feel that the presence of these two deceased women overshadowed Diana in the room. It seemed as if she was an interloper into another past, into these very women's lives. No wonder Diana had a tendency to shrink away when her very slumber was overpowered by long dead ancestors.

Diana was sitting before her dressing table, combing her hair in a slow fashion that suggested it was not because her hair was untidy that she brushed it, but rather because she had nothing better to do. Her door was open. Clara knocked anyway.

"Hello Miss Fitzgerald," Diana glanced over her shoulder, her tone dull and sombre.

"Might I come in and talk with you?" Clara asked.

"What about?" Diana frowned and fidgeted with the hair comb.

"Your father wants me to continue investigating the reasons why Harvey pretended to be dead."

"Are you looking into his murder too?"

"Only to ensure those who are innocent are not condemned," Clara promised, she hoped with such words to gain Diana's trust, to demonstrate that she was not about to accuse anyone of murder without good reason. "I would like to ask you about what happened last night?"

"Is that necessary?" Diana turned away and started to rearrange perfume bottles and lotion jars that stood on the dressing table. She had quite a collection of skin creams. Clara could not fathom why, as Diana's skin was flawless, or at least to her eyes. Perhaps the girl saw things differently.

Clara quietly closed the bedroom door.

"May I be blunt Diana?" the girl made no motion either of consent or denial, so Clara carried on. "I found it all rather odd that you rose from your bed last night to investigate a strange noise."

"Why?" Diana still toyed with the bottles and jars on the dressing table.

"It struck me that you would prefer not to risk confronting Harvey, whether he be alive or dead," Clara explained. "I struggle to imagine you gladly rising to investigate a sound in the middle of the night. Personally, I would prefer to ignore the noise and hope it would go away."

"I might be braver than I look," Diana countered, but not very vigorously.

"You might be," Clara agreed. "Then again…"

"You think I am lying? That I shot Harvey?" Diana suddenly turned in her seat and her eyes flashed with a hitherto unexpected fury.

"I just think there is something missing from your tale. It might be that it is not of any great importance, then again, it might be that it has a bearing on Harvey's death. I am not accusing you," Clara replied, keeping her tone light.

"Jolly good, because I had no reason to harm Harvey."

Clara waited, letting the silence stretch out and act on Diana. She knew there was something else to Diana's story, she just had to be patient. Diana's fury evaporated as swiftly as it had come. Her determination went with it. She was a naturally honest girl, hopeless at keeping secrets. Now she shut her eyes and sighed.

"I can't sleep in this room," Diana said, her voice barely a whisper. "Please do not laugh, but I am convinced it is haunted."

Clara did not laugh. Surrounded by the belongings of

the previous occupants of the room, it was entirely possible to feel as if they were present, just a hair's breadth away and looking over one's shoulder. Clara understood.

"Last night I felt certain something was in here with me. I suppose I was so worked up about Harvey my imagination was overwrought. I was convinced someone was stood behind the curtains at the window. Only, not an actual someone, if you understand?"

"A ghost," Clara elaborated.

"Exactly," Diana nodded. "It is not the first time, either. Some nights I don't sleep a wink because I believe there is someone else in the room with me. I have asked mother if I can move rooms, but she says there is none other I can go into. You see, though this house has many bedrooms, most are not fit for habitation. The beds in most of the rooms are so fragile they would break at the slightest touch, or the rooms have developed damp and the air is bad for the constitution. There are only a handful of rooms that are actually liveable, this is one of them."

"Then you are stuck here?" Clara said.

"Until I marry, or perhaps Genevieve marries and I have her room. You don't know what it is to live in a house that is dedicated to the people who came before you. I can hardly call it home."

"What happened last night?" Clara asked. "With the person behind the curtain?"

"I suppose there was no one there really, though it felt as if they were," Diana chewed on her lip. "I never am sure when morning comes whether ghosts exist or not, but at night I am certain. It is so peculiar. Last night, as I lay in bed, I just knew there was someone hiding behind the curtains. And then I heard this dreadful bang. The hall echoes a lot and, in my fright, I thought the bang came from the window and something was coming to get me. I panicked, leapt from the bed and raced out into the hall."

Diana paused.

"You have probably noted that the spot where Harvey died is not far from this room?"

"I had noticed that," Clara agreed. "As you ran you would have nearly stumbled over him."

"Everything was dark when I came out. The corridors are pitch black in places. But there was enough light coming in through the dome in the great hall for the staircase and part of the corridor ahead to be illuminated. My nerves were so stretched that I seemed to see more than usual and when I saw this lumpy bundle on the floor ahead of me I came to a complete stop," Diana was breathing fast, as if the panic of the night before was returning. "I didn't at first know what it was. Then my eyes seemed to work it out like a puzzle, and I realised someone was lying on the floor. I hardly thought they were real at first! I screamed because I thought this was some ghostly shadow from the past!"

"Then you realised it was Harvey?" Clara asked.

"No. I never realised it was Harvey. I was paralysed with fear. All I could think to do was scream and hope someone would come. Then daddy arrived with a torch. It was he who saw that it was Harvey," Diana shook her head. "So, you see Miss Fitzgerald, it was not bravery that forced me from my bedroom, but terror. I was running from an imagined nightmare only to stumbled into a very real one."

Clara did see, and everything made much better sense.

"When you heard the bang, what was it like?" she asked.

"I suppose it was like a gun shot," Diana shrugged.

"No, that is what you think it sounded like now you know what caused the noise. But what were you thinking when it actually happened?"

Diana frowned again, the question clearly a little too probing for her.

"Why did that bang make you run?" Clara pressed. "What did you think was going to happen?"

Diana pursed her lips, digging back into her memory. She looked up at the watercolours on the wall.

"It made me think of a door slamming," she said at last. "I think, in that instant, I thought someone was…"

She turned her eyes to the other side of the room where the wardrobe and the porcelain dolls stood.

"That was it, I remember now! I thought someone was coming out of my wardrobe! The bang sounded just like a door being opened and closed!" Diana pointed at her wardrobe. "I was sleepy, not asleep, but sleepy nonetheless. And I thought the noise came from the wardrobe because it was strangely muffled. Now I know it was because I was hearing something further away in the hall."

Clara nodded.

"I heard Harvey being shot!" Diana gasped.

"Perhaps, perhaps not," Clara responded. "You heard what sounded like a door slamming. Perhaps it really was a door? The killer had to go somewhere after they murdered Harvey."

"It is true he was shot with Richard's Webley?" Diana asked suddenly, her eyes tearful now.

"Richard's Webley is missing. Whether it is the murder weapon, I cannot say."

"Poor Richard," Diana groaned. "But, no! He arrived after daddy! He came up the stairs…" Diana hesitated. "Now I think of it, that was rather odd. Richard's room is on the same floor as everyone else. Why was he downstairs… unless he was getting his gun?"

Diana looked panicked. Clara quickly moved to reassure her.

"Richard would not have been downstairs getting the gun after Harvey was murdered. And since the gun was not replaced, it does not seem that that was the reason he was downstairs," Clara could see Diana was not convinced. "Think if you saw anyone, anyone at all, when you came upon Harvey."

Diana was still thinking about the possibility of

Richard being a killer. She was not listening anymore.

"Diana, did you see anyone other than Harvey in the corridor?"

Diana blinked as if she had just heard Clara. She opened her mouth, her lips quivering.

"Nothing. I saw nothing but Harvey. Oh! If I had seen the murderer, stumbled upon them, would they have shot me too?"

"Let us hope not," Clara could see the girl had already persuaded herself that her brother was a killer. "Richard would have no reason for killing Harvey."

Diana gave a strange laugh.

"Really? Richard hated Harvey!"

"But not enough to kill him, surely?" Clara had suspected Richard's hate, but she wanted to act astonished to try and wriggle some more information from Diana.

"Richard was so angry after the war, I never could understand it," Diana stated somewhat naively. "I mean, he survived, so why was he angry? Then one day I heard him have a blazing row with Harvey and threaten to shoot him. And Harvey responded, 'just like you tried to shoot me that day in France.' And Richard did not deny it!"

Clara had not heard this story before and she pricked her ears.

"Whatever could he have meant?" she said aloud.

"I don't know, I never asked. But they were bitter enemies after the war," Diana sighed. "They should have been like brothers, but Harvey could never accept that he was the overlooked son. It made him so sour."

"Did you like Harvey?" Clara asked.

Diana took a long time to mull over a question that should have been simple to answer. Most people, when asked if they liked someone, could easily answer yes or no without hesitation. Clara thought the girl's pause for thought rather curious.

"I think I could have liked Harvey, if he had let me,"

Diana said at last. "But he did not want me to like him. He wanted to be hated by everyone, because that was the way it ought to be. He could only hate all of us if everyone was indifferent to him. If one of us actually liked him it would spoil things, you see? Harvey was complicated. I was a Howton and therefore I was not allowed to like him, according to his own rules. Harvey gained a sort of power from imagining he was resented by us all."

Clara worked that idea around in her head and slowly gained understanding. She did see.

"What a shame," she said. "He spoiled his own life by harbouring resentment."

"He had reason to," Diana shrugged. "I can guess how he felt. This house reeks of the past and of the people who came before. Harvey didn't just feel resented by his living family, I think he felt resented by his dead ancestors. His mother wasn't an aristocrat, that was the trouble. Harvey never considered himself a true Howton, and all those dead eyes staring down from the portraits on the wall made it worse, not better. This is a place where the dead are never truly gone."

Diana gave a shudder and looked around her room with its furnishings from two ladies of the past.

"Nothing is ever your own here," she said.

Clara rose from the bed, her questions done. She had her answer and she was reassured that Diana had not shot Harvey. It was time to move on.

"Thanks Diana," she said. "Try to keep strong and remember the past is just that – passed. The dead cannot hold anything over you."

Diana gave a bitter little laugh. Her face curled up into an unpleasant grimace and she suddenly looked many years older.

"You really never have lived in a house like this, have you?" she groaned.

Chapter Twenty-two

Clara went in search of Richard next. With so many accusations flying about, and the missing revolver, he was shaping up to become the prime suspect in the case. Now there was Diana's revelation that Richard had appeared at the crime scene from downstairs. It was becoming harder to find innocent explanations for all these worrying incidents. Clara wanted to hear Richard's side of things.

Richard was in his study. Lord Howton and Richard both had their own private studies, Harvey made do with a writing desk in his room. Had he been denied a study of his own or had he never asked for one? Was this yet another blow to his fragile sense of self-worth? The man was dead and could not be asked.

Clara walked into Richard's study as the door was open. He was not sitting at the table in the middle of the room, but was by the window looking out into the grounds. He turned his head and gazed over his shoulder as he heard her approaching footsteps.

"I never thought I would see policemen in the grounds," Richard said in a detached tone.

Clara walked into the study and glanced around. The walls were lined with bookshelves and the volumes were largely on history, Richard's passion. The sons of lords rarely have to work for a living. Lord Howton was one of the wealthiest men in the country, even if that wealth was largely tied up in land. Richard had no need to earn his own money, he was free to work on whatever attracted his attention. This appeared to be the history of the country and the estate.

Richard turned from the window and noted Clara's interest in his books.

"I am writing my experiences of the war," he said. "Probably won't publish them, but I felt the need to jot them down."

He motioned a hand to the table upon which sat a typewriter. There were various papers scattered around it.

"I'm sorry to disturb your work," Clara said.

"I can hardly work with all this going on in the background," Richard waved a hand at the policemen outside. "I know they are looking for my revolver and when they find it I shall be wearing handcuffs."

"If they find it," Clara corrected him. "And just because your gun is missing does not mean you shot Harvey. Anyone could have used it."

"True," Richard nodded. "But it doesn't look good."

He pulled a face.

"Everyone knows my relationship with my uncle was difficult."

"Could we talk about that?" Clara asked. "You father wants me to conduct my own investigation alongside the police. If you are innocent, it would be wise to speak with me, so I can prove it."

"If?" Richard frowned.

"I cannot read your heart or go back in time to see what really happened. I don't know you well enough to judge whether you could do such a thing as this. Which is why I would like to talk to you, maybe then I will know."

Richard gave a short snort, it was somewhat like a stifled laugh.

"Let us begin with the simplest of questions. Could I

176

kill a man? Why, yes," Richard shrugged. "I have shot men in the war. I have been in nasty trench skirmishes where you were virtually on top of the enemy. You didn't need to aim, they were so close, and you could see the life draining from them before your eyes. Am I a killer? The answer is obvious."

Richard tapped carelessly at a key on his typewriter. The letter A pinged forward on its little arm and marked the clean sheet of paper in the machine. Ping, ping, ping. Three As appeared in rapid succession.

"I think it more prudent to ask if you could kill someone you knew? Someone who you had grown up with? That is a very different scenario to killing a stranger in battle," Clara countered his statement. "Cold blooded murder is not the same as killing for self-preservation during a war."

"Why don't you just ask me if I hated Harvey enough to want him dead?" Richard snapped, tiring of the typewriter and marching back over to the window.

"All right," Clara agreed. "Did you want your uncle dead?"

Richard stared out the window, his hands clasped behind his back. The autumn sun fell on the side of his face and he looked more like his father than at any other time. He also looked younger, he was, after all, still in his youth. The wisdom of experience and age had yet to come, though the rush of war had forced him to grow up a lot faster than normal. It had also tainted him for life. He was a scarred man, only the scars were on the inside.

"When we were little boys we were pals," Richard began. "Being near enough the same age we played together and acted like brothers. We were inseparable. No one seemed to mind, well, maybe my mother a little. But my father said nothing. We swore to take care of one another, always. Then we went off to school and things began to change."

Richard tilted his head forward and breathed deeply.

"That was when the competitiveness started. I can't

remember whether my mother or Angelica was the first to compare our school results, but what began as one cruel remark about one boy doing better than the other, became a terrible feud between our mothers," Richard briefly shut his eyes, as if the memory pained him. "Slowly, without us realising it, the words of our mothers infected us. Harvey and I started to perceive ourselves as rivals. We wanted to do better than each other, so we could make our respective mothers proud and victorious over the other's mother. Before long, our friendship was nothing but ashes. We did not even talk to one another."

"And that rivalry continued after school?" Clara asked.

"Certainly. We were bitter enemies through university. I studied history, Harvey the classics. Despite our differing subjects we still compared marks. It carried on into the war. You wouldn't believe how petty it became. If we had both been in battle and I came back with more men than he did, well that was a victory to me. If his platoon had managed to gain a fraction more ground in a push than mine, that was his triumph. It went on and on. Whatever we could compete over, we did."

"Harvey was very popular with the men," Clara said, bringing up something the under-gardeners had said. "Did you compete over popularity as well?"

Richard hefted his shoulders.

"Harvey would always win that one hands down," he answered. "I never had the way with the ordinary soldiers. Harvey said I acted too aloof, but I knew no other way to be. He could walk among the men handing out cigarettes and telling stories and they still respected him. If I had done that, I would have looked a fool.

"Whatever anyone has told you, however, I cared about those under my charge as much as Harvey. I might not have sat by the bedside of wounded soldiers or commiserated with the troops about lost brothers, but I cared," Richard stood a little more proudly. "What no one will tell you is that the men under my command had a far better survival rate than those under Harvey's. I was the better military leader. I brought more of my men home, but, because I did not swap stories with them and share nips of whisky and rum, I am perceived as the worse leader. Ironic, isn't it?"

"The human mind is a complicated thing," Clara agreed. "We don't always see the truth."

"Well, it hardly matters now," Richard watched the dust motes dancing in a beam of sunshine coming through his window. "The war is over. Let Harvey have his glory, I know my conscience is at peace for the efforts I made to keep my men alive."

Richard fell silent. He became very still as he stood in profile to the window. For an instant, he could almost have been a statue.

"Did you hate Harvey?" Clara asked him bluntly.

Richard moved his head a fraction, the only indication he was still a live man and not a figure carved in stone.

"I was angry with him," he said. "I suppose, sometimes, that made me hate him. But not in a way that would wish him dead. I have seen enough death to last me this lifetime and several more. In any case, I thought he was dead…"

"Yes, that raises another possibility."

Richard turned to Clara, his eyes narrowed.

"Another?" he said.

"Perhaps you thought you were shooting at a demon?"

Richard almost laughed and then he realised he would effectively be laughing at himself.

"I did think he was something supernatural," he said, his words abashed. "I feel a fool now, but at the time it made a sort of sense. I suppose, had I been in such a frame of mind and had come across Harvey in the hall, I might have reacted badly. But then, I would not have had the gun on me, would I?"

"Unless you were worried Harvey's spirit would enter the hall and you wanted to protect yourself?" Clara suggested.

Richard shook his head.

"But I wasn't."

"Shooting a man in self-defence is different to murder, at least in the mind of the shooter."

"Miss Fitzgerald, I may have been bloody stupid thinking my uncle was roaming the grounds as a woken corpse, but I did not remove my revolver from its case. I, better than any in this family, know how foolhardy it would be to shoot at someone in the darkness of a corridor. How was I to know it was Harvey and not another member of the family or a servant who had been summoned? Many people walk about the upstairs corridors without candles or torches. They know them so well they don't need them."

That was a fair point. The corridor had been pitch black and it would have been impossible, even when right on top of a person, to know for sure who they were. Only a person in a panic would shoot out and risk hitting a genuine member of the household. Richard did not look like a person to panic.

"I have been in some dangerous situations," Richard continued. "I know how to keep my head when trouble brews."

Clara believed him, but that still left her with one problem.

"Diana tells me that when you ran to her last night, you did not come from your bedroom, but from downstairs."

Richard showed no sign of being fazed by the question, he truly was a person in full control of himself. If he had shot Harvey, it would not have been some rash act, but something he had planned in advance. The coolness of his demeanour was somewhat disturbing.

"Diana was paying more attention than I would have thought," Richard's response to the question was mild, he did not seem worried. "Yes, I was downstairs. Because, you see, Diana was not the one who actually found Harvey."

Clara was paying full attention now.

"I heard a pistol shot," Richard explained. "There is nothing plainer to a man who has heard such noises day-in and day-out for two years of his life. I was lying awake in bed, mulling over the fact Harvey had not appeared that evening, and then I heard the crack of the shot. I jumped out of bed and was out of my room in an instant.

"My room is not far from the corridor where Harvey was found. As I came upon him I saw someone hurriedly closing one of the doors that leads to the old bedrooms. I knelt by Harvey first, saw he was dead and then went into the room. It was empty and I saw the window was open. That told me all I needed to know. I ran out of the room, in my haste slamming the door so hard it must have echoed about the hall. I headed for the stairs hoping to get outside and catch the interloper. But I was out of luck. By the time I reached the back of the hall, they had vanished."

"Then it was the sound of you slamming the door that spooked Diana," Clara realised. "She said the bang was like a door being closed. She assumed it was the revolver being fired, but I see now it was not."

"I can't have been outside more than a moment. Long enough to realise the shooter had gotten clean away. I came back into the hall and as I ran up the stairs I saw Diana and father, so I joined them. I think only then did it dawn on me that it was really Harvey on the floor. That he could not have been dead at all before then."

"What of the person who fled? The real shooter?" Clara demanded.

Richard spread his hands in an apologetic fashion.

"I saw a glimpse, that is all. They were a shadow moving fast."

Clara was disappointed. Here was her first clue to the real killer and it was no more than a glimpse.

"Do you believe me?" Richard mistook her grim look for doubt.

"Your story is plausible," Clara reassured him. "I also find it hard to imagine you would use your own revolver to shoot your uncle, knowing full well that would place suspicion on your shoulders."

"Despite it all, I never wished Harvey dead," Richard told her. "He was family, at the end of the day. I wish I knew why he played this strange game on us all. It was a cruel thing, and so very odd. Why did he wish to be thought dead and to play the spectre? Why scare us?"

"I don't know," Clara could offer no other solution for the moment. She hoped to get to the bottom of the mystery, but for now she could only guess. "Harvey had a very dark mind, it seems."

"He was obsessed with death, you know," Richard explained. "During the war, I was told he had acquired this charm that would protect him from harm. He believed in magic. Sometimes it seemed like a madness with him."

Angelica had said the same. Harvey's passion for the supernatural was a factor they had all noticed.

Suddenly there was a shout from outside. Richard glanced out of the window and grimaced. Clara quickly joined him. Down in the grounds a police constable was holding something up in the air and others were rushing to him.

"They have found my gun," Richard said bleakly. "Now will they arrest me?"

"It proves very little," Clara reminded him, though she could not say that in the policeman's mind such a find might lead to unfortunate connections being made.

She was hopeful Inspector Park-Coombs would not be so blind to the other facts in this case.

Chapter Twenty-three

Clara left Richard and walked into the corridor, intending to head downstairs and speak with Inspector Park-Coombs about the discovery of the revolver. She had barely gone a few steps when Genevieve confronted her in a state of panic.

"They have found a gun in the garden!" she declared, wringing her hands together, her usual self-confidence utterly evaporated. "I know what people are thinking, I have heard the servants whispering!"

Clara placed her hand on Genevieve's shoulder.

"Calm down, what are they whispering?"

"That I shot him! I know I said all that stuff about winging the fellow and I won't lie now by saying I didn't mean it, because I did, but I had no intention of killing him!"

Genevieve appeared not to have slept since the discovery of Harvey. She looked to have lain wide awake, fretting about the possibility of being considered a murder suspect. Her eyes were darting back and forth, starting at any hint of a footstep on the stairs that might indicate a policeman's arrival to arrest her.

"I really talked some rot, I know, but I am not a murderer," Genevieve insisted to Clara. "I would never have harmed Harvey. He was family."

"Where were you when everything happened?" Clara asked her.

"In bed. Asleep. I never heard a sound. My room is some distance from where Harvey was…" Genevieve clutched a trembling hand to her mouth. "I keep thinking that someone among us all killed him, murdered him. Perhaps it was by accident; a wild, fearful shot in the dark. Or maybe it was by design. That scares me the most."

"Try not to upset yourself," Clara told her gently. "The investigation is barely begun. It will soon become plain who is innocent and who is not."

"I am innocent," Genevieve repeated, assuming Clara was suggesting otherwise.

"I never said you were not. Besides, I believe you stated you were going to wing the intruder with a shotgun blast?"

"Yes," Genevieve nodded. "I never would have thought of using the revolver. It is not my sort of weapon. And you can do such damage with a thing like that. A shotgun, at a distance, would be unlikely to kill someone, but would give them a nasty shock."

Clara saw her point.

"Be assured, I am looking into this matter also and will find out the truth, even if the police do not," Clara promised. "As long as you are innocent, you have nothing to fear."

"Thank you Miss Fitzgerald," Genevieve breathed deeply.

Then she gave a start as they both heard a voice echoing up the staircase and the tread of feet.

"They are coming!" Genevieve hissed dramatically, rather like she was in a stage play. "I am going to my room and will be locking the door!"

She started to disappear, then turned back to Clara.

"Protect us, Miss Fitzgerald, please!"

Clara watched her disappear speedily around the

corner of the hallway, before looking back to the main stairs. Inspector Park-Coombs appeared at the top a second later. He looked worried, which was never a good sign. There was a police constable behind him and, carried in a handkerchief, he was holding a gun. Even at a quick glance, Clara was fairly confident it was the same gun that had once been proudly sitting in the display case downstairs.

"Hello again Clara," Park-Coombs said as he neared her. "I don't suppose you know where Richard Howton is?"

"The study," Clara pointed down the corridor. "I will show you."

She led the inspector to where she had last seen Richard. He was still stood by the window staring out into the grounds. His hands were clasped behind his back and he tipped his head forward like a man deep in his own unhappy thoughts.

"Richard Howton?" Inspector Park-Coombs addressed him.

Richard turned around.

"Might this be your revolver which went missing?" Park-Coombs held out the gun towards Richard.

Richard stepped forward and gave it a brief look.

"Yes, Inspector. That is my Webley."

"It seems to have recently been fired. I hear it was still loaded when put in the display case?"

"Yes," Richard answered simply. "In a rather superstitious moment, I decided it should retain the last bullet ever loaded into it. Barring that one bullet, the gun was empty. I developed a morbid obsession about the fact I heard of the Armistice a second before I fired that last bullet. I found myself unable to remove it. It seemed... poignant."

The inspector made no comment on this oddity.

"Who knew the gun was still loaded?" Park-Coombs asked.

"Anyone who cared to read the label in the display

case. My father is very thorough about recording the history of the objects in this house and he types out notices to be displayed next to them. He wrote up the story of the last bullet in my revolver and mounted it in the back of the case."

"Anyone could know the revolver was loaded, then," Clara observed.

Richard shrugged.

"I suppose, over these last three years, quite a number of people have visited the hall as guests and read the notice. It was not a secret," Richard's eyes wandered to the revolver, a strange look coming into them. "I never thought my revolver would ever be fired again. I feel as if some sort of private bond has been broken. As if this will herald a time of terribleness for the family."

"It is just a gun," Clara reminded him. "The bullet had no more magic to it than any other. It was a thing, made in a factory by very ordinary hands. Don't fear the future over something so mundane."

Richard had turned grey. Clara's words had not reached him. He stared at the gun as if it was the catalyst for the end of the world. It might as well have been pointed at him for the horror in his face.

Inspector Park-Coombs flicked his moustache side-to-side with a twitch of his nose.

"We will be taking the gun with us. It is evidence," he said.

"Yes, Inspector," Richard's voice sounded dry and distant. "Take it, the thing only fills me with dread now."

The inspector nodded solemnly, then he left the room, handing the revolver to his constable.

"Get that to the station, Riley."

The constable took the gun carefully and departed in a hurry. Clara appeared by the inspector's side.

"Curious lot, this family," Park-Coombs remarked to her. "Rather obsessed with death."

He cast his eyes around the corridor they were in. The walls were lined with old paintings of people long dead, some were family members, others were strangers. They were interspersed with landscapes, but even they seemed to be harking back to a time long gone. The sensation of mortality was not helped by various cases of stuffed animals that had infiltrated the hallways of the house when the great hall became overwhelmed. Dead pheasants strutted alongside wide-eyed hares, and a great number of squirrels. Some had been placed into whimsical scenes of tea parties or duels, dressed in the fashions of the day. It was all extremely grim.

"Superstitious too," Park-Coombs pointed to a rabbit's foot, ancient and moth-eaten, that hung from the picture frame of a painting depicting the hall. "Folks like this spend too much time lost in their own worlds. They stop living and moving forward, too impaled by the memories of the past. I'd clear the whole place out."

"Probably that is why people like you and I do not have titles and live in great houses," Clara smiled at him.

"Hmm," Park-Coombs made the sound almost under his breath. "You can see why in a place like this people would start to believe in ghouls."

"You've heard the story of Harvey's resurrection, then?" Clara asked.

"At great length, from various members of the family and also the more talkative servants. What is your take on it?"

"Harvey played the hoax for a reason and knowing full well the family would believe in it. I still haven't worked out his motive, but I have a good idea who within the house was assisting him."

"Faking one's own death, just so you can play-act as a ghost, is pretty bizarre. I swear there is a streak of insanity running through these noble families," Park-Coombs twitched his moustache again and dropped his voice. "A little too much inbreeding."

Clara was amused.

"Harvey certainly went to great lengths to scare his relatives. I don't think he intended to genuinely die, however."

"No, I would guess not. And we still don't know why he came into the hall. It's all very sinister, however. A man who can think up something like that must have considerable darkness in his soul."

Clara had no response to that observation. Instead, she asked;

"Do you think Richard a suspect?"

"The gun is his," Park-Coombs stated the obvious. "Many would consider that proof enough."

"But you?" Clara asked.

"Hmm, I rather think a man like Richard would not pick up a weapon he knew would be linked to him so easily."

Clara was glad to learn the inspector was thinking along the same lines as her.

"My thoughts exactly, and I feel this event was all prearranged by someone who knew Harvey was going to enter the hall. Just the act of getting the gun required time, not something done in haste when faced by an intruder," Clara paused. "Richard said he saw someone going into a room where Harvey was shot. I don't think Richard is lying when he says he saw another intruder about the hall and they gave him the slip."

"He would like us to think the murderer is an outsider," Park-Coombs pointed out bluntly. "No one, especially not an aristocrat, wants a member of their family labelled a killer."

"It would explain the gun in the bushes," Clara replied.

"I could also argue that Richard threw the revolver from his study window. The bushes are in a direct line and it would not be so hard a throw."

"Just bear with me on this one," Clara countered. "It will only take a moment to look at the room Richard mentioned and to see if anything can back his story."

Park-Coombs huffed to himself, but he made no further argument as Clara led the way to the murder scene.

The servants had worked hard on the rug and floorboards to remove the unsightly blood stain, but Clara could still see a vague outline and thought that the rug would certainly need to be replaced. The floorboards might be sanded and freshly waxed to remove the mark from them, but it would take considerable effort. Better to just get a new, larger, rug to hide the spot.

"Richard's bedroom is on the far side of the stairs," Clara explained. "He came along and saw someone disappear into one of these four rooms near where the body was. Since Harvey fell close to the two rooms on our right and Richard was able to step past the body to follow the intruder, I would suggest we narrow our inspection to these two rooms on our left."

Clara opened the doors to both rooms. One, as she had noted before, was a forgotten bedroom, the other was being utilised for storing items not wished to be displayed, but still wanted within easy reach. This included empty trunks, wooden skis, some wintry paintings and a dusty full silver dinner service. The room was so full of such items that it was impossible to reach the window on the far wall easily. Park-Coombs shook his head.

"No one came through here," he pointed to the dust on the floor which was unmarred but for their own footsteps. "Clearly this room is not on the cleaning rota."

They exited the room and went into the one next door. This had the feel of the realm of a ghost. The bed was still made as if awaiting its occupant and the old mementoes of a forgotten life sat silently watching Clara and the inspector as they entered. There was a nasty damp patch on the ceiling and Clara recalled what Diana had said about many of the bedrooms no longer being habitable. She wondered, if she were to touch the old bed, whether it would fall to pieces in her hands. There was a draught in the room and Clara shivered.

"The window is just a little open," Park-Coombs spotted. He went to the window and lifted it up to its full height. He was going to look outside, so he let go of the window, the pane instantly crashed down to within an inch of being closed. "The sash is worn. The window won't hold open."

"Which explains why I did not see an open window when I was pushing the doors of these rooms open to let in light," Clara came to the window. "That drainpipe just outside would be fit for climbing, if you were nimble."

Park-Coombs snorted. He did not do a lot of climbing.

Clara cast her eyes about the room further. The marks of the intruder might be minimal, but she was sure they would be there. She stepped forward and hesitated.

"A leaf, Inspector," she picked up the orange leaf, still damp from the dew outside. "Fallen off the intruder's shoe."

"Or blown through the gap in the window."

"Why was the window open at all?" Clara argued. "This room is damp enough as it is without leaving the window ajar all year round."

Park-Coombs could not object to that. He started to look around the room with fresh eyes. Like the other room, this one was rarely cleaned and there was a thin veneer of dust over the surface of the furniture. However, there was a large rug on the floor which, though also dusty, did not show footprints like bare boards might. Park-Coombs traced the path an intruder would make from window to door.

"Look at that," he said, somewhat amused. "I think you may be right, Clara."

Clara joined him to look at a spot on the rug. There were indentations in the pile, as if something heavy had stood there. They both looked around them and Clara pointed out a small round table, now stood against the wall.

"Does that not look awkward there?" she asked the inspector.

Inspector Park-Coombs went to the table and examined it.

"Finger prints in the dust," he observed, before picking it up and moving it back to the rug. It fitted the indentations perfectly. "So, in the dark our intruder stumbles into this table which would have been blocking the direct route to the door, and they moved it to one side."

Park-Coombs smiled.

"Well, well, Clara, someone did come in from outside."

"More importantly," Clara replied. "Richard Howton was not lying."

Chapter Twenty-four

Clara headed downstairs and to the back of the hall. It took her a while to figure out which window connected to the room upstairs where they had found evidence of an intruder. The windows had a tendency to look all the same from the outside, but when she noticed the large drainpipe, she knew she had found the right one. She had been hopeful of glimpsing footprints in the ground below the window. Unfortunately, this part of the hall had a gravel path running flush with the walls. There was no trace of footprints. Only some torn tendrils of ivy still clinging to the wall, and a broken piece of drainpipe, indicated where the intruder had been.

Clara turned her back to the hall and looked out across the grounds. The grass had been wet last night, but the autumn sun had dried it and with it any lingering tracks left by someone running away. Clara was disappointed. The killer had evaporated into the night, like the demon Harvey had pretended to be.

She was about to go back inside and continue questioning the family, when she heard the crunch of feet on the gravel path. Looking right, she was in time to see Jimmy and Charlie coming around the corner of the house with big rakes. They both looked sombre and were silent as they trudged along. Clara moved from the wall and stood in their path. The brothers paused moodily, clearly not appreciating her presence.

"I think you both have some explaining to do," Clara placed her hands on her hips and faced them squarely. Her tone was stern. "You lied to me."

The brothers exchanged a look with each other. Charlie started to open his mouth, a squeak of an excuse coming out.

"He seemed dea…"

"Don't even try that one," Clara interrupted him sharply. "Because I won't believe a word of it. If this had all been a genuine mistake, Harvey would not have been masquerading as a dead man. You witnessed him drown, you told me you pulled him ashore and informed Mr Crawley. You carried him to the house. And in all that time, you really want me to believe you could not tell he was alive? He may have fooled those who never came near him, but not the two men who carried him. You had to know he was alive."

The under-gardeners dropped their heads in unified shame.

"You both served in the war. You know what a dead man looks and feels like," Clara persisted. "It is time you admitted the truth."

"What truth?" Jimmy muttered petulantly.

Clara sighed crossly, annoyed she was going to have to spell things out for him before he would confess.

"The truth that you helped Harvey to fake his own death. For what purpose I don't know, but you were key members in the hoax. You could witness the 'drowning' and report it to Crawley, who was also involved in the plan. Then you would make sure you carried Harvey to the hall, preventing anyone not initiated in the scheme from touching him and realising he was still alive," Clara glared at them both. "There are policemen here. If you will not confess to me, I can soon enough tell them what you did and have you confess to them. You were involved in a conspiracy with Harvey, I am sure the inspector would like to hear about it."

The two men dropped their heads lower and shuffled their feet.

"Did we commit a crime?" Charlie asked.

"That very much depends on Harvey's intentions. What did he hope to gain by this charade?"

"We really don't know that," Charlie quickly replied. "I swear to that. So will Jimmy. Harvey asked us for help and we gave it."

"We owed Harvey an awful lot," Jimmy interrupted.

"Because he saved Charlie's life," Clara nodded. "I do understand your loyalty to him."

"It was more than loyalty, we owed him," Jimmy insisted. "He asked a favour and we were glad to help him."

"What precisely did he ask you?"

Jimmy glanced at Charlie and the brothers started to clam up again. Clara was growing impatient.

"I am going to fetch a policeman!" she declared.

"No, miss, please!" Charlie begged, almost dropping his rake. "Our mam would break her heart if we got in trouble with the police."

"Then talk to me!" Clara demanded. "You owe Harvey nothing now, except to help me find his killer. You want justice for him, don't you?"

The two brothers nodded simultaneously.

"Well, it seems his faked death was intrinsically linked to his murder, one way or the other. Explaining how he played this hoax might help solve the question of who killed him too."

"What happened to Harvey, miss? All we know is he is dead," Charlie looked bleak.

Clara relented a fraction.

"Harvey was shot outside the room above us," Clara pointed upwards. "The person who did so appears to have climbed up this drainpipe to enter the room and shoot Harvey. They left the same way."

The brothers followed her arm as she pointed up to the window. Jimmy chewed on his lip.

"That window has been a nuisance for years. Mr Jenkins, the handyman for the estate, is always trying to fix it. He moans about it a lot. Needs a whole new frame, but his lordship won't pay for that," Jimmy hesitated. "Everyone knows that window can be opened from the outside."

"Everyone?" Clara asked.

"All the servants and family members," Jimmy clarified, then he shuffled his feet anxiously. "Master Harvey used to sneak in and out of that window when he was younger. Sometimes, he would have his lady friends enter the hall that way too, so his mother and brother would not see them."

"Why did Harvey fake his death?" Clara returned to her original question.

Both brothers failed to answer her. She groaned.

"He must have told you something to gain your help?"

"Master Harvey said he wanted to play a trick on the family," Charlie explained slowly. "He said he was going to pretend to drown, to scare them all. Said they deserved a fright after the way they treated him."

"That was a cruel trick," Clara said.

Charlie shrugged.

"He asked us to help him and we couldn't refuse. I didn't quite understand the joke," Charlie pulled a miserable face. "We honestly didn't know he was going to pretend to be a demon. Had we, we would have talked him out of it."

Clara doubted that, she didn't think either Jimmy or Charlie would have had the courage to stand up to their former commanding officer, but if it made them feel better to imagine they would have stopped him had they known the truth, she was not going to disabuse them of the idea.

"He never was in trouble in the water, I presume?"

"No, he just went for his normal swim," Jimmy agreed. "Then we had to run to the house and ask for Crawley and pretend to tell him Master Harvey had drowned. Crawley knew about the joke too."

"And you carried Harvey into the hall?"

"Right up to his room," Jimmy said, his brother nodding his head in agreement. "We laid him on his bed. Before we left the room, he thanked us and gave us a wink. That was the last time we saw him."

"We weren't involved in the rest of the plot," Charlie added. "Not in the demon part. We knew nothing about that."

Clara believed them. She doubted Harvey would have involved the brothers further than he needed to. They were loyal to him, but did not have the guile to be active in the grimmer details of his plot. There was too great a chance they would let something slip by accident. They knew the barest details, of that she was certain.

"I can't really believe he is dead," Jimmy mumbled, his words choked with emotion. "I can't believe someone killed him!"

Clara had no answer for him. She thanked them for their help, promised she would say nothing to the police, and went back indoors. She had talked to nearly everyone involved in the case, at least within the family, except for Lady Howton and Angelica. She was now convinced the murderer was an outsider, but it would not hurt to hear what those two ladies knew of the events of the previous night. They might have heard or seen something important.

She did not have to go far to find Angelica, because she was stood in the drawing room, gazing sadly at the terrace door. Her thin, tragic figure was silhouetted against the light coming through the windows. She was as still as a statue, her light breathing the only sign that she was alive at all. Clara walked quietly into the room and hesitated. What did you say to a person who had lost their son, only to recover him and lose him again? It was confusing enough to Clara, let alone to the woman who had birthed and loved Harvey with all her heart.

"Do you believe in heaven, Miss Fitzgerald?" Angelica was the first to speak, her voice sounding frail and distant as it broke the silence.

"I don't know," Clara admitted. "I don't really think about it."

"Hmm," Angelica sighed softly, the murmur barely audible. "Harvey was like that. He had these strange ideas and a fascination with the Occult, but he could not quite get his head around traditional religion. I fear for his soul."

Angelica started to weep. Her shoulders hunched and tears fell down her cheeks. For a brief moment the emotion brought colour to her face and she seemed less like a ghoul herself. Clara walked to her and slipped an arm around her shoulders, hoping the woman would not find the gesture improper. Angelica seemed a woman who had endured a lot, and for whom there was little comfort or joy in life. She shrugged Clara off. Her small body shivered. Finally, the emotion failed, and, exhausted by it all, she dabbed her eyes with a handkerchief and let Clara guide her to one of the sofas in the room. She sat down and took a shaky breath.

"He has done me wrong," she said aloud. "That boy of mine. He has treated me so cruelly."

Clara could not deny that. Harvey had played a wicked trick on his mother.

"I do not understand why he did it," Angelica continued. "What did he hope to gain? I would have given anything to speak with him once more, to ask him why he hurt me so."

"I assume he was coming to your room last night," Clara said.

Angelica pressed her handkerchief to her lips.

"Perhaps he was. Did he intend to scare me? I would have welcomed him with open arms, dead or alive. I hope he knew that."

"Did you hear anything last night?" Clara asked. "Anything at all?"

"I have tried to think back and remember," Angelica said, her reddened eyes meeting Clara's. "Sometimes, I think I heard his footsteps coming along the corridor, but I am not sure, it might have been a dream. I might be telling myself I heard him."

Angelica shook her head.

"I try to remember if I heard a shot, but I can't…" she clenched her lips together. "Who did this to him? Who did this to me? Was I not tormented enough without taking my son from me again?"

Fresh tears rolled down Angelica's face.

"When I heard he had drowned, my heart broke into pieces. He had survived the war, been brought back to me, only to drown? I had prayed night and day for his safe deliverance from the battlefields of France and Belgium. How could he die on English soil?" Angelica gasped. "I thought my heart could break no more, but then I was given hope, the hope that his shade was returned to speak with me again. I should not have clung to that idea, but it sustained me. And now I learn he was alive all along and for a second I was filled with joy at the thought and then I was crushed because someone has killed him. What am I supposed to do?"

"I don't know," Clara admitted apologetically.

"My heart is broken once again and this time it shall not be repaired, and yet," Angelica cringed bitterly to herself, "and yet, there is this part of me that sings and reminds me that he faked his death once, why not again?"

"Don't torment yourself with such false hope," Clara told her gently, but Angelica was not listening.

Her grief had started to take on the form of madness. She was clutching at hopes that were not rational. Her mind was too stricken by sorrow to think straight and there was a real risk she would not come back from the brink of madness, not this time.

"Angelica, please, as hard as it is, you must accept that Harvey is gone," Clara talked to her, a little desperately now.

She had seen something change in Angelica's eyes. It was as if her vision had glazed over and her mind had shut down a corner of itself, the corner that dealt with reality. Now a strangeness was come over her and with it a sort of peace. The peace which detachment from the real world can bring.

"Mrs Howton?" Clara tried to grab her attention again. "Angelica?"

The woman did not answer. She instead sat and gazed at the empty fireplace, her lips parted a fraction and a slight smile graced them. Slowly a hum came to her lips and she sang a lullaby to herself, oblivious to Clara's presence.

"Angelica!" Clara demanded, but the absent gaze remained. The woman was gone.

Clara found herself afraid. She had never seen a person's mind crack before her very eyes before. Angelica had been normal, but grief-stricken, one moment, then completely lost the next. She had vanished into some deep inner self, where nothing could hurt or disturb her. In that place she was safe.

Clara bit at her lip, she reached out and touched the woman's hand, but there was no reaction. Angelica Howton had disappeared into an abyss and it would take more than a kind touch to restore her. Harvey Howton had destroyed his mother, whether that was his intention or not who could say? But she was destroyed nonetheless.

Clara rose from her chair and walked out of the drawing room. She spotted Mr Crawley counting the silver knives and forks in the dining room – he had a low opinion of policemen – and went to him.

"I think a doctor ought to be called for Angelica Howton," she instructed the butler.

He glanced up in surprise, but Clara did not want to explain.

"She is in the drawing room," she told him, before heading for the front door, determined to get out of the house and away from the festering atmosphere of death that infected the hall.

Chapter Twenty-five

Clara walked away from Howton Hall and down the long drive. She had an idea in mind of where she ought to go next. In the midst of all the confusion, she doubted anyone had remembered poor Betty staying at the nearby inn. The woman needed to know that her husband had not been dead, but now he was. Exactly how that was to be explained Clara tried to devise in her head as she walked.

The day was clagging in. There was a hint of rain in the sky. Clara momentarily wondered if the inspector might find something on the gun to point to a suspect. A fingerprint would be useful, especially if it could be used to rule out family members. It might not lead to the actual killer, however, as only criminals had their fingerprints taken and on file. Clara didn't think this was the work of a hardened criminal. Maybe there would be something else on the gun, just a small fragment that would provide a clue?

Or was that clutching at straws? The trouble was, Clara felt there was so little evidence, there was a real risk the killer might evade capture or, worse, someone innocent might be accidentally implicated in the crime.

The inn was set back from the road, it was a quaint old

place made of wooden timbers and thatch. The sort people take pictures of for postcards. It was still early in the day and, while the front door was open, there were not a great many customers present. Clara passed by a man and a woman sitting on an outside bench and clearly on a walking holiday – their sturdy footwear and rucksacks told her that. She smiled at them as she passed into the inn.

The building was as rustic on the inside as it was on the outside. The ceiling was low and there were beams running across it. They had been ornamented with horseshoes, horse brasses and drinking tankards. There was a hearty fire roaring in a large hearth on the left side of the room, taking off the morning chill which slipped in through the open door. Behind the bar stood a cheery woman wiping dry some freshly cleaned glasses.

"How may I help you, my dear?" asked the woman, the landlady of the property.

She was a voluptuous lady in all ways, with glistening red hair and a broad smile. She was the sort of person who is cheerful on the darkest of days.

"I was hoping to speak to one of your guests? Mrs Betty Howton?" Clara said.

"Oh, yes. Mrs Howton has been quite the talk of my little establishment," the landlady winked mischievously. "Who knew that Master Harvey had found himself a wife? Well, clearly no one! Quite the mystery. I dare say the family is as surprised as the rest of us! Sweet little thing though. Poor girl, not knowing her husband had drowned."

"Quite," Clara said, realising that the latest news from the hall had yet to filter this far. It would soon enough, but for the moment she was not going to be the one to reveal what had happened. "I thought I better see how she is. It has been a difficult time for her."

The landlady nodded sympathetically.

"Can't think she got much of a welcome at the hall when she arrived. At least Harvey's mother should have known better, having been in the same boat once," the landlady dropped her tone conspiratorially. "Mind you, she is the sort who quick enough forgets all her own faults when it comes to dealing with others. She had fine ideas for that boy of hers, or so I am told."

"What sort of ideas?" Clara asked, briefly distracted from her mission.

"She wanted him to marry this American heiress. The girl visited here once with her father and mother. They came into the inn and kept remarking how positively darling it was and so very English. The regulars started to get annoyed," the landlady pursed her lips. "The talk I heard was that this young lady was the heir to a considerable fortune, her daddy being involved in oil. She was worth more than the entire Howton estate. If Harvey married her, it would be quite the snub to his brother. He could buy Howton Hall and still have a fortune left over. I can imagine Angelica liking the idea of her son being worth more than England's wealthiest lord."

"You knew Angelica?" Clara asked, wondering how the landlady had such insight into the woman.

"Before his former lordship died, they would come here quite often on a Sunday. Partial to a pint was his lordship," the landlady explained, a smile returning to her face. "He was a right sort, as comfortable among his workers as he was among the aristocracy. He liked being among the ordinary folk, he used to tell me it made him feel grounded. I was but a girl then and my mother was the landlady here. He seemed a nice gentleman. I can see why he married a stationmaster's daughter."

"And what about Angelica?" Clara asked.

The landlady twitched her nose.

"Funny sort, that one. But then, must have been hard being trapped between worlds. She was not an aristocrat, but she no longer fitted in with the ordinary folk either. She looked to have everything and yet there was a deep unhappiness to her. It came out as arrogance, but I saw through her," the landlady paused for a moment, a wet glass twisting between her hands and the drying cloth. "I always had a feeling the rumours were true, that she married his lordship purely for his wealth and then regretted it. She didn't seem very fond of him."

"That's a shame," Clara said. "I had liked to imagine there was a fondness between them."

"Maybe she got what she deserved, after all," the landlady pondered. "She married for all the wrong reasons and ended up miserable. I always had the impression she was ambitious, not just for herself, but for her son. She never would have condoned him marrying a London maid."

"That would explain all the secrecy surrounding the arrangement," Clara agreed. "Such a shame."

"It is, but who am I to mull over the mistakes of my betters?" the landlady gave a chuckle, indicating she did not take much heed of her own statement. "I put Mrs Howton in my best room, it was only right. She came here looking like the world had fallen down about her ears. I could see she had been weeping. Poor thing. The young break their hearts so easily."

Clara could only agree. Betty had been through a terrible time, and what she was about to hear was not going to make things any better.

"She is in room one, just at the head of the stairs," the landlady nodded to a staircase that ran up the far wall, close to the blazing fire. "I took her up some breakfast earlier, but I doubt she touched it. She looked so pale and ill. I'm glad she has someone to visit her."

Clara didn't think Betty would be so glad once she learned the reason for Clara's visit, but she did not elaborate on that to the landlady. She thanked her for the interesting information, then proceeded up the stairs.

Room one took up most of the rear of the building, and was really a small suite with a bed and sitting area. It was reserved for better quality guests. Clara knocked on the door and waited impatiently for a response. Betty took a while to answer and, when she did, Clara found herself looking at a pale imitation of the girl she had met earlier.

"Miss Fitzgerald," Betty said in a dull tone. "This is unexpected."

"I needed to see you," Clara said, wondering how she could tell this wretched creature that her husband had been murdered. The man she already thought dead. "May I come in?"

Betty pulled back the door without a word and Clara entered the room. It seemed Betty had just crawled out of bed. The sheets were rumpled and Betty was dressed in a shift and with bare feet. She gave a shiver as the chill of the day found her and grabbed up a cardigan to drape about her shoulders. There was a fireplace in the room, but it was not lit. Clara set to work lighting the kindling and bringing the fire alive. The room slowly drew warmth from the burning logs and became cosy. Betty watched her without saying a word.

"Sit by the fire and get some warmth into you," Clara instructed.

Betty obeyed silently. Her face was ashen, as if she was sick with some dreadful disease. Clara sat in a chair opposite her.

"This has been a dreadful week for you," she said softly. "I wish I could make it better, somehow."

Betty shook her head.

"You can't make it better," she mumbled. "My husband is dead. My poor Harvey."

Betty's lower lip trembled, but she did not cry. She drew a deep breath and composed herself.

"I have some further upsetting news for you," Clara said, not knowing how best to break this latest horror to her and thinking it was better to get it over with. "A terrible thing happened at the hall last night. Harvey was shot."

Betty blinked, for a second a flush of colour came to her cheeks, then she shook her head.

"I don't understand."

"No, I explained that badly. You see, Harvey was not

205

dead, he was pretending. I don't know why. Last night he entered Howton Hall and was shot in one of the upstairs corridors. I'm afraid that now he is no longer pretending," Clara waited for the reaction, it did not take long.

Betty frowned, her lips worked but no sound came out. Then her head dipped and she fainted. Clara groaned to herself. She was not handling this well, at all. She decided it would be best to summon the landlady with a warm pot of tea and some smelling salts.

Betty had started to recover before the smelling salts arrived, but they were wafted under her nose nonetheless and the landlady assured Clara that the tea was on its way.

"Now, what has happened?" she asked, guessing Clara was not there on a purely social visit.

"It is somewhat complicated," Clara forewarned her. "Harvey Howton did not drown in the lake. He faked his death. As yet we don't know why. Last night he entered the hall in his ghostly costume and someone shot him. Now he really is dead."

"Oh my!" declared the landlady.

Betty gulped hard, she was shivering violently from the shock of the news.

"Harvey was never dead?" she whispered, the information slowly sinking in.

"What a dreadful thing to do! To fake his death!" the landlady exclaimed. "And someone shot him? Who?"

"That remains a mystery," Clara answered her. "Someone climbed in through a window, took a gun from the hall, and murdered Harvey. But no one is really sure why."

"One of the family did it!" Betty's pallor temporarily lifted as she became angry. "They all hated him! Genevieve said she was going to shoot him!"

"Oh my!" the landlady repeated.

"The evidence points to someone entering the hall from the outside," Clara persisted. "That would exclude the family who were already in the hall. Possibly it was a servant..."

"Why are you defending them?" Betty interrupted sharply. "Every member of the family had reason to want Harvey truly dead. They could have made it look as if someone came in from the outside!"

"That is true," Clara admitted, quietly noting to herself that that would put Richard back in the picture for the crime. He was the only one who had seen the intruder, after all. "At the moment, it is very uncertain what occurred."

"My poor Harvey," Betty started to weep. "They all treated him so badly! He used to tell me how Richard wished him dead, as did Lady Howton. He knew it, he had overheard things and he felt their hate. I tried to comfort him, I really did. He must have faked his death in revenge!"

"Possibly," Clara replied, not really sure what sort of revenge Harvey had hoped to achieve. "I know this is an awful shock for you, Betty, but I had to come and tell you. It would have been worse if you had heard about it through local gossip."

"That is very true," the landlady sided with Clara. "It's a terrible thing, but it would have made it worse if you had heard about it through rumours. I am so sorry, my dear."

Betty sniffed, tears still on the brink of falling.

"I don't know what to feel," she said to them. "I am so confused. I thought he was dead, I was already grieving. But he was actually alive all this time? Oh Harvey, what a wicked thing to do!"

Betty rubbed at her temple as if she was in pain.

"It was a wicked thing," the landlady spoke. "To make everyone grieve like that. Poor Angelica!"

"Don't talk of her!" Betty snapped. "That woman was as bad as the rest of them! She never spoke a word to me! I knew she hated me the second I saw her! There was something so bitter inside her!"

"She was grieving too," the landlady countered.

"People act strange when their hearts are breaking."

Betty was not convinced. Her despair had turned to anger.

"It is their fault! All of it! He would never have faked his death had they been nicer to him! And then he would never have been shot!" She gasped as she spoke the words, the reality of them sinking in. "I feel faint again. I think I need to lie down."

She was helped to her bed by the landlady and tucked under the covers. More tea and a light lunch was promised before Clara and the landlady retreated to leave her in peace.

"What a terrible business," the landlady tutted to herself as they walked downstairs. "I have never heard the like!"

"It is hard to imagine what drove Harvey to do such a thing," Clara agreed.

"I shall never think of him the same way. I used to feel sorry for him."

"You should still feel sorry for him," Clara countered. "He was ill-used. The atmosphere in that hall was poisonous."

"It was still a wicked thing to do," the landlady said staunchly. "When I heard he drowned I draped black crepe over the windows and everything."

Clara could see she would not be convinced. In any case, it was time she returned to the hall and saw what progress was being made there. She said her farewells and departed the inn. It was beginning to rain outside and Clara wasted no time in hurrying for the Howton's home.

Chapter Twenty-six

Clara managed to reach the hall before the rain tipped down on her. She was just in the front hall when the heavens opened and water fell down in sheets. Clara watched the rain for a moment, relieved she had been able to avoid it.

"Clara? Any news?" Oliver appeared from the great hall, a camera tripod under his arm.

"Not really," Clara replied. "Have you finished your photographs?"

"Almost. The Inspector wants pictures of the smashed gun case. I've developed the ones I took of the crime scene," Oliver pulled a face. "Grim old thing. What with the maggots squirming everywhere, it didn't seem as if he had just been shot."

"Well, he was," Clara said swiftly, not wanting Oliver to go down that line of thinking again. "You know, now we have proof Harvey was always alive, it would be interesting to know how the switch was done. I mean, someone, or something, was buried in the mausoleum. If I can't find someone to answer that for me, I may just have to break into the place."

Oliver shuddered. He hadn't quite shaken off his feelings about the strange events at Howton Hall.

"I'll not be present for that one," he said.

"What? In case a vampire dives out at us?" Clara raised an eyebrow at him. "Honestly, Oliver, what could possibly be in that tomb that we should be scared of?"

"I've already had enough of the heebie-jeebies over this case," Oliver shook his head. "I don't need tomb robbing added to it."

Clara was amused, but she didn't push him further.

Oliver was just moving into the Gun Room, when Mr Crawley appeared from the door to the servants' quarters. He glanced suspiciously at the camera under Oliver's arm.

"What is he taking pictures of now?" he asked, looking for all the world as if the camera was some sort of evil device that could potentially harm the antiques in the hall.

"The police want a photograph of the broken gun case," Clara told him.

Mr Crawley was clearly not impressed.

"I was intending to clear up that mess personally, but the inspector informed me I was not to touch it. Evidence, he said. Quite how a pile of broken glass is evidence I cannot imagine," Crawley glowered at the retreating figure of Oliver. "I can't abide the hall in a mess."

"For the time being, I fear you will have to suffer it," Clara told him calmly. "Might I have a word Mr Crawley? About Harvey?"

"What about him?" Crawley said mildly. "The poor man has paid the ultimate price for the cruel hoax he played upon his lordship."

Clara found it difficult to keep a straight face before the butler's self-righteous indignation. An indignation that was obviously forced considering he was part of Harvey's scheme.

"But he didn't fool you, Mr Crawley, did he," she said.

The butler hesitated for just a fraction of a moment.

"I beg your pardon?"

"You knew all along that Harvey was not actually dead. You assisted him."

The colour drained from Mr Crawley's face and he had some difficulty looking Clara in the eye as he replied.

"You are mistaken, Miss Fitzgerald. I was at his funeral."

"And at his bedside during the entire time he was feigning death," Clara added. "You, Mr Crawley, played a vital role in this charade. You kept the family at a distance, and the old doctor at bay. Only with your help could Harvey pull off this hoax."

"That is a terrible thing to say!" the old butler declared. "Quite where you got this idea from…"

"Please, Mr Crawley, we both know you aided Harvey, you are the only person who could have helped him. Denials are pointless," Clara took a step closer to him. "Who, after all, over-saw Harvey's 'body' being brought back to the hall?"

Crawley blinked rapidly, but the game was up. He had been foiled and he knew it. His denials were pointless. He either had to admit to being involved, or admit to being so dreadfully stupid that he could not tell that the man who he laid out on his own bed and stood vigil over was alive.

"Harvey had help from someone inside the hall," Clara repeated herself. "There is only one likely possibility for that help. You, Mr Crawley."

The butler started to say something, but the words died on his tongue.

"Shall we go somewhere private to discuss this?" Clara asked him. "I still have a lot of questions."

Crawley gave a sort of moan, then he conceded defeat.

"Please accompany me to my private parlour," he said in a deflated tone.

They walked through the servants' quarters, Mr Crawley with his head bowed like a monk. He seemed to have lost all his bluster and usual self-confidence. Clara wondered if his conscience was pricking him, or whether it was just the misery of discovery that made him hang his head in shame.

They entered his private parlour, which was a cosy room with two armchairs and a small folding table. The room was pristine, not a speck of dust in sight. Mr Crawley offered Clara a chair and then asked if she would take tea. The formality of it all made Clara want to laugh aloud. She had just accused the man of conspiracy in a prank that had ended in death and here he was politely offering her tea. She declined, she didn't want to waste any more time.

Mr Crawley sat in the opposite armchair and clasped his hands together. He seemed to become terribly still, as if he had turned himself to stone.

"How did Harvey persuade you to assist him?" Clara tried to bring the butler back to life.

"Oh, it was my duty," Crawley said sadly. "Before his late lordship passed, he made me promise I would take especial care of his son. I fear he realised the terrible situation his new wife and boy would be in once he was gone. He sensed the resentment from the rest of the family. I swore to him I would serve the boy as if he was my only master and do anything I could for him."

Mr Crawley's face twisted into unhappiness.

"Over the years, Harvey has imposed upon my oath many times and I have obeyed. I felt I could not break the promise I made his late lordship. This last request, however, brought me to the brink of my resolve."

"You almost refused?"

"Almost," Crawley winced, pained by his failure to stand up to Harvey. "I wonder how different things would have been had I stuck to my principles? Harvey, however, knew exactly how to persuade me."

Clara sensed something behind those words, something more.

"How did he persuade you? He was asking you to disregard your duty to the current Lord Howton, after all."

"Please, do not ask me," Crawley shut his eyes.

Clara was not satisfied.

"A young man is dead, Mr Crawley. I have to ask. How did Harvey persuade you?"

Crawley rubbed a hand over his face. He was now as pale as a ghost, and looked like he might be joining Harvey in his corpse performance, if this torment carried on any longer.

"Confession is good for the soul," Clara quoted to him. "And I think you have a lot to confess."

Mr Crawley raised his head and fixed Clara's eyes with his own.

"May I ask that whatever I say stays between you and I?"

Clara nodded.

"You may," she said, carefully making no promises.

"I have spent a lifetime serving the Howtons. I consider them as much my family as any flesh or blood kin. It pained me deeply to trick his current lordship. I don't think I shall ever forgive myself, and I cannot defend my decision by referring to my duty to Harvey, for, in reality, I agreed for very selfish reasons," Mr Crawley sighed. A clock on the mantel over his fire chimed the hour and, for a second, they seemed in a space removed from the rest of the house and the recent dramas. For a moment there was a pause in time and Mr Crawley could reflect on what had occurred.

"I am fond of all the family," the butler continued. "But I found myself deeply attracted to Angelica Howton the moment she came to the hall. Naturally I shut away these feelings while his late lordship was alive, even after his death I was loyal to his memory. But, poor Angelica was desperately lonely, and felt resented by the family. I was able to provide her with solace."

Mr Crawley's breath caught in the back of his throat. Emotion was threatening to overcome the masterly command he usually had of himself.

"Seeing her today, brought to madness by the actions of her son, breaks my heart. Knowing that I have been a part of that, that I helped with this, destroys me,"

Crawley gasped. "I love Angelica and I believe she loves me, or perhaps I should say loved, because I am not sure she knows herself, let alone anyone else anymore."

"Were you lovers?" Clara asked bluntly.

"Miss Fitzgerald, you offer me no reprieve," Crawley rebuked her miserably.

"I have to ask, I have to understand why you became involved in this hoax. Just loving Angelica would not have been enough. Harvey must have known there was more and could hold that against you."

Crawley ducked his head in shame once more.

"You are right. We were lovers, for many years. I am not much older than Angelica and when she was widowed her loneliness became heart breaking. I offered her consolation. It became something much more. Of course, it went against all the rules of etiquette and it was disloyal to his late lordship. Had the family learned of it, then I would have been dismissed and I would never have seen Angelica again."

"That is the sort of secret Harvey could use to make you do anything for him," Clara understood. "That and the promise you made his father, a promise you were driven by guilt to keep, made you the ideal stooge in Harvey's scheme."

"Yes," Mr Crawley agreed, ashamed of how far he had fallen from grace. "I was trapped. I agreed to help Master Harvey. I honestly did not know what his intentions were. At least, not at first. He told me he wanted to make the family regret the way they had shunned him. He wanted to make them feel guilty by suddenly appearing to die. I believed him."

Clara was intrigued.

"There was more to it?" she asked.

Crawley took an unsteady breath. He was trembling as he confessed, the words having to be dragged from him.

"It was only after Harvey's wife turned up on the doorstep that I learned the truth. I told Harvey about her, I had to. But, he had already seen her when he came to the hall one night."

"He looked shocked when he saw her," Clara remembered.

"I demanded the truth from him. Why, if he had a wife, was he playing this silly charade? Harvey was so stunned to see his wife here that he made no effort to lie to me. He confessed that he had genuinely married the girl and that he loved her. Unfortunately, his mother was insisting he marry an American heiress. He had told his mother about his wife and she had refused to believe him. She told him he must cut the girl off and carry on with her schemes," Crawley ground his lips together in distress. "Apparently they argued on the matter regularly. Angelica would not be moved. She told Harvey that if he ever brought the girl to the hall or acknowledged her publicly as his wife, she would change her will, disinheriting him from her portion of the estate.

"When my lordship died, he divided his wealth between his wife and two sons. Harvey's lifestyle had eaten through a large portion of the money he inherited, and the estates and the income they produce are solely owned by his brother. Harvey was reliant on his mother's generosity, and she knew that all too well.

"When Harvey said he wanted to make the family regret how they had treated him, he was being truthful, but it was only his mother he really wanted to make feel guilty. Harvey explained it all to me, how he would play on his mother's superstitious mind and make her believe her son was visiting her from beyond the grave. He would convince her that if she would only relinquish her desire for him to marry an heiress and consent to his existing marriage, then her son would be restored to her."

Clara was amazed at the audacity of the scheme, but then she had met Angelica and had seen how she believed in the supernatural and things of a magical nature. It was a far-fetched ploy, but, considering how desperately Angelica longed for her son to be alive again, she could see how it might have worked.

"That was why Harvey came into the hall last night?" she asked.

"Yes. He planned to act like a ghost and make the proposition. Depending on how his mother responded, he would have the under-gardeners knock through the wall of his mausoleum and act as if they had found him alive inside."

"Instead, someone shot him," Clara mused.

"I wish I had never agreed to the whole thing. I betrayed Angelica," Crawley berated himself.

"You unwittingly betrayed her," Clara reassured him. "Let us not excuse Harvey's part in all this. He was behind this wicked plot."

"And I felt so sorry for his wife," Mr Crawley continued. "She, out of all of them, did not deserve to be afflicted by false grief. It was breaking my word to Harvey, but I had to tell her he was alive."

Clara almost jumped with this new piece of information.

"Betty Howton knew her husband was alive?" she asked.

"I informed her as she was leaving the hall yesterday. I could not let her go on imagining her husband dead. Harvey had been so unfair to her also, even if his intentions were to secure their future together."

Clara wasn't listening anymore. When she had spoken to Betty earlier, the girl had acted as if she had not known her husband had faked his death. Why would she hide that? A terrible feeling came over her.

"Miss Fitzgerald, you will tell no one about this?" Mr Crawley insisted.

Clara glanced at him.

"No one," she agreed hastily. "At least, unless I have to."

Chapter Twenty-seven

Clara went straight from her conversation with Mr Crawley to the room upstairs used by the intruder to gain entrance. There were still too many unanswered questions. She stood in the middle of the room and took great care to look about it, examining every portion so it might reveal any secret it held. Nothing jumped out at her.

Damn!

Everything was so circumstantial. She could place several people in the vicinity of the murder and give them a means and motive for the crime. While her instinct was to believe Richard and Genevieve when they said they had not killed Harvey, and Diana seemed an unlikely candidate, the truth was they all had the opportunity. They all knew about the loaded revolver in the display case. She only had their word they had not done it. Genevieve swore she would not have used a revolver and would certainly not kill someone, but she might have done just that to throw suspicion off her and onto her brother.

Richard might have used the revolver as a double-bluff. Why would a clever man use a weapon that would incriminate him? Perhaps, for the very opposite reason; to make it appear he could not have possibly done it. And then there was Diana, first to the scene and only her story about running from an imagined ghost to explain her arrival.

Richard had thrown the story of an intruder into the mix. He alone had seen this stranger and there was tantalising evidence in the forgotten bedroom to suggest someone had used it as an entry point. Clara walked to the window and turned around, examining the room as if she had just secretly entered it. The window was still slightly raised. To close it properly required a lot of force. And there was the shifted table with the marks of fingers upon it. Sadly, they were just smudges and could not be identified as belonging to anyone in the family or otherwise.

Clara shook her head. The evidence was vague; a person wanting to make it appear that an intruder had entered could have staged everything. There was no sign outside of an intruder, except for a broken piece of drainpipe. Who knew how long that had been damaged? Everyone in the house knew the room's window was loose and that for years it had been a secret way for Harvey's ladies to enter and exit. That was the sort of secret that was poorly kept. No, if you were clever enough, and Richard or Genevieve were both that, you could arrange this room to look as though someone had come in this way. Throwing suspicion off the family entirely.

Clara was worried. There was nothing concrete to prove the existence of an intruder. She had been so certain when Richard had first told her his tale and she had gone to the room and found seemingly clear evidence that he was telling the truth. Now she was questioning herself. Could Richard have been lying to give himself an alibi? Conjuring a mysterious intruder who snuck in to kill Harvey for no obvious reason?

Clara's mind turned to those who would have needed to break in from the outside to get to Harvey. There was only one real candidate for that; Betty. She had been staying away from the hall and now Clara knew that she was aware her husband was alive. Had that made Betty angry enough to murder him? Did she think he had betrayed her? A broken heart can be a powerful motivator. But there were flaws in that argument too. How had Betty known to climb into the house and confront her husband? And how had she slipped in and out of the inn?

Clara was starting to feel this case was getting away from her, that the killer had vanished into thin air like, well, a ghost. This was all becoming too bizarre!

Clara started to leave the room and then found herself pausing once more. Two other suspects had sprung to mind – first, Angelica, the distraught mother who had seemed so keen to have her son, even when dead, returned to her. But what if she had started to question that determination after dark when things always seem more sinister and evil? What if she started to wonder about Harvey's real motives for apparently returning from the dead? Maybe, thinking she ought to be prepared, she stole the gun and lay in wait for her son's shade? She would have heard his footsteps and come out to the hallway rather than wait for him to come to her.

Harvey's intentions towards his mother were not benign. According to Crawley he meant to scare her, to convince her that she had failed her son by not acknowledging his marriage to Betty. He wanted to play on her grief and guilt. What if he took the act too far and terrified his mother so badly that she shot him in self-defence? Angelica was clearly of unsound mind. Perhaps she had taken drastic action in those brief, dark moments in the hallway? If she was the killer, the odds were they would never know it.

Then there was Crawley. The butler had helped Harvey out of a sense of duty and guilt. Harvey was blackmailing him, that was plain enough. He held a secret over the butler and was willing to threaten to use it when it suited him. Had Harvey gone too far when he used Mr Crawley's guilt-ridden assistance against his own mother? Crawley was obviously distraught that he had been part of a plot against his beloved Angelica. Had something snapped inside the butler? Had he been pushed beyond his limits? All those years of deceit and fear because Harvey knew his secret! Had they suddenly overwhelmed him so that he plotted the downfall of Harvey?

He would have known about the gun, and he could have access to the whole house any time he wished. He was even aware of the exact moment Harvey would be in the house, since he had been instrumental in letting him in and out. Supposing he shot Harvey in anger, not thinking of the consequence it would have on Angelica? People, even pompous, self-controlled people like Crawley, can act irrationally on impulse. He had every reason to want revenge on Harvey, to put an end to the torment.

Yet, in his moment of triumph, what if he was almost discovered when Richard had come running down the corridor? Crawley, with his extensive knowledge of the house and its residents' habits, could have fled through the forgotten bedroom and out of the broken window. Then, instead of running across the grounds as a real intruder would have done, Crawley would have turned back to the servants' quarters once he was outside. No wonder Richard had been unable to follow the escaping intruder – he was already back in the house!

Clara clutched her head in her hands and growled to herself. Too many possibilities! There had to be some further clue! Something that would point her in the right direction.

She walked along the hall where everything had occurred and stopped at the precise spot Harvey had fallen. The hall had been thoroughly cleaned, the rug removed. She stared about her, just in case, looking for a hint of what had happened in the dark of night.

Had it all been a terrible accident? That was a new thought. It had not before occurred to Clara that someone had shot the revolver at what they imagined was a genuine burglar. With all that had gone on in this hall recently, tensions were high and the fear of a living person entering the house at night could easily have led to drastic actions being taken.

Clara shook her head. She didn't think the killer could have been in any doubt as to who they were shooting.

She knelt down and looked along the edge of the skirting boards, hoping to spot something insightful. There was not a speck of dust in the tiny groove where the skirting met the floor. The maids had been exceptionally thorough. What was she really expecting to see? A button or cufflink that had somehow fallen from the killer in their haste? A fingerprint that revealed all? No, there was nothing here. She stood up and looked about at the glass cases with their displays of stuffed animals. Dozens of eyes had been on this spot at the moment Harvey died, and not a single one of them could act as witness.

Clara was beginning to feel despondent. She had been asked to the hall to prove Harvey was a resurrected demon, and she had at once set about disproving that assumption. It seemed, in the process, she may have acted as the catalyst for his death. After all, proving he was a live man gave several family members, including his secret wife, good reason to want his blood. But she could not have known someone intended to murder him.

Clara headed downstairs. Just as she was walking along the first landing that led into the great hall, she heard voices talking quietly. She found herself pausing to listen, her instinctive curiosity overriding her sense of decorum at eavesdropping.

"The woman is in a state of catatonic shock," a man's voice spoke softly.

Clara could guess who he was talking about. It seemed this was the doctor who had been called for Angelica.

"I cannot say for how long this state will last. It may be hours or weeks. Whether she will recover entirely from it is in the hands of God."

"What is to be done for her?"

That was Lord Howton's voice. As always, he was taking responsibility for the members of his household. Of all the residents, he was the one Clara could least imagine murdering Harvey.

"She will need to be nursed. I can recommend some very reliable people for the position," the doctor continued. "I am very sorry I can offer you nothing more."

"Hardly your fault," Lord Howton replied. "How soon before we know if her state will be temporary or permanent?"

"That is a difficult thing to determine," the doctor admitted cautiously. "Nothing is certain in these cases. I have known of one where the person was in such a state for years and then made a full recovery. However, in general, the first few weeks are telling."

Lord Howton thanked the doctor and Clara heard them leaving and heading for the front door. She sighed to herself. Poor Angelica, surely the woman did not deserve this? Had Harvey really despised his mother so much that he had been prepared to inflict such torment upon her?

The great hall was now empty, and Clara walked through it and into the front hall, thinking to go look at the gun display case one last time for inspiration. Lord Howton was walking back inside from seeing the doctor off, ushering along with him the two walkers Clara had seen earlier at the inn. Lord Howton gave Clara a nod.

"Spotted them sheltering from the rain in the porch. I insisted they come inside."

The walkers gave Clara abashed smiles, clearly embarrassed they had been discovered sheltering in an aristocrat's porch.

"The rain came on so heavy," the female walker

explained, "we were desperate to get out of it."

"Might I leave you to show them the drawing room, Miss Fitzgerald? A fire is burning in there, so they may dry themselves off. I have so many things to attend to," Lord Howton did not wait for a reply from Clara, but hurried off on his errands.

Clara would have liked to have reminded him that she was busy too and was not one of his servants, but he was already gone. Since she was somewhat stumped as to what direction to take next with her investigating, she was not entirely unhappy to be distracted by the walkers.

"Come this way," she instructed them, showing them to the drawing room and the cosy fire.

"We really are grateful," the woman kept speaking. "One of the perils of a walking holiday is being caught in the rain. We generally carry on, but my husband has a cold and did not want to get too wet."

The male walker nodded to Clara and she now saw that his eyes were streaming and his nose sore and red from being blown. She settled them both by the fire.

"We saw you earlier at the inn?" the man spoke up, his voice hoarse.

"You did," Clara nodded. "I was just checking on Mrs Howton who is staying there."

"She is the young lady I pointed out to you, Alfred," Alfred's wife told him. "She looked so lonely her first night there that I asked her to join us for dinner."

"She has been through a dreadful time," Clara agreed, not wanting to add that things might soon get worse for her.

"I sensed that, not that she spoke much. Mainly she listened to us rambling on about our walks. We are bird watchers, you see."

Clara smiled, but was only half-listening.

"I invited her on one of our night-time walks. We go looking for owls," the woman carried on blithely. "The inn's landlady is very good and leaves a key on a ledge over the door so we might let ourselves in and out. It is very considerate. I explained all this to poor Betty, but I could not persuade her to come with us. I think it would have done her good."

Clara glanced up. A thought had occurred to her, but she needed to speak to the inspector and see what he had come up with. Maybe something had turned up with the examination of the gun, though she was not hopeful.

Excusing herself from the damp walkers, she departed the drawing room, her mind whirring. An idea was forming; it was risky but she thought she knew of a way to draw out the murderer. Because, otherwise, she had a nasty feeling Harvey's assailant was going to get away with murder.

Chapter Twenty-eight

The inspector had turned the hall's library into his temporary headquarters while investigating the murder. He would return to Brighton soon enough, but while the search of the grounds for clues was still underway, he had opted to find a space within the hall from where he could oversee things. The rain had delayed the search and threatened to wash away any visceral clues, such as footprints. Inspector Park-Coombs stood at the window of the library and sighed to himself.

"Good afternoon, Inspector."

"Clara," the inspector turned around. "Is it that time already?"

He glanced at his watch.

"Do you suppose if I ring one of those service bells I can have someone bring me some lunch?"

"I should think so," Clara nodded. "If not, I shall speak to his lordship."

"No need for that Clara, I shan't disturb him over trifles," the inspector winked at her. "I am causing him enough distress at the prospect of arresting one of his family."

"Do you have any leads?"

"Nothing further to what we have already discussed,"

the inspector shrugged his shoulders. "Clues are thin on the ground. Oh, but we did find where Harvey had been hiding during the performance of his prank."

"Really?"

"Yes. There is an old ice house at the very edge of the grounds. The family rarely use it now. Harvey had turned it into his den. We found everything inside; changes of clothes, further tubs of maggots, stage make-up. Quite the performance he had going on."

"And I can tell you why, inspector," Clara responded. "Harvey wanted to play on his mother's superstitious nature to convince her to acknowledge his marriage to Betty. He had told his mother what he had done and she had reacted badly, insisting he continue with her plans to marry an American heiress."

"He faked his death to haunt his mother and make her feel guilty?" the inspector asked incredulously.

"Something like that," Clara agreed. "I imagine he had tried every other means he could think of and was becoming desperate. He pretended to die and, with the connivance of the under-gardeners and Crawley, the butler, orchestrated this charade. Once he had the family convinced he had returned from the grave, he intended to call on his mother, play on her grief and anguish to persuade her that if she only would agree to his last wish – his marriage to Betty to be acknowledged – then her son would be miraculously returned to her.

"Quite frankly Inspector, it is preposterous, and any rational person would not be fooled. But, as you have no doubt seen, Angelica's mind is not what it once was, and her madness could be played upon. It was a cruel thing for her son to do, but then he might argue it was cruel for Angelica to deny him his love for Betty because the girl was of working stock. Especially when his mother was from that same class. I suppose he convinced himself it was the only way, and that his mother deserved it, somehow."

The inspector still looked amazed by it all.

"I tell you, Clara, these folk live apart from the real world in these big houses and they go a little peculiar. Even his lordship tells me he was convinced Harvey was dead and still prowling the grounds."

"I know, Inspector, it beggars belief. But not all souls are as grounded and rational as us."

Clara grinned at him and he laughed.

"Well, at least we know Harvey is dead for real this time. I had Dr Deàth summoned. He confirms Harvey was shot at close range with a revolver similar to the Webley. Further tests will confirm if the gun from the display case was the weapon, though, I suspect it was. It had been recently fired and I can't see the killer wasting time with two guns."

"Unless they wanted to throw suspicion on the family?" Clara suggested.

"Let's not make this more complicated than it already is," Inspector Park-Coombs' good humour evaporated. "I have too many suspects, Clara. I can make a case for half a dozen people to want to have Harvey dead and the circumstantial evidence could be used against them all. But none of it would hold before a good defence lawyer. He would rip it to pieces, point out that the facts used against one person could be equally used against another. Without something definitive, I fear I am stumped."

"I feel the same," Clara admitted. "I have been over the whole thing in my head and still I can't narrow my suspicions down. There were no fingerprints on the gun?"

"Nothing usable. I had that checked at once, but the only ones on it were badly smudged. Luck, of course, the killer did not have the sense to wear gloves."

"It was a hasty act, whoever did it was not thinking clearly," Clara paused. "Have you told anyone apart from me that the gun had no usable fingerprints on it?"

Park-Coombs shook his head. Clara paced across the room and back again.

"So, the killer doesn't know the gun is an almost worthless piece of evidence?" Clara continued.

"What are you thinking?" Park-Coombs watched her curiously.

"I am thinking, inspector, that we might lure the murderer out by convincing them the gun holds the key to the mystery."

"Tempt them into a trap?" Park-Coombs stroked his chin thoughtfully. "Yes, we could try that. Only, I have sent the gun back to the station."

"We shall use the second gun from the case," Clara shrugged. "They are identical, and we can cover the case with a cloth to disguise that both are absent."

Clara moved to the long table in the library and placed her hand on its polished surface.

"We shall let it slip that fingerprints were found on the gun. All the family will need to be fingerprinted for comparison. We shall make it plain that this will solve the crime."

"And the gun will be here, in this room," Park-Coombs followed her line of thought. "We shall say that Oliver is going to take photographs of the fingerprints."

"By sheer fluke, Oliver will briefly absent the room and the gun will be left unattended for a significant span of time. During which, if our killer has any sense, they will try to steal the gun and remove the one piece of evidence that could convict them," Clara concluded.

Park-Coombs grinned from ear-to-ear.

"I like it. But we must set to work at once. We shall gather everyone in the dining room, it is opposite the library and will give the suspects a good view of proceedings here."

"And we must have Betty Howton and the butler Crawley present," Clara added. "They are suspects too and there will be no harm, if they are innocent, of letting them know it."

The inspector was keen now.

"Give me an hour to arrange things. I'll have one of my constables hidden in here to watch the trap," Park-Coombs glanced about, planning how to arrange the room to suitably conceal his constable. "And I'll have to brief Oliver."

"I'll gather everyone in the dining room," Clara assured him. "And I'll pretend to let the cat out of the bag concerning the fingerprints on the gun."

They went to their respective tasks, eager to set their plan into action.

~~~*~~~

Genevieve clasped her hands together anxiously.

"I don't understand why they need my fingerprints," she said for the third time.

"Miss Fitzgerald explained all that," Richard replied to her crossly. "They found fingerprints on the gun that killed Harvey, and they want to compare them to ours."

"But, why mine?" Genevieve insisted. "I never touched the gun!"

"Then the fingerprints they take off you will prove that!" Richard growled at her.

"Aren't you worried, Richard?" Diana turned to her brother. Unlike Genevieve she was acting calmly and unconcerned by the whole affair. "It was your gun. Surely your fingerprints will be on it regardless?"

"And I hope the police are clever enough to see that," Richard grumbled. "In any case, the newest fingerprints will sit over the older ones. It will be those top ones they are interested in, and since I haven't handled the gun in years, they will not be mine."

"Nor mine!" Genevieve squeaked, her terror seemingly mounting.

Clara placed a clean fingerprint card before Betty Howton and explained how she should ink her fingers on an inkpad and then press them onto the card in order. Betty was looking stunned by the whole thing.

"This will tell us who killed Harvey?" she whispered to Clara.

"I hope so," Clara replied, her uncertainty genuine.

The murderer still had to fall for the trap.

"Then I shall gladly give my fingerprints," Betty inked her fingers and pressed them onto the card.

Mr Crawley was being more recalcitrant. He was standing aloof from the others with a look of disdain on his face.

"Mr Crawley, if you would oblige?" Clara held out a card to the butler.

"I do not see the relevance of all this," Crawley snapped. "And I do not like the idea of getting my fingers covered in ink. I have my appearance as the most senior servant in the house to think about. I can't go around with inky fingers."

"The ink will wash off," Clara told him. "This is a standard police procedure."

"It may be that, but I am affronted by the indignity of it all. To be cast under the suspicion of being a murderer is offensive alone, but to be asked to give my fingerprints like a common criminal goes beyond the grain! I am offended on behalf of the family too!"

"We are not bothered, Crawley," Richard rumbled from his seat at the dining room table. "Better to have the suspicion cleared from us, don't you think? Unless you have something to hide, old boy?"

"Nonsense, Master Richard!" Crawley looked appalled by the thought. "I must protest at such implications. I have been nothing but loyal to your family."

"Yes, yes," Richard brushed off his excuses. "Just give your fingerprints, will you?"

Reluctantly the butler sat at the table and, with great distaste, dabbed his fingers into the inkpad and pressed them onto the card. Clara wondered if his hesitation was purely out of revulsion at being even considered a suspect, or whether he had other reasons for his uncertainty?

Park-Coombs entered the dining room to see how proceedings were fairing.

"How are we doing?" Park-Coombs asked casually.

"I think everyone is done," Clara replied. "Has Oliver managed to take the photograph?"

"He was just about to," Park-Coombs answered. "Something about getting the light just perfec..."

Timed to perfection, there was a smashing sound and a hushed voice cursing himself for his clumsiness. Through the open door of the dining room it was possible to get a clear view of the library. Oliver emerged from the far room, leaving the doors wide open. He was carrying shards of glass in his hands.

"Everything all right, Oliver?" Clara called across from the dining room, drawing the attention of everyone present.

"Smashed my last glass plate!" Oliver replied, annoyed with himself. "I'll have to fetch some more from my studio. Sorry Inspector, I'll try not to be too long."

"Never mind Oliver," the inspector shrugged. "I'll give you a lift in the police car, that will save time and I wanted to drop by the station."

Park-Coombs and Oliver conveniently removed themselves from the hall. The library doors were left open, the gun plainly visible on the table with Oliver's camera mounted on a tripod next to it. Clara shrugged her shoulders.

"Oh well, looks like we will have to be patient a while longer," she said, then she started to gather up the fingerprint cards, ensuring they were correctly labelled with the names of everyone. Her suspects started to filter out of the room. Crawley walked straight across to the library. Clara had been bending over the dining room table, labelling a card. Now she stood bolt upright and watched the butler. He stopped at the door of the library and peered inside, tutting loudly to himself.

"More broken glass," he could be heard mumbling then, apparently satisfied that Oliver had left no fragments of the smashed plate behind, he turned and walked back to the servants' quarters.

Clara relaxed. The trap had not yet been sprung.

She remained in the dining room, pretending to be working on some notes. She had pushed the doors ajar, so she would be invisible to anyone approaching the library. She didn't want to put off the murderer from stealing the gun by her presence. She had been sat alone for ten minutes, when she heard footsteps in the hall outside. Someone was pacing about.

Clara could not resist. She went to the door and peered through the gap. To her surprise, Genevieve was stood before the library doors, walking back and forth agitatedly. Genevieve had been low on Clara's list of suspects – until that moment. Now Clara wondered if she had misjudged her. Maybe she had been cunning enough to steal her brother's gun and murder Harvey?

Genevieve paced for several more moments, then she went into the library. Clara braced herself for the shout of the constable watching over the gun. Any moment she expected the trap to be sprung, but just as she was certain Genevieve must be the culprit, the woman reappeared with a book in her hands. It seemed she had not been after the gun, but after a volume from the shelves of the library. Her reluctance to enter had been a natural response to the room being taken over as the inspector's domain for the time being. She walked away and Clara could see that the revolver remained exactly where it had always been.

Returning to the dining room table, Clara started to wonder if the killer would walk into the trap at all. Perhaps they were prepared to take a chance with the fingerprints? What if the killer was the one person they had not had into the dining room to take fingerprints from? Angelica was a suspect, but her current state of catatonic shock rendered her incapable of knowing about, let alone stumbling into, the trap Clara and the inspector had set. If she was the murderer, then Clara would have to accept she had already been punished by her own remorse and grief.

Clara glanced at her watch. The inspector and Oliver

would return soon. It looked as though the trap had failed. Clara felt a wave of despair come over her. She had no idea how to proceed beyond this point, no idea how to solve the riddle of Harvey's death. Surely she would not have to leave this case unsolved?

The churning of the gravel on the drive outside told her that the inspector was back. It was over.

She was just rising to her feet, to explain to the inspector that they had failed, when a shout rang out from the library.

"I have them! I have them!"

Chapter Twenty-nine

Clara rushed into the front hall. She nearly collided with the inspector, who had just entered through the front door as the cry went up. He muttered an apology without breaking stride. They both entered the library at the same moment.

The constable had emerged from his hiding place. He was holding the arms of the person who had stumbled into the trap. The revolver was lying on the floor, dropped in haste. Oliver's camera had been knocked over and he gave a cry as he ran to rescue it and check it was not damaged.

Inspector Park-Coombs paused for a moment, confronted with the scene. Then he gave a long, serious sigh.

"Mrs Howton," he said. "Looks like you need to explain yourself."

Betty Howton had dropped her head down as the young constable held her arms. She was trembling, knowing that any feeble excuse she might attempt would not be taken seriously. Her lip wobbled and she gave a tiny sob. Clara was reminded of Betty's youth and couldn't help but feel sorry for her. She stepped closer.

"Best you come clean Betty," she said softly to her.

"You can only have been picking up the gun for one reason."

Betty bit at her lip.

"I've made a right mess of things," she groaned to herself. "I couldn't let them see it was my prints on the gun."

"You took the revolver from the case," Park-Coombs joined Clara facing Betty. "Did you know it was loaded?"

"There was a little sign that said as much on the case. The last bullet Richard never got to fire," Betty sniffed. "I don't know what I was thinking, I was just so angry."

"Why don't you start from the beginning?" Clara suggested.

Park-Coombs motioned that the constable could let Betty go, and they sat her in a chair and brought two more for themselves. Then the inspector told the constable to watch the doors to the library, so they were not disturbed. In the calm privacy of the room, Betty slowly relaxed. The reality of her situation was sinking in and, with it, a sense of resignation had come over her. Her fury at Harvey had been spent, now there was only the realisation that she had killed the man she loved.

"Mr Crawley told you Harvey was alive, didn't he?" Clara asked.

Betty nodded her head.

"Mr Crawley thought I ought to know," Betty mumbled. "He saw me as I was leaving the hall. I suppose he thought I was going home and didn't want me to leave without knowing the truth. When he told me I was dazed. I found my way to the inn and rented a room, hardly aware of anything, my mind was spinning!

"I sat in the room and I started to piece things together. Harvey was alive and at first that made me so happy! But then I asked myself why he had not contacted me in all those weeks? Why had he not let me know? The more I thought on it, the more I was convinced he had abandoned me."

Betty pulled a handkerchief from her pocket and wiped

at her eyes.

"I won't cry for him anymore," she told them stoutly. "He isn't worth it. I saw that letter in his room. The one from that other woman, talking about their engagement plans. I realised then how things were."

Clara said nothing. She had seen the letter too, and on its own it appeared damning, but when you knew the background of the situation between Harvey and his mother things became a little clearer. Not that Harvey was a gentleman for stringing along two women, but he was presumably thrust into a dilemma by the overwhelming power his mother had over him.

"I realised, in that moment, that I knew something secret that only a handful of people knew. That Harvey was actually alive!" Betty had focused her attention on Clara, she seemed happier talking to another woman than the inspector. "I don't know, but, in that moment it seemed I had a sort of power over Harvey. I was angry and upset, I wasn't thinking clearly. I thought I would go after him and I would confront him and… and I would tell him that I would reveal what I knew if he didn't come back to me!"

Betty, despite her previous statement, had tears running down her cheeks. She wiped them again with a hanky.

"I knew about the spare key for the inn door. I could slip out and then get back in without anyone knowing I had been gone. And so I came to the grounds of the hall and I watched for Harvey. I knew the time he would come to the drawing room window. Only, that night, he didn't come," Betty pursed her lips together. "I was so confused. I started to wonder if Crawley had told him that I knew he was alive? Maybe he would no longer come at all? I was so upset. I thought maybe he had gone for good!"

"Betty, did you not wonder why he was playing out such a charade?" Clara asked as the girl fell into silence.

Betty hefted her shoulders up and down miserably.

"Harvey was always playing games. I didn't give it any

thought. I was too worried about why he had lied to me, abandoned me," Betty closed her eyes and gave a shaky sigh. "I was, sort of, paralyzed by my own anger and hurt in that moment. I just stood, hidden in the bushes, my mind revolving over and over again what had happened. I lost track of time, I even stopped noticing the cold. I should have gone back to the inn, everything would have been better if I had done that. But I didn't move.

"Then, as if I had conjured him up from his hiding place, Harvey was suddenly there, at the drawing room door. I don't even remember seeing him appear. Maybe I closed my eyes for a bit, I don't know. But then he was at the drawing room door and he was letting himself in. I hesitated for just a moment, long enough to see him go through into the front hall and then I made my mind up to follow him.

"I was angry again. So very tired and so very angry. I had meant to confront him, ask him for the truth, but suddenly that didn't seem as important as making him suffer for how he had treated me. I mean, I knew why he had abandoned me, why should I waste time listening to his excuses? I picked up the poker from the fireplace first. It was heavy and I felt such a great desire to hit Harvey, to make him know what it felt like to be hurt that badly..."

Betty's emotions got the better of her again. She had to stop for a moment to control her tears, she was choking on her own grief – grief for both herself and Harvey. She had never stopped loving him, despite her words.

"When I got into the front hall, I realised I could not see a thing and the poker suddenly seemed a bad idea. I went to put it back, but I couldn't see where I was and I went into the gun room rather than the drawing room. My eyes fell on the display case with the revolvers. I remembered what Genevieve kept saying about 'winging' the intruder. I thought... I don't know... in that strange moment, it occurred to me that I could shoot the gun at

Harvey to scare him, to make him realise how upset I was. I never meant to kill him…"

Betty opened her eyes and looked first at Clara and then at the inspector.

"Never. I never meant…" she pressed her handkerchief to her mouth and made a sort of retching noise, as if she was now truly grasping what she had done and it sickened her.

Without a word, the inspector rose, departed the room and returned moments later with a glass of brandy. Betty sipped the alcohol, slowly recovering herself enough to carry on.

"It was easy to smash the case with the poker. But, oh, it made such a noise! I thought someone would hear me, but I guess I forgot how vast this place is," Betty looked around her, as if seeing the many corridors and rooms of the hall from where she sat. The enormity of the building seemed to scare her. "I put the poker by the fireplace in the gun room and I took out Richard's gun, the one with the last bullet…

"After that everything seemed to be happening to someone else, like it was all a dream and I was not a part of things at all. I went upstairs after Harvey. I didn't really know where he had gone, but I could guess. I came across him in the corridor. I actually startled him. For a moment he didn't realise it was me.

"I waved the gun at him. 'You've done me wrong, Harvey!' I told him. He just stood staring at me, he seemed stunned I was there. 'I want you to know what it feels like to be hurt!' I said, and I was waving the gun about and he said, 'Don't be silly, Betty!' And it was his tone! The way he patronised me! I just snapped! And it was so dark, I really only meant to graze his shoulder, but I've never fired a gun before and I didn't realise how close he was to me…"

Betty gave a wail.

"I killed him! I pulled the trigger and he fell to the floor! I was so shocked! I bent down and told him to get up, and he didn't move! Then I heard someone coming down the hall and I panicked! I was near all these old rooms and I thought I would hide in one. I stumbled through the nearest door, but I could hear the person behind me running and I thought they had seen me.

"It was awful! I stumbled into this small table and quickly moved it aside, then I ran to the window and just grabbed at it and, to my amazement, it flew up! I have never moved so fast as in that moment! I climbed out the window and was lucky there was a drainpipe below. I clambered down it and ran as fast as I could when I hit the ground. I threw away the gun at the nearest patch of bushes. I should have taken it with me, I suppose, but I didn't know what to do and I was so upset!

"Please, please understand, I never, ever meant to kill my poor Harvey!"

Betty scrunched the handkerchief in her hands and her face contorted into a picture of anguish.

"I told myself he wasn't dead," she gulped in air as she spoke. "I told myself I had stunned him. I believed that too, until you came Miss Fitzgerald and told me the truth."

Betty snuffled and gasped, her throat tight with her intense feelings of guilt, remorse and terrible, terrible grief.

"You... can... arrest me... now," she held out her hands, each word requiring a moment to squeeze out through the sorrow. "I did it!"

Inspector Park-Coombs twitched his moustache. He looked downcast and Clara knew exactly how he was feeling, because she was feeling just the same. Betty had been ill-used. Whichever way you looked at it, Harvey had played a cruel hoax on her as much as the family and had brought her to the brink of despair. He didn't deserve to die for it, but it was easy to see how Betty had been pushed to the limit by his actions and had struck out without thinking. After all, Angelica had been driven to madness by the events of the last few days. Surely what

Betty had done had also been an act of madness?

"The constable will escort you to the station," Park-Coombs said to Betty. "Then we shall need all this in a statement and I shall have to press charges."

"I understand, Inspector," Betty had calmed a fraction. "I shall not protest anything."

Betty rose with a surprising amount of dignity and the inspector walked her to the door of the library, where she was handed over to the constable's care. Once they were gone, Park-Coombs turned to Clara.

"Not an arrest I take any pleasure in," he muttered.

"The shame of it all is that Harvey was doing this masquerade for Betty. Admittedly, he did clearly court the American heiress under his mother's instructions, but only until he could figure out a way to change her mind about his marriage to Betty," Clara shrugged.

"What a mess," Park-Coombs grabbed up the gun from the floor. "Sometimes I wish I hadn't solved a case."

He put the gun on the table.

"At least his lordship will be relieved it was a not a member of the immediate family," he said.

"Cold comfort," Clara remarked. "But the matter is resolved. We know how and why Harvey was killed and also the mechanics of the charade he played on his family. It will not make things any better, but at least we understand."

"Hmm," Park-Coombs stared at the gun thoughtfully. "Has it crossed your mind that things would have been a lot simpler if Harvey had actually been a corpse returned from the dead?"

"Now you are being silly, Inspector."

"You know, some of the lads were quite worried they might find a hoard of the undead on the estate. I really despair," the inspector huffed. "I blame it on watching too many of these horror movies that are on at the picture house nearly every week."

"How do you explain the reaction of the Howtons?" Clara chuckled.

"Oh," Park-Coombs considered for a moment. "That is due to too much heritage."

He wafted his hand about at the books on the shelves, some of them several centuries old.

"Yes, too much heritage. A man must live in the present and always be looking forward," he was satisfied with his answer and looked it.

Clara smirked to herself.

"As you say, Inspector," she said.

They walked to the gun room and replaced the revolver in its case. It looked slightly sinister on its own, without its partner.

"Harvey was a fool. A clever fool, but a fool nonetheless," Park-Coombs said. "He made life extremely complicated for himself. Whatever happened to just talking to people?"

"Some people will not be talked to," Clara thought of Angelica.

"Well, he paid a high price for his jest," Park-Coombs stroked his moustache. "The newspapers will have a field day with this one. Just the sort of thing to whet their appetite."

"If Angelica had not lost her mind already, I fear this would have done it," Clara agreed.

Chapter Thirty

Clara was packing her bags when Lord Howton found her in the guest bedroom.

"Miss Fitzgerald, I would like to thank you for your efforts in this affair," Lord Howton stood in the doorway, hands in his pockets, looking somewhat baffled by the whole business, but, nonetheless, satisfied. "My wife and I would like to extend a final dinner invitation to you and the inspector, as an acknowledgement of your work and discretion. Will you accept?"

Clara closed the lid of her suitcase. She was looking forward to getting home and being among sensible, sane people who did not believe the dead could rise from their graves. However, she could see Lord Howton was offering a genuine gesture of thanks and it would be rude to decline for no good reason.

"Of course I will accept," Clara answered. "I am sorry the outcome was not a happier one."

"I am not so much sorry for us," Lord Howton said, "excepting Angelica, but I am sorry for the girl, Betty. I think she was ill-used."

Lord Howton became downcast.

"I have already decided that I shall pay all her expenses. I know of a very good barrister I hope to persuade to represent her. I think there are many mitigating circumstances and she should avoid the death penalty," he confided.

"I think that is a very generous thing to do," Clara nodded. "And, I agree, this was an extreme situation. Betty did not mean to kill Harvey."

"No, that has been explained to me," Lord Howton walked across the room and picked up a little trinket box that sat on a dresser. "While Harvey is at fault in all this, I find myself questioning my own actions, or rather my failings. I clearly did not make him feel at home here. He would not have gone through this ridiculous charade had that been otherwise."

"There was a lot of bitterness about Harvey," Clara said. "Bitterness instilled by his mother, as much as by the rivalry between him and Richard."

"They were like brothers as boys," his lordship sighed heavily. "I should not have allowed the tension between their mothers to destroy that. I had a duty to Harvey, but I overlooked it. I might excuse myself by saying I was extremely busy, my father's death placed great burdens upon me, and I discovered the estate was in an alarming degree of debt. But that does not really excuse me."

"You are in debt?" Clara said in surprise. "I thought the Howtons were the wealthiest family in the country?"

"On paper," Lord Howton gave her a wan smile. "On paper, when our assets are put together, we are indeed the wealthiest. But the wealth is tied up in land and things, not actual money in the bank. I have worked these last two decades to reduce that shortfall and make the estates profitable again. It is still an ongoing process."

"So, the inheritance from your father..?" Clara asked.

"I inherited many debts and a title," Lord Howton answered. "Angelica's inheritance proved very disappointing to her."

"Harvey thought she had a fortune, it was why he kept in her good graces."

"She convinced him of that, I know it and I suppose I

should have disillusioned him," Lord Howton gave a gruff snort. "But, I was annoyed by his attitude to his mother and I rather felt it would serve him right if he discovered all his efforts had been in vain one day. If only I had not been so churlish these events might not have occurred."

"The reason Angelica wanted Harvey to marry an American heiress was not just one-upmanship over the rest of the family, it was because she knew without such a wife he would be thrust into poverty."

"There would always be a place for him here," Lord Howton promised. "He was my brother, after all."

"But he would have been reliant on your charity, much like his mother. Oh, now I see why she was so angry about his marriage to Betty! It was not just pride, it was the desperate knowledge that one day her son would be penniless because she had connived to fool him over her own situation!"

"Our lies always come back to haunt us," Lord Howton nodded sadly.

"Is Angelica still the same?" Clara asked tentatively. Insanity was always something to tiptoe around.

"Her condition is unchanged. The doctor can give me no firm answers as to whether she will recover or not. I hope for the former, I hate to think of her spending the remainder of her life in such a state."

Clara could not say for sure what would be the better option for Angelica. It all depended on precisely where her mind was at the moment. If it was somehow at peace, restful, then would it be a kindness to rouse her when all that awaited her was great despair and unhappiness?

"Naturally I shall see that everything that can be done, is done for her," Lord Howton continued. "My wife feels very aggrieved about the situation too. I think she feels she, in part, drove Angelica to this state. She now feels guilty over her antagonism towards her. She has said she will tend Angelica as dearly as if she were a beloved sister. I think she looks upon it as a penance."

Clara could not help feeling that the Howtons were a

very troubled family, with a lot of anguish and anger running among them. But she said nothing.

"While I am thinking of things, I should pass on the appreciation of your assistance felt by my children. I am certain they will express their gratitude to you at some point, but just in case, rest assured they are very grateful of your actions in this matter."

Clara wondered if they would have felt so grateful to her had one of them proven to be the killer. She couldn't help feeling that everyone was most relieved that the killer was someone outside of the family.

There was a sudden heavy thud outside the window. Clara walked across the room and peered out into the grounds. A cluster of workmen were stood about Harvey's mausoleum and were in the process of removing its roof.

"You have wasted no time!" Clara said, somewhat amazed by the rather unseemly haste with which the monstrosity was being removed.

Lord Howton joined her at the window.

"It was never really meant to house him," he said. "It was a prop in his game and it seemed wrong to leave it standing. It is a reminder of all the bad things that have happened these last few days. Worse, it is a reminder of the cruel prank Harvey played on us. No, I thought it best it go sooner rather than later."

Clara could see the logic, but she still thought it was a very sudden thing to do under the circumstances. The next moment, her curiosity got the better of her sense of priorities.

"Excuse me a moment, Lord Howton."

Clara headed downstairs and outside. The autumn wind whipped leaves about her legs and there was a chill in the air that made her regret not grabbing for her coat as she hurried outside. Oh well, she would not be long.

She walked to the mausoleum and paused near the group of estate workmen bringing about its destruction. They had so far removed a portion of the roof and were adjusting their ropes to remove the next portion. One man was up a ladder, using a chisel to work lose the cement holding the roof stones in place.

"I would like to look inside," Clara declared to them.

All the workmen turned and stared at her in astonishment.

"Look inside?" an older man stepped forward and looked Clara up and down as if she was a mad woman. "Whatever for?"

Clara smiled at him.

"I want to know how he did it," she answered. "What went into the mausoleum in the place of Harvey Howton."

The older man now looked around him at his crew, clearly astounded by Clara's request.

"Actually," one of his workmen piped up. "I was wondering the same."

The workman on the roof put down his chisel.

"I hadn't liked to say before," he spoke, "but I had been thinking the same and had been somewhat concerned at what we might find. Now, as we know Harvey was never in this here tomb, I have to ask myself, who is?"

"You lot are not suggesting there is another body in this here crypt?" the head workman glowered at his men.

"Would it be so hard to switch a dead tramp for himself?" the rooftop workman pondered. "Don't we all remember there was that vagrant wandering about just a few days before Master Harvey's supposed accident. But we saw no more of him after the funeral."

"Tramps move on," the head workman grumbled.

"I am just pointing out, how it might have been done. Got to be said, Master Harvey was clearly not averse to getting his hands dirty."

"It is one thing to pretend to be dead and another to kill a man to act as your corpse," the head workman declared sharply. "That is a very dangerous thing you are saying up there, George!"

"Master Harvey was clearly up to no good," George, the man on the roof, stuck to his guns. "What was he doing sneaking about the hall at night when everyone was abed? I heard tell he was going to kill his mother!"

"That is silly gossip!" the head workmen snapped, trying to stop the unhealthy talk.

"Is it?" George said. "Then what was he about, then?"

"The laundry maid told me that she heard he was going to smother his lordship in his bed and then Master Richard, so that he could miraculously be discovered alive and inherit the estate!" said the young workman on the ground.

The head workman was growing red with indignation at the talk. Clara decided to intercede.

"Whatever Harvey intended, it cannot be done now. All I want to know was what he substituted for himself in that coffin," she said. "Could we take a look?"

"I'm not opening it!" George announced, hastening to clamber down his ladder. "I'm not being confronted by a dead tramp!"

"For crying out loud!" the head workman snarled. He wrenched the chisel and hammer out of George's hands and set to work on the door of the mausoleum himself.

The cement that held the front piece of the tomb in place slowly chipped away and fell to the grass. A carving, halfway between a lion and a gargoyle, accidentally broke loose in the process, but it hardly mattered now. The weird, meaningless script on the stone would soon be gone, along with it the ugly decorations, purloined from a dozen cultures in a mismatched fashion. A stone suddenly jerked loose and was pulled free. More followed, the plaster that had masked their joins cracking and crumbling to dust. The more that the mausoleum was hacked down, the plainer it became how cheaply and shoddily it had been put up in the first place. It would probably not have lasted a year or so exposed to the English seasons.

"Who put up the mausoleum?" Clara asked George who was now stood beside her.

He shrugged.

"Some men Harvey had hired. He didn't get any of us estate workmen to do it."

Clara could see why. Had the estate workmen put up the tomb they would have learned of the poor quality of its component parts and would have wondered why Harvey was allowing his final resting place to be built so crudely. Harvey didn't need those sort of questions circulating about the estate.

The last of the stones that comprised the door came free and Clara was able to step inside. She glanced up suspiciously at the roof, now missing a section, just in case it looked in danger of falling on her. She noted at once that the inside of the tomb was built of wood, the walls were not made of stone like the external ones, but plastered and painted to look like it.

"Yes, I noted that when we pulled down the first piece," the head workman saw her gazing around. "This place is just a façade, nothing more."

But there was a coffin. It stood in the middle of the mausoleum on a plinth. It was elegant and stylish, paid for by Lord Howton and therefore the one thing in this place that was not a stage prop. Harvey had no doubt smirked at seeing his brother pay a fortune for this smart coffin when he was not actually dead.

"Open it carefully," Clara said to the head workman who was about to insert a crowbar under the lid of the coffin. "It might as well be reused."

He caught her tone and called out for a screwdriver instead. Then he carefully removed the screws that held down the lid of the coffin. Once they were all gone, he paused and looked at Clara.

"Don't lose your nerve now," Clara said. "I don't think he killed any tramps. Harvey was not a murderer."

She placed her hands under the lid on one side, the head workman placed his hands under the other and then they lifted together.

The coffin revealed its 'corpse'. It was full of red bricks. Just enough to give it the right weight when carried. Sitting on the top was a scrap of paper. It had been glued to several bricks so it would not move. There was a message on it from Harvey;

"If you expected to find me dead, you'll have to try harder!" It stated in bold letters.

Clara sighed to herself.

"Sorry old boy, but I won't."

Printed in Great Britain
by Amazon

75777974R00151